Stick to the Deal

A Billionaire Marriage of Convenience Romance

R.S. Barry

RILEY PAWS PUBLISHING

ISBN 979-8-9901858-4-5 (Ebook Edition)

ISBN 979-8-9901858-5-2 (Paperback Edition)

Cover Art by Lily Bear Design Co — www.lilybeardesignco.com

Interior Design by R. S. Barry

1st edition 2025

To anyone who's made themselves smaller to fit society's box.

Knock down those walls!

July

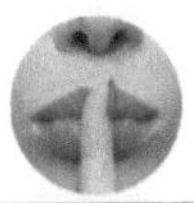 **Whisper Wire** ○ ○ ○

The end of all the gorgeous June weddings is leaving me quite blue. So here's my pick for the most eligible bachelor and bachelorette of London's society.

Class, cash, and the chance to be a countess? Reginald Bancroft, 34, current Viscount Ravenscourt and future Earl of Silverbrook, tops our list of men to marry this year—and inside sources hint this may be the year he's finally taken off the market. So go ahead ladies and shoot your shot. You'll have to find him, though. When he's not representing his family at charity functions, he's been quite mysterious jetting off to who knows where. Boys will be boys, but at his age, it's time to man up and face matrimony.

For you gentlemen, may I suggest Miss Nicolette Atherton, 29, the sole heir to the late billionaire Edgar Atherton. A bit of a party girl in her teens, this bachelorette has managed to stay out of the spotlight in recent years. She's hardly ever seen in London, but sightings are constantly reported around the globe. What is this enigmatic beauty up to? Perhaps there is already an equally mysterious man, and you've all lost your chance? With all the other eligible bachelorettes vying for attention on the marriage mart, I'm dying to know what makes Miss Atherton tick.

Send me your hottest gossip! Where in the world is Nicolette Atherton?

TTFN
Wendy

CHAPTER ONE

The Naked Truth

NICOLETTE

A bead of sweat trickles down his neck. It grabs my attention as it slides across perfectly sculpted pecs and washboard abs. Even naked, the heat of the lights can be intense. You'd think he'd be used to it. I lose sight of the droplet as it falls behind the guitar he strategically holds in front of his groin.

"Ok, I think we got it. Go ahead and take a break and I'll review the images," I yell. Perspiration beads at my temple, I dry it with a towel and then guzzle from a nearby water bottle.

Turning my back on the giant lights, I check the monitors to make sure I've captured the image as I imagined it. I've photographed for hundreds of magazines and designers over the past decade, but this project is special. This is for Time magazine!

"Whoa, that's fabulous." Kenzo Star, now safely wrapped in a robe, stares at the monitor over my shoulder. With his spiky, jet-black hair, tattoos, and guyliner he looks every inch the rock god he is. Even in fluffy white terrycloth and bare feet. "I have to admit I wasn't sure about the whole naked with a guitar thing, but your vision is incredible."

My lips quirk. Yeah, I'm fucking good at what I do. "Well, the article is called *The Naked Truth.*" I flip through a few more images, hitting keys to mark my favorites for editing later. "Just be glad you got to pose with a guitar. The female novelist with the tiny paperback was a real challenge."

A sexy chuckle rumbles through his chest. "I thought this was too on the nose or cheesy. You managed to make it look like art."

"Thank you. Coming from a fellow artist, I appreciate it." I smile at him over my shoulder.

Kenzo's eyes rake over me with appreciation. "You are a fascinating lady, Miss Kato-Atherton. Have dinner with me."

Turning towards him fully, I prop a hip on the table behind me. His eyes darken as they take in the long line of my body. At five-ten, I'm tall for a woman. And mostly leg. Even in a simple black tee and cotton shorts, I know I look good. "Tempting. But no."

His brow raises in surprise. Probably doesn't hear 'no' often. Especially from women. When his eyes snap to mine I see a challenge flicker, confirming my initial read. "Oh, come on. It's only dinner. You do eat, don't you? You've seen me naked. I want to find out what makes you tick."

"I do eat. What I do not do is paparazzi, and you, sir, are practically infested with them."

He hums agreement. "They are a bit like parasites, aren't they? Ok, then answer me three questions here in the safety of your studio."

"Not my studio, but go ahead."

"Even more interesting. Where is your studio then? You must have one."

"I go to my subjects, not the other way around. There's a mini space in my apartment in Florida. If I'm not shooting at an event, I rent spaces like this for the assignment."

"A bit of a nomad. I hear that. It gets old, though." Creases appear by his eyes for a moment, then he blinks and the confident man returns. "Question two, where can I see more of your photos?"

"You've probably seen my work before and didn't note the photographer. Non-commissioned photos are on my website or Instagram." I pull a card out of my camera bag and hand it to him. On the front it simply says 'Nic Kato-Atherton, Photographer' in bold script. The back has my contact information and social handles.

"No gallery showings?" His inky brows pinch as he studies the simple card.

"Does that count as question three?" I smile at Kenzo. "No galleries. Too busy with work to curate a show." The well-rehearsed excuse I use for my friends slips easily. "Go ahead, what's your last question?"

His lips spread in a full grin, showing straight white teeth. It's a look that screams sex. There's no doubt why the ladies throw their panties at him on stage. "How long are you in New York for?"

"Flattered, but not going to happen. Don't need to catch your parasites. I'm only here until Monday, then flying out."

"Oh no, while I would happily take you back to my hotel for dinner and breakfast," his black eyes twinkle, "I can take a hint. I had more professional pursuits in mind. My new album is coming out and I haven't liked a single photo the label has provided. I want something grittier. More passionate." He points to the monitor beside me. "I think you're exactly what I've been looking for. Come to my show Saturday night. Take some photos. If one works for the cover, you get credit and royalties. If it doesn't, I'll still post them on my socials and tag you. Either way, it's a free rock concert with VIP access."

My teeth gnaw at my inner cheek as I debate his offer. It is an amazing opportunity for more exposure. Not that I'm hurting for work, I've had multiple shoots a day since I flew in almost a month ago. I have been working too hard though, and a night out would be a nice break. It's not like I have other plans. Most nights, I've been grabbing a quick bite on my way back to the apartment. Usually sitting at the bar with some smutty novel on my Kindle.

"Sure. You have a deal." I hold my hand out for a shake.

His warm fingers surround mine, the calloused pads caress the sensitive skin of my wrist. Guess fuckboy just can't turn it off. It really is a shame about his paparazzi infestation. I'm certain he'd be good for a night, or three. Lord knows I haven't had time for such distractions since I got to town, and back home is too small a pool for meaningless dalliances. Sorry lady bits, but even this dry spell isn't worth the unnecessary attention he draws.

I'd slip back into his dressing room with him for a quickie, but a chemist is arriving in an hour and I still don't know how I'm going to hide her tits behind a microscope and test tubes.

More's the pity.

After promising to courier over the passes and details, Kenzo heads off to change, closely trailed by his assistant. No rest for the wicked, I dive right back into setting up for the next shoot.

CHAPTER TWO

Meet Reginald

REGINALD

As the car inches along the busy streets of New York City, I gaze out the windows at the noisy life around me. Maybe I should have walked. It'd certainly be faster. After a day of pounding the pavement from Chelsea to Brooklyn and back, my Armani loafers couldn't take another step.

My heart quickens at the colors and sounds outside. Vendors shouting, taxis beeping, storefronts, and billboards. In many ways, it's similar to my native London. We do share common ancestors after all. In others, so very different. Especially from the upper echelons of society I grew up in. Here, I can disappear. Both cities may sport over eight million people, but here I'm one of the throng. Back home, I'm Reginald Bancroft, Viscount Ravenscourt, favored son and all around golden boy.

My phone vibrates in my pocket. I pull it out, revealing a text from my best mate Daniel.

Daniel

So what do you think? You in?

The morning had started off well, meetings with lawyers and accountants, reviewing contracts and business proposals. Everything looks good, but looks can be deceiving. My gut is screaming yes, jump in with both feet on this venture with Daniel, but something is holding me back.

Me

> I want to, not sure how I can make it work though.

Getting away this week was tough enough, but I don't want to admit that to him.

Daniel

> How many charity events is one man expected to attend?

Me

> More than you can possibly imagine.

Daniel

> You deserve this, Bancroft. Do something for you for once. Most parents would be happy their son is starting a business!

Me

> I guess you're right.

Daniel

> Of course I am. When are you going to stand up to him?

One block down and twenty or so to go, I collapse back against the seat with a tired sigh.

When am I going to stand up to him? That's the problem, isn't it? I've never raised my voice, pushed back, or said a cross word. I've simply gone along with my father.

Am I crazy? My brother certainly thinks so. Montague is more than happy to play polo and live off the family name. He's told me more than once I should do the same. Hell, as the oldest, I have more reason to stay home.

I'm thirty-four years old, and I've never had a job. All of my money is from my maternal grandparents. I want something that's mine. Something I built with my own two hands. Something... meaningful.

Twenty minutes later, we finally arrive at my hotel and I shuffle through the lobby, still deep in thought.

We're in good shape. True, media, especially publications, is an incredibly competitive industry. Daniel and I have done our homework, though. We've identified a clear gap in the market and are working to fill it with an extremely conservative and risk-averse plan.

Feeling a little lighter, I hurry to run a bath to soak my aching feet while I consider room service. A crime in NYC I know, but there's no way I'm heading back out for takeaway. Even if they'll deliver to the lobby.

My cell blares from the desk. With a wistful glance back at the steaming water, I limp into the main room to answer.

"Reginald, you need to come home immediately. I've had Foster book you the first available flight, but it's not until Monday." Leave it to Edward Bancroft, Earl of Silverbrook, to jump straight to the punchline. No 'hello, son. How is your trip going?'

"Whatever for, father? Is mother alright?"

"You're getting married."

I couldn't have heard him correctly. "Pardon?"

"It's time you do your duty by this family and marry. We'll arrange it all when you arrive."

Bloody hell, I did hear him correctly. My legs give out and I sit on the edge of the bed as my heart pounds in my temple. Through gritted teeth, I ask, "And to whom am I getting married? Have you already picked my bride?"

"Don't be cheeky, boy. You can choose the young lady. As long as she's rich."

"Rich?" I snort. "Why the hell does she need to be rich? The Silverbrook holdings are vast. How much money does one family need?" The silence is loud. "What did you do, father?"

"Don't take that tone with me. I'm still the bloody Earl of Silverbrook, and you will show me respect. Just a spell of bad luck," as in bad luck at the gambling tables I'd wager, "but we can fix it with your marriage exactly as we've done for generations."

My jaw aches from grinding my teeth to physically hold back words I long to say. Words a proper British son would not.

He must take my silence as obedience, because he continues on. "Luckily, there's a top matchmaking firm with an office in New York. Foster has engaged them for a list of acceptable brides. They'll send a dossier over to your hotel and you can review it. When you arrive at Silverbrook Hall, have your final candidates selected and we'll take it from there. This is happening, Reginald, or so help me, I will disown you and ensure the title goes to your younger brother. Monty would be delighted, I'm sure."

I hold the phone in my hand long after my father has disconnected. It's not lost on me, I'm always Reginald where my brother is *Monty*. The sound of rushing water penetrates my mind and I rush to shut off the still running bath before it overflows. I'm certain my father would have something to say about those damages.

Rolling up my slacks, I hiss as my aching feet touch the steaming water. The edge of the tub is cool under my ass, but it does little to distract me from the cyclone of thoughts in my head.

Marriage.

It had to happen eventually. Raised the heir to an earl, I never had illusions of marrying for love. Even in this modern day. At least he's letting me have a say in my potential bride rather than a blind arrangement. The timing is so bad. Daniel and I could actually make our idea work. I don't need the distraction of courtship, negotiations, and wedding arrangements. I need to be focused on networking, staffing, and logistics.

By the time the water turns tepid, I'm no closer to solutions. There are still two days before my life sentence. That's two days to focus on my fledgling business with Daniel. The dossier can wait for the flight home. What else am I going to do with seven hours?

Resigned to my fate, I decide to mourn my loss of freedom with a loaded pizza and scotch.

CHAPTER THREE

Pastry in the Park

NICOLETTE

My sunglasses slip down my nose as I strut down the empty streets. Well, empty for New York City, anyway. Sunday mornings bring a strange mix of folks out. There are the brunch goers in a variety of fashions and social standings rushing to cafes to gossip over mimosas and Bloody Marys. The working class scrambling to open shops and stalls. Wide-eyed tourists, snapping photos and staring at the skyscrapers overhead rather than where they're walking. And my favorite, the walk of shamers who own the raccoon eyes and rumpled clothes in hand. Chin high and strutting like they're on some couture runway. You go, girl.

Even at ten a.m., the streets echo with the sounds of horns and trucks bouncing over construction plates. Every corner features a trendy restaurant, gallery, or boutique. It is a city of artists and my heart swells as I breathe in the talent. Ugh. And the constant smell of piss and garbage.

As Grandmama always reminds me, everything comes at a price.

My smile fades at the thought of my grandmother. Refusing to dim my last day in the city, I take a sip of my iced chai and take the final turn to Bryant Park. This is my favorite spot to eat alfresco in the city. I can read, work, or people-watch all while enjoying a delicious panini or giant croissant. Everything about this place feeds my soul. From the modern turquoise glass skyscrapers, to the ancient white marble of the New York Public Library. The hard bronze busts and the soft dripping periwinkle wisteria. It is an absolute delight to the senses.

So why does a photographer like me live in a small town in central Florida instead of this bustling hub? I come here for commissions and to refill my creative battery, but my heart lives in Friendship Springs with my family. Well, not technically family. My only blood relation lives in England. I'm talking about my two best friends, Brianna Chance-McLeary and Annabel Bennet. They are the sisters of my heart. Photography gigs keep me traveling a lot, but missing them always brings me home to Florida.

Grabbing a free table, I perch on the green slatted chair and unpack my pastry bag. The first bite explodes in my mouth, eliciting a lusty moan. An older woman at the next table looks at me reproachfully, but then smiles as she spots my croissant in hand and chipmunk cheeks. Smiling an apology, I pull out my cell and open an email from Time.

Ms. Kato-Atherton,

We are absolutely thrilled with the initial images you've provided. This is exactly the tone we were hoping for. I've marked which photos we would like to select for the article and look forward to seeing the final edits. We'll definitely be looking to work with you again in the future.

Regards,

Rebecca Green

Senior Editor, Time Magazine

With a mental fist pump, I take another bite of my pastry. The rest of my inbox is easy to sort through, mostly inquiries or spam.

I scroll through the photos from last night on my phone. Most are still on my camera memory card awaiting editing, but I'd snapped a few candids on my cell. Choosing one, I send it to my bestie group chat. The reply is almost instant.

Breehive

> Holy shit! How did you find front row seats to Kenzo Star? Did you drain your trust fund?

I chuckle as I take another healthy bite of my pastry. Oh, the dreaded trust fund. While I appreciate not being the stereotypical starving artist thanks to my family's generational wealth, I don't appreciate all the strings that come with it. More than once, I've thought about telling Grandmama exactly where she can shove her money. My Jimmy Choo sneaker taps the gravel under my feet. I like nice things, though, and a deal is a deal.

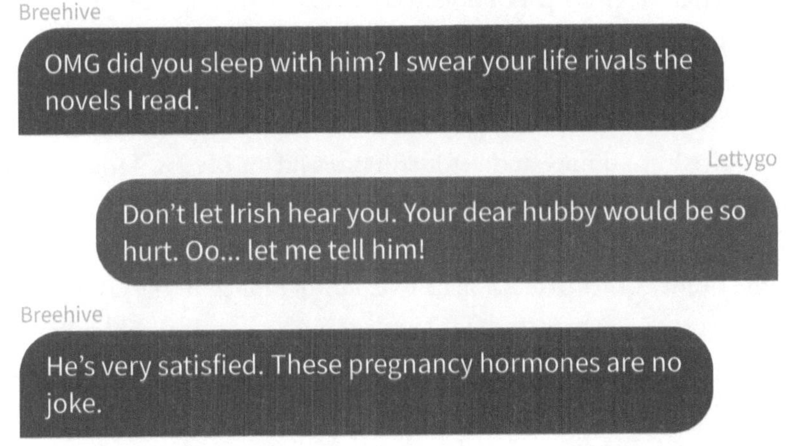

Anna is the head chef of the restaurant, Pop, we co-own. She's sweeter than chocolate and one of her four brothers is an aspiring musician.

I like to give Bree's husband, Colin, a hard time, but I can't dislike a guy who makes my best friend so happy. In one year, he's managed to loosen her neurotic, tightly wound persona better than I have in a decade. He's kind of like the brother I never had. Not that I'd ever admit that to him.

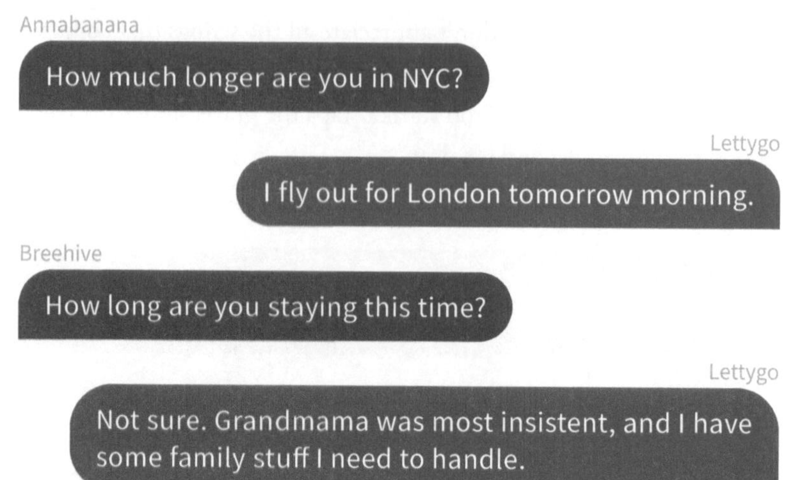

My phone vibrates in my hand as the Wicked Witch Theme softly plays. I sigh and curse under my breath. It's like the woman has me under constant surveillance. Begrudgingly, I answer, "Hello, Grandmama."

"Nicolette." Her crisp London accent echoes through the line. "When are you arriving? What are you thinking being photographed with rock celebrities? Was I not clear you are expected to keep a low profile?"

With a slow breath through my nose, I count to five. This is exactly why I didn't give in to dinner and yet it still bites me in the ass. "You have been most clear. I was attending a concert for work. Kenzo Star is a client, I met him while doing a piece for Time Magazine. He's apparently more interesting than the twenty other professionals I've photographed in the last month."

A faint tut sounds over the line. That's about as emotive as the ever proper Vivienne Atherton gets. "Really, Nicolette. I know I agreed to give you some space to find yourself, but gallivanting with rock stars and landing in the gossip columns is unacceptable. It's about time you grow up and accept your place in this family. Need I remind you that you'll be thirty in a few months?"

My delicious pastry turns to lead in my stomach. "No, Grandmama." There's no use defending myself or trying to shock her with how 'inappropriate' I could have been. "I fly out in the morning and will be at the estate by supper."

"Very well. Do wear something appropriate. I'm sure the paparazzi will be waiting outside Heathrow after your latest dustup." Without so much as a goodbye, the line goes dead in my ear.

Appetite lost, I gather my breakfast and dump it in the bin. Four hours later, after extensive retail therapy and a visit to my favorite stylist, I once again have a spring in my step. Or maybe that's the bounce of my new chin-length bob? Nothing can get me down now!

"Ms. Atherton."

Dammit. Spoke too soon.

I turn towards the doorman. He's worked here as long as I remember, yet still calls me by my grandmother's last name despite my staunch insistence on including my father's surname. That's the downside of using the family apartment, I guess. "Yes, Peter?"

"Package arrived for you, miss." He steps around the imperious desk and hands me a packet wrapped in brown kraft paper and tied with twine, my name and address written on the front in a majestic, feminine hand.

"Thank you, Peter. I'll need a car at nine a.m. for the airport, please." I may rebel against my socialite standing, but I'm not an idiot. Why haul my suitcases through the subway when I can afford a town car?

He dips his head as he returns to his post, fingers already flying across the keyboard to mark the request. "Shall I send a cart up at quarter of for your luggage, miss?"

I thank him again and drag my bags and parcels into the elevator. Very quickly, I realize my love of fashion has outgrown my luggage capacity over the last month. Sorting through the clothes I've accumulated during my visit, I sort them into two piles. Unfortunately, the more casual or daring outfits won't be welcome in London. Those I box up and ring Peter to ship them back to my penthouse in Friendship Springs. Once every Grandmama Dearest-approved item is carefully packed and my carry-on ready, I eye the parcel over a slice of cold pizza.

Beneath the plain wrapping is a cerulean blue folder with the words "Something Blue" embossed in gold foil. Atop the file is a single white Post-it note.

Miss Kato-Atherton

Included you will find all profiles matching your specifications. Please let me know which are acceptable and I will arrange meetings.

J. Kelleher

My chest tightens as I tuck the packet into my carry-on and stare out over the city before me. The lights dance as I picture a dozen futures, each full of what-ifs and make believe.

Everything has a price, and now my bill has come due.

CHAPTER FOUR

Up in the Air

REGINALD

I tap my loafer on the carpeted floor of the first-class cabin. Both anxious to be off and dreading being one minute closer to this homecoming.

"Sir, your coffee." The attendant gives me a radiant smile.

My answering expression is polite but dismissive. "Thank you." I'd much rather be having a scotch, but it's only five a.m. local time. With a seven-hour flight, there'll be plenty of time to numb my senses before we land.

The first-class cabin is nearly full. As a last-minute ticket, Foster wasn't able to secure a solo seat, but luck is on my side and the adjoining spot is empty. I hadn't thought about prying eyes when I'd planned to review my potential blushing brides on the plane.

A glance behind me confirms that the stream of boarding passengers has slowed to a crawl. A giant pastel green backpack lands on the seat next to me, jerking my attention back to my row.

The woman standing in the aisle is tall and slim, dressed in black leggings and one of those shruggy sweaters over a tank. Her inky hair twists into two haphazard buns on the top of her head and the little of her face I can see is absent of makeup. She looks wholly out of place among the suits and high-end clothing dotting the cabin, but she certainly draws the eye.

The hostess must agree, because she rushes over. "Miss, may I see your boarding pass?"

I almost expect a scene, but the woman simply pulls her ticket from the side pocket of her backpack and hands it to the attendant with a smile. A bright pink key chain that resembles a champagne bottle swings from the bag zipper.

The air hostess's eyes scan the ticket and grow wide. "Apologies, miss. May I get you anything? We should be taking off shortly."

"Mimosa, please." I'm not sure which surprises me more, her low sultry voice or the fact she had the guts to order alcohol when I did not. Now that she's facing me, I can study her face from the corner of my eye. Clear skin on an oval face with high cheekbones and dark almond eyes. A straight, slightly button nose over full lips. She is beautiful.

My seatmate settles in and secures her seat belt. The attendant quickly returns with the requested drink. Her first sip is followed by a satisfied sigh. The sound sends a curl of heat through my belly. I rub at the spot and drink my coffee.

"If you insist on judging me, this is going to be a long flight." Her voice startles me and I turn to find her regarding me with a raised brow. Amusement and maybe a little annoyance glitters in her eyes. This close, they're not as dark as I first thought, more hazel than brown.

"Jealous, actually." Now why the bloody hell did I say that? She laughs, and the sound is smooth as silk. Who the hell is this woman?

Any further discussion is staunched by the pilot announcing our preparation for takeoff. We both focus on finishing our beverages before the attendant whisks through the cabin to collect them. My stomach drops as the plane picks up speed and I fist my hands on my legs. It doesn't matter how many times I do this, it never gets easier. Man simply wasn't made to fly. I focus on the safety video until the aircraft levels out.

"Not much of a flier, huh?" She's scrolling on her phone, looking as if she hasn't a care in the world. My lip curls as I read the title of the website: Whisper Wire. The gossip rag is the very thing I hate about media and so-called journalism.

I merely grunt and concentrate on my breakfast instead of the human chaos factory beside to me. The meal is over all too quickly, and with no more excuses, I pull the dreaded dossier from my bag. A snort next to me stirs the festering annoyance within.

"Can I help you?" I turn my best sardonic peer of the realm look on her.

Nonplussed, she draws an identical bright blue folder from her backpack. "Small world." Her lips twist in a carefree smile full of amusement. At my sake?

I've never had cause to doubt Foster before, but what the hell kind of second-rate matchmaker did he engage if little Miss Nuisance is also a client?

My silence only amuses her more, a mischievous glint sparkles in her eye. "You know, I could probably help you weed out some of those profiles."

"Is that so?"

"The shit debutantes say behind closed doors would amaze you. At the very least, I can steer you away from the batshit crazy ones. I don't know you, but we obviously run in the same circles."

I'm about to cut her down, ask her what she could possibly know about my circles when my eyes narrow on her shoes. She's taken to curling up in her chair, like a cat settling in. The white sneakers I'd dismissed clearly say Jimmy Choo on the heel. Scanning the rest of her outfit, I realize that while casual, every article is a luxury brand. Guess my nanny was right about not judging a book by its cover. "What's in it for you?"

Her smile spreads, sensing impending victory. "You can do the same for me, review my file and tell me who to avoid." She holds the folder out to me, holding my gaze confidently.

"And what exactly are you looking to avoid?" I take her folder and hand her mine before I can have second thoughts. There is no downside to her offer. I'll still examine every profile, but she can help me prioritize the order of that investigation. Narrow it down a bit.

"Hmm." She takes a sip of her sparkling wine as she thinks. "Obviously your closet abusive types, megalomaniacs."

My lips quirk despite myself. "Obviously."

"But also the ones looking for a Suzy Homemaker."

"You're not the stay at home type? Don't want children?"

"It's not that. Kids are great and all. I simply have my own aspirations and I refuse to give them up because I'm expected to marry."

My eyes narrow hearing words I've thought a dozen times in the last 72 hours. "Parents pressuring you?"

The energy around her dims slightly and I'm almost sorry I said the wrong thing. Just as quickly, the emotion flickers away. "Grandmother. You?"

"Father. Ok, you have a deal, miss...?"

"Call me Nic." She extends her hand.

My hand engulfs her long, thin fingers. Her grip is cool and surprisingly firm for a socialite. My palm tingles lightly as I retract it. "Bancroft."

She salutes me before turning to my folder in front of her.

What have I done?

As she reviews the pages, there are occasional snorts or muttered comments as she makes piles on the tray. I turn my attention to the file in my hands, committed to carrying out my end of the bargain. Exactly as Nic predicted, I find pages with familiar faces smiling up at me. Almost all these men I've met at school, the club, or at numerous social engagements. There's a mixture of titled and untitled men ranging from thirty to forty years of age. Varied professional backgrounds and net worths. All of them are members of British upper society, though.

I quickly rule out three bachelors—they're too old-fashioned and full of themselves to expect anything less than a stereotypical trophy wife. Trystan Kensington I move to the maybe pile. I'm pretty sure he's gay, but he's a nice enough chap and he'd be more likely to give her space. A couple more go into a stock of prospective choices.

"Holy shit." Nic's bald reaction draws my attention back to her. She's sitting forward with a single sheet clutched in her hand. The paper shakes slightly.

My eyes snap to her face. Her cream complexion practically matches the paper. "You ok?" Maybe that second mimosa went to her head. I glance around for the attendant—we need a soda or a sick bag. As I lean closer to check the other aisle, the face on the profile smiles at me. It's Nic.

Holy shit is right.

I shuffle through the remaining pages in my hands, and sure enough, I find myself.

Reginald Edward Montgomery Bancroft, Viscount Ravenscourt, Age 34

Parents: Edward and Penelope Bancroft, Earl and Countess of Silverbrook

Siblings: Brother, Montague Edward Alexander Bancroft, Age 27

Schooling: Eton, Oxford

Hobbies and Interests: Horsemanship, Patron of the Royal Opera House, Supporter of the World Literacy Organization, Bancroft Red Hearts Foundation

Profession: None

Net Worth: £10.0 M

Sourness rises up my throat. I might be the one in need of an airsickness bag. No wonder she turned pale. To have one's entire life summarized down to a handful of statistics is embarrassing. So cold. So impersonal. Is this what my life amounts to? This is so misleading. Especially those last two lines.

How am I going to face the remaining five hours trapped here when it feels like the walls are closing in?

CHAPTER FIVE

A Terrible, Brilliant Idea

NICOLETTE

When I suggested this exchange, I never expected to find myself in that damn cerulean folder. I truly thought it could be a mutually beneficial arrangement. It's true that women and men are more open with their peers than potential suitors, and why wouldn't I use every tool at my disposal? A part of me wanted to see Mr. High Society squirm, though.

I read people. Years of juggling bitchy socialites and Grandmama's expectations taught me how to survive. From the moment I put my bag down, I clocked him as an elitist with his panties in a twist. After the side eye at my mimosa, I decided I wanted to twist those panties a little more.

What can I say? I love to stir the pot. Well, when I'm sure I can get away with it.

Color me surprised at the humorous response. Figured a human might actually reside in that Tin Man costume.

Handsome costume, to be sure. Piercing steel gray eyes over an aristocratic nose with a slight bump at the bridge. Umber hair, so dark a brown it must look black in most lighting. Skin with golden undertones but too pale to be considered tan. His designer suit is obviously custom, perfectly chosen to highlight both his coloring and shoulders. Not overly muscular, but clearly fit.

I shake my head and return my focus to the paper in front of me. My gut churns.

Nicolette Sen Kato-Atherton, Age 29
Parents: Genevieve Marie Atherton and Hashi Kato; Granddaughter of Edgar Atherton II and Vivienne Atherton
Siblings: none
Schooling: Sacré-Cœur Hall Boarding School in France, University of Florida
Hobbies and Interests: Art, Fashion, Patron of the London Ballet Company
Profession: Photographer
Net Worth: $1.5 B USD / £1.2 B

While flipping through profiles of old schoolmates and acquaintances, it hadn't honestly occurred to me how barbaric this was. How cold. Sterile, even. Is this all I am?

The ding of the call button draws my attention. Bancroft, who is waving down the attendant, has turned a bit green. The perky blond arrives at his elbow in a moment, all teeth and eager eyes.

"Scotch." Bancroft turns to me. "Another mimosa?" There's no judgment in his eyes, if anything, he almost seems... supportive? Well, as supportive as a stranger can be.

"Better make it a vodka." I'll need something stronger to get over this twist.

"Double," we say in unison.

The attendant's eyes pinch in confusion as they dart between us briefly before she rushes back to the galley. We sit in charged stillness until she returns with our liquors, lingering at Bancroft's elbow and staring at us. "Will there be anything else?" She's probably wondering what our connection is.

I shake my head no. Normally I'd be worried about gossip getting back to Grandmama, but right now I have bigger issues. The silence is thick as we both nurse our drinks.

"So..." The man clears his throat, still looking lost as he stares into his drink.

"So, apparently we're a match." My sharp tone drips with sarcasm.

"Why do you need a matchmaker?" he asks baldly. I arch a brow at him and he has the grace to wince. "Apologies. That came out badly. You're a beautiful woman, seemingly from a good family. Why haven't you found someone on your own?"

"As in, what's wrong with me? I could ask you the same." He grunts and takes another swig of his scotch. Sarcasm and dry wit won't help me through this one. If he's in that damned folder we'll most likely be running in the same circles.

Taking a deep breath, I modulate my tone and try again. "My family has always been clear on their expectations of me and my future partner. I bought a decade of freedom with the promise to marry by thirty. I've been focused on my career instead of looking for a husband. A matchmaker seemed like the fastest solution."

His brows pinch again. "Fastest? How long do you have?"

"November." I toss back another gulp and wince as the vodka burns down my throat.

He whistles. "Nothing like leaving it to the last minute." He plucks the paper from my numb fingers and scans the page. "What kind of photography?"

"Mostly portraits. I was in New York for a shoot for Time. Freelancing lets me pick and choose my assignments, but I travel up to fifty percent of the month."

"The rest of the time you are in London?" His eyes are serious as they study me.

"Florida, actually. My grandmother has an estate in Surrey, but I spend as little time in England as I can manage."

"Do you object to England in general, or Surrey in particular?" His lips purse, eyes still glued to my sheet.

The question catches me by surprise. I inspect the planes of his face, trying to read him, but for once my gift fails me. Rolling the dice, I go with honesty. "Surrey in particular, I suppose. It's less about the geography and more about the company. I find society's expectations stifling."

"Hence the no-Suzy-homemaker requirement. You would prefer to keep working."

Annoyed, my fingers snake out and grab his profile from in front of him. "What is this? The Spanish Inquisition? Two can play this game, Colombo." As I scan his name, my lips quiver. "Reginald?"

His face is thunderous to match the stormy eyes. "Don't start. It's a family name, after my grandfather."

"Ok, Reggie." I've never understood the appeal of the broody hero type before, but his glares are definitely amusing. "No job, aristocrat hobbies... and a title. You're a trust fund kid. So what? Looking for your future trophy countess to continue the line?"

A muscle ticks in his jaw, and I have the strangest urge to touch it. Seems I hit a nerve.

"Overseeing my family's charitable contributions isn't simply a hobby. Yes, I have an inheritance from my grandparents, but it's not funding my lavish lifestyle, if that's what you're thinking." A sardonic brow raises as he stares into the amber liquid. "Like you, marriage has been the farthest thing from my mind. My father has decided its time for me to marry." As he salutes me with his drink, he mutters under his breath. It almost sounds like "and no one goes against the earl."

I hum in condolence. "How long do you have?"

"He needs a name by the time I land." Those gray eyes meet mine with a swirl of emotion.

The vodka I'd just sipped burns my throat and the back of my nose as I gasp, choking. A warm hand rubs my back as another shoves a water bottle into my hand. "Thank you." I wheeze a few more times. "So, what are you looking for? Besides, not crazy, that is."

Reginald sighs. "Preferably someone who isn't high-maintenance or hunting for a title. Someone I could hold a conversation with over the dinner table. Contrary to what you think, I don't particularly enjoy the high life. I suppose it's too much to hope for a partner in all this."

A partner. That sounds nice.

When I watch Bree with her husband, it's not the looks of adoration that make me jealous. It's the way they act as a unit. How he supports her dreams and she his. Love may be a major inspiration for art, but the pictures don't show when passion fades and the work begins. Love alone doesn't make miracles.

"So not a petite blond who smiles at galas or in Easter photos with three perfect kids?"

That ghost of a grin plays around his shapely lips again. What would it look like for him to smile for real? "Well, I would need to have children—eventually. But otherwise, that sounds dreadful. If I'm to spend my life with this person, I'd like to have a conversation without dying of boredom."

Hmm, good answer. "What if she has a career? Would you expect her to quit her job to support your family name?"

"Of course not. That's antiquated." Reginald's brows pinch, making him look adorably insulted. "There will always be expectations and some required events, but what you describe sounds like a recipe for resentment."

Surprisingly insightful for a silver spoon prince. I take a breath to ask about his family, but what comes out is: "We should get married."

He jerks back. "Just like that? I could be the next Jack the Ripper for all you know."

Amused, I fight a smile and lean into his space. Sandalwood invades my senses. Flicking my eyes back and forth, I whisper, "Are you?"

"Am I what?" he whispers back, those stormy eyes darting between mine and my lips.

"A historic serial killer with a thing for ladies of the night?" I bite my cheek to keep from laughing.

He blinks. Once. Twice. Then his lips spread into a smile. My heart speeds up. It's small, showing the slightest hint of white teeth, but it's real—unlike the polite ones he's given to the flight attendant. "No, haven't had time around my polo matches."

I let out a surprised snort and sit back slightly.

"Seriously? Let's get married, just like that?" His brows knit again and I find myself missing his smile.

"Just like that. You haven't done anything particularly objectionable in the two hours I've sat beside you. If you're in the file, that's good enough for my needs. With," I check my watch, "five-ish hours until you have to decide, you don't have time to be choosey. So, are you in, or should I give one of these other lucky bachelors a call?" I wave the folder at him.

Reginald's jaw clenches as he snatches the packet from my hand.

I'm half convinced he'll say no—I haven't exactly proven myself countess material in the last few hours. He says he doesn't want a simpering socialite, but I've acted a complete shrew. I can't seem to help goading him, even knowing the lecture I'm bound to get from Grandmama on my behavior.

It takes me a moment to notice his hand stretched out. I return the gesture and his warm palm and fingers engulf mine, sending a zing up my arm. There's a curious callous on his second and third finger, not the buffed and smooth hands I expect.

"It's a deal." His words echo with finality.

My eyes raise to his and find determined steal. Those full lips stretch into a confident smile, and I'm left wondering if I finally bit off more than I can chew. I swallow, pushing down the rising tide of uncertainty.

Don't let it show, Nic. "Just like that?" I mock his earlier question, glad my voice is steady.

His head tilts. "As you said yourself, you're in the folder. That's good enough for my father. You're certainly not boring. That's good enough for me. What else matters?"

"Ok, I'll bite." I lean in, curving my lips into the femme fatale smile that leaves men eating out of my hand. "What about physical needs? Confident you're up for the task? Not sure I'm you're usual type."

"I think we'll get on fine." He leans forward. His nose whispers against the sensitive skin of my jaw, erupting tingles down my neck. When he continues, his voice is a growly whisper, pitched only for my ears. "But if you need a hands-on demonstration, I'm up for slipping into the lavatory. With or without biting."

Heat uncurls in my belly. I think he may be right.

My thighs press together to ease the sudden ache in my core, and I force a bored look on my face. "Fair enough. So realistically how does this work?"

"We'll have to make this seem legitimate. A few public dates, maybe some staged paparazzi photos. Then an engagement announcement and a society wedding before your birthday."

His effortless shift from flirt to business leaves me dizzy. Have I met my match? "Ok, but what about after? We don't even live in the same country."

"I've been spending a lot more time in New York, but I can honestly work from anywhere right now. When you are in the city, I can meet you there. Or in Florida. When necessary, you can come here. Let's say a week a month, otherwise our lives are our own."

I arch an inky brow at him. "Our own? As in complete autonomy? An open marriage?"

Emotion flickers over his face before he smooths it out. "If you like. Absolute discretion is required. There can't be even a hint of scandal."

"Agreed. The last thing I want is to read about my husband's mistress in the tabloids." My teeth gnaw at the inside of my cheek as I debate. "To that end, we do not bring anyone to our homes. Shared spaces are to be respected."

He grabs a cocktail napkin from under his drink and writes out a few lines of text. His handwriting is bold and confident with harsh slashes. "Of course. Anything else?"

I study his face, looking for any hint of insincerity. Any whisper of him not being exactly what he appears to be.

His gaze is level as it meets mine. Not an ounce of doubt. He might just be a kindred soul in this glittering world we were both born into. Diamonds are beautiful when they sparkle, but they're hard and cold.

"Don't go falling in love with me, Lord Ravenscourt." I give him my best smile, the one that always gets me my way.

His lips quirk more, but still no signs of a full smile. "I think both of us are safe on that account." He adds onto the napkin, then thick fingers slide it to me.

The Deal:
Make It Believable
Get Married Before November
Together 1 Week a Month
No Scandal
Respect Shared Spaces
Don't Fall in Love

Across the bottom, his signature is already inked. I study the man in front of me one last time. I wait for that sinking feeling in my stomach. For my gut or head to scream this is a bad idea.

His easy posture in the chair looks calm, but a tension about his shoulders contradicts it. This is important to him. Intelligence and sincerity shine in his steely eyes. God help me, but I trust this man. I may not know him yet, but his body language is open.

With a flourish, I sign my name next to his.

His lips quirk into a wolfish smile, and he raises his drink. "To us." The clink of the glasses is followed by the dry burn of vodka down my throat.

This isn't a great love affair, but I never wanted that. I only wanted a partner in life, and my gut tells me I've found him.

CHAPTER SIX

Mother May I

REGINALD

There's a renewed spring in my step as I make my way through Heathrow. It might be the scotch, but I can't deny that flight went better than I could have ever hoped.

With no checked baggage to claim, I'd said goodbye to my new fiancée before breezing through immigration and customs. As I exit the doors to the car line, the sight of a familiar figure with gray hair and suit clad shoulders has me changing my path.

The older man smiles as I approach. "Welcome home, sir. Was your flight satisfactory?"

My lips twitch as I think of the last few hours with Nic. "Quite." With her quirky style and smart mouth, she is absolutely not the bride my father had in mind—which may be half of her appeal. He only set one requirement, after all. Perhaps he should have been more specific.

"Good to see you, Foster. Did father send you to make sure I didn't skip town?" I clap him on the shoulder and wave him off as he goes to grab my bag.

Rupert Foster has been my parents' butler for as long as I can remember. He drove me to school, picked me up for holidays. Hell, he's probably my favorite part of visiting home. "He did seem most insistent on you coming straight to the manor, sir."

The constant hum of voices around us escalates in pitch as the doors behind me open and a woman emerges. Lights flash and the crowd is practically titillating, and I can't quite blame them.

She's tall, her black-and-white heels making her even more so. The white sheath dress is conservative, hitting a couple inches below her knees with a demure walking slit, but it's expertly cut to highlight her toned figure. Shiny black hair lies perfectly, grazing her delicate jaw. Large black sunglasses obscure her face, and burgundy lips—the only trace of color—lift in a smirk before blowing a kiss in my direction.

My body tenses as I stand frozen by my father's car. What was that? A familiar green backpack perches on the top of the luggage trolley, pushed by the attendant closely following her.

Nic.

I swallow and pray it's not audible. The woman is Eris, Greek goddess of chaos, incarnate. I think I've opened Pandora's box, but what a way to go.

Despite the slow traffic, the gates of Silverbrook Hall come into view all too soon. I'm still reeling over Nic's transformation as I climb the front steps and cross the marble foyer. My feet carry me to the parlor on autopilot even before I hear the murmur of voices inside. Nothing about this place changes. It's frozen in history, devoid of progress. Or humanity.

"Reggie-bear!"

Up to now, I'd still enjoyed a slight buzz from the scotch. Just enough to soothe my frayed nerves and amp myself up for the conversation ahead. Hearing the shrill voice of Serena Wentworth instantly sobers me up and sucks any remaining warmth from the room.

"Serena. What are you doing here?" My teeth creak as I bite back more words as my mother shoots me a look of rebuke.

Undeterred, she steps into my space until the hem of her Pepto-Bismol pink dress brushes my slacks and her matching manicured claws rest on my shirtfront. "Don't be cross, darling. Your mother spilled the beans about the engagement and I couldn't wait a moment longer. Of course I'll marry you."

My eyes dart to my mother. The joy in her smile tempers my rage. With significant effort at gentility, I remove Serena's hand as I side-step past her. "I'm afraid you've misunderstood." Giving her my back, I stride forward to sit beside my mother on the antique love seat.

Blue eyes flare, showing a hint of the demon within the debutante. "Are we not getting married?"

Holding her gaze, I let my lips curve into my most gentlemanly smile. It's a look I practiced for hours as a child—after the first time my grandfather backhanded me for being an ungrateful lad. "I am getting married, but not to you."

Both women gasp at my proclamation. "Married to whom?" Serena's eye twitches and her pouty pink lips pinch like she swallowed a lemon.

My decision to marry Nic keeps looking better and better.

Footfalls echo through the foyer moments before father appears behind a still seething Serena. "Reginald, about damn time." He does a double take at the young woman, his dark brows pinching in confusion. "Excuse us, Serena, dear, but we have family business to discuss. You'll have to continue your tea with Penny tomorrow."

I have to bite my cheek to stop from laughing as Foster closes the heavy doors in a sputtering Serena's face.

"Reginald," Mother turns to me with confused blue eyes, "I don't understand. Why wouldn't you marry Serena? I thought you were sweet on each other. You know it's been my fondest wish to see you two married."

My merriment evaporates. Poor Mother. Serena is the daughter of her dearest friend. Yes, I've known for decades what my mother planned for my future. I even went along with it for a while. Until I couldn't anymore.

"Now, Penny. Serena is a nice girl, but as the heir, Reginald needs to marry someone who can bring something to this family. Social clout, a sizable inheritance, business connections."

"And why is that again, Father?" At his glare, I simply walk to the decanter in the corner and pour myself a scotch.

"Are we in trouble, Eddie?" My mother's tremulous voice and bright eyes send an arrow of guilt through me. Although my father has always been ruthless, my mother has always seemed too delicate for this world of social warfare.

Claiming my emptied seat, Father takes her hands in his and kisses the backs. "Of course not, my dear. It's true, some investments are not growing as I'd hoped, but Reginald's marriage will fix all that. Plus, it's expected for the eldest son. Why don't you set Serena up with Monty?" The scotch burns in my throat as I choke on my sip, earning yet another glare from my esteemed sire. "So, boy, have you narrowed it down? Or must I do everything myself?"

My knuckles whiten around the crystal glass and I carefully place it on the sideboard before it cracks in my grip. "No, sir. I have spoken to Miss Atherton, and she has agreed to be my bride."

Gray eyes, a perfect match of my own, widen. It's the closest to emotion I'll see from him. "As in Edgar Atherton? Real estate mogul, Edgar Atherton?" I nod. "Yes, the Atherton heiress will do quite nicely. Well done." His lips pucker as if the flavor of the compliment is vile. Must be a surplus of lemons going around.

"Well, when do I get to meet her?" Mother whines. Her pout almost matches father's.

I repress a sigh. "Soon, Mother. We'll have to arrange a public courting before announcing the engagement. We'd like to marry early November."

"This all seems very fast, Reginald." Mother's hand flutters about her pearl necklace.

Swigging back the rest of the scotch, I paste my practiced smile back into place. "When you know, you know, Mother."

The dinner bell sounds and I follow my parents into the formal dining room. As they fall into their own world discussing my life as if I'm not sitting right here, I pull out my cell phone. I wonder if Nic is getting on any better.

CHAPTER SEVEN

A Thorny Rose

NICOLETTE

The shock on Reginald's face was a welcome distraction from the impending confrontation as I left the airport. Ugh. I am so not calling him that. The bustle of the city has long given way to tree-lined motorways and then to narrow country roads. The scenery constantly flickers between rural towns, cow pasture, modest homes, and mini mansions as we make the trek to Surrey. To the house I once called home.

To Grandmama.

As the driver passes through the gates leading to the gargantuan house, my pulse quickens. I blink and find myself staring down the giant oak doors of Rosevale Manor, so named for the pink English roses that climb the white stone facade of the imposing house. A less jaded individual would describe this place as a fairy tale castle, but to me, it's more like Maleficent's lair, the thorns a malevolent barricade to my freedom.

The house looks huge as I stand on the steps clutching my tiny suitcase. The social worker smiles down at me, urging me forward. Inside is like nothing I've ever seen, is this really a house?

At the bottom of the stairs stands a woman in beautiful clothes, her dark hair with a shock of white by her temple pulled into a bun. I approach her, expecting her to smile, but her firm expression doesn't change.

"Gr-Grandma?" I ask

"It's Grandma-ma," she corrects, then sweeps up the staircase, leaving me confused.

A heavy woman with tight black curls and a friendly face rushes over to me. Her hands are soft and she smells vaguely of spices and sweets. "Welcome, Nicolette. Let's get you settled into your new home."

"Nobody calls me that. They say it's a mouthful."

She smiles and her eyes crinkle at the edges. "Then I'll call you 'Letty.' My name is Gloria, but you can call me 'Glo.' Are you hungry? I've got ravioli and fresh grated cheese in the kitchen." She spends the afternoon showing me my new room and filling my stomach with pasta, bread, and cookies.

With one last breath of clean air, I square my shoulders and open the door. The tinkling sounds of piano draw me to the dining room. Like a queen, Vivienne Atherton sits at the head of the ten-foot table. She is resplendent, wearing a black-and-white tweed jacket with white silk ruffles frothing at her throat and diamonds twinkling at her ears and fingers. Though her face has lined and her hair is white, the beauty of her youth still shines.

Her green eyes are still sharp as they snap to me, scanning my appearance from head to toe. "Nicollette, come sit. Supper is already growing cold." She rings a bell at her elbow and a young man immediately appears from the kitchen doors with a covered tray.

I sit as quickly but demurely as I can. Not next to her. Oh no, why would we want to be able to have a polite conversation over a meal? No, we must yell from across the room, over monstrous vases overflowing with roses and gladiolas in a pompous display. "Apologies, Grandmama. Customs took longer than usual."

"Yes, well, it's good you're here now. I've had Gloria freshen up your old room. Then tea with the hospital charity fund committee is on Thursday. There's a dinner party on Friday with your grandfather's old business partner. I took the liberty of buying you an appropriate dress. I also got us tickets for the ballet on Saturday, *Swan Lake*, your favorite."

The whole monologue is delivered in crisp tones with no pauses for response—not that she expects any. These are simply her expectations of what a young lady is to do. It's not all bad. The dinners and teas are mind-numbing, but I do enjoy the evenings at the ballet, theater, or opera.

My stomach drops as I realize the room has gone quiet. Glancing up, moss green eyes stare into mine. A perfectly plucked white brow wings slightly overhead. A clear indication I missed something. "Pardon?"

"I asked, dear, how have things been in America?"

Stalling, I pat the soft cream napkin to my lips. "Very good. Time Magazine was thrilled with my photographs. I've gotten so many new inquiries I've had to turn away clients."

"You'll have to cut back on your photos, anyway. Courting takes effort. Plus, your husband will expect you to take on social responsibilities. Chair a few fundraisers and such." Her eyes narrow on my face. Maybe I wasn't schooling my features as well as I thought. "I know you think it's all silliness, Nicolette, but it is a wife's duty to support her husband. Forging connections and philanthropic commitments in his name is hard work."

Under the table, my nails dig into my palms. The pain grounds me in this moment until I can swallow my emotions. My phone vibrates against my thigh, and I find a text from Reggie—nope, not calling him that either, need to keep brainstorming. I shoot back a thumbs-up with two wine glass emojis. "I've actually already met someone, Grandmama. He's asked me to coffee tomorrow."

A surprisingly unladylike clatter echoes as she lowers her silverware to her bowl. "Nicolette, you better not be talking about that rock star again. I was quite clear on my expectations when you begged to go to America for college. You agreed to marry a man from an old English family, with an impeachable reputation. Someone your grandfather would be proud of."

I never knew my grandfather, but I'd hope he'd want more for me than that. Good breeding is no guarantee in show dogs, let alone husbands. He died from a heart attack before I came to live in this mausoleum. It was quite the culture shock from the California apartment I shared with my parents. A few intense weeks spent with etiquette tutors and then shipped off to boarding school in yet another new country.

"I told you, Grandmama, he was only a client. Your requirements were quite clear, which is why I engaged the top matchmaker in New York." As she opens her mouth to argue, I rush on. "It's a firm with a strict non-disclosure agreement who caters to only the most exclusive clientele. I shared your list of dem... requests and received a file of matches. One of the candidates happened to be in New York on business and we met before I left. We hit it off, I wouldn't be surprised if he proposed soon." With effort, my lips curve into the semblance of a polite smile.

Her mouth shuts and she blinks rapidly, the only reaction I'll receive. "Well, it's good to see you are taking this seriously." She returns her attention to her soup, all conversation now over.

I lift the steaming spoonful to my lips. Butternut squash, typically a favorite of mine, but the creamy soup turns tasteless on my tongue. She didn't even ask for a name? After twenty years, I shouldn't expect any warmth from the woman across from me, yet I find myself disappointed by her indifference.

Look at me, I want to scream. *Can't you see me drowning under your expectations? Don't you care what I want from my life? When will you realize I'm not her, and I'm definitely not you.* I want to hurl that ridiculous vase against the marble hearth and storm out the door.

But I won't.

I'll sit here, silently suffocating. Pushing down every thought and feeling. Snipping off every part of my personality that does not fit the perfect little box Vivienne Atherton has set for her only grandchild.

My friends think I'm Nic Kato-Atherton, this fearless woman who speaks her mind freely, and maybe I can in Friendship Springs. Everywhere else I'm Nicolette Atherton. I wear a carefully crafted mask of who society wants me to be, because I'm desperate to gain the love of my only living relative, and absolutely terrified I never will.

August

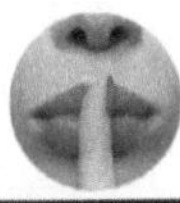 **Whisper Wire**   o o o

She's back! Maybe Miss Nicolette Atherton is a reader as well, because no sooner did I highlight her as the bachelorette of the year and she returned to London.

Miss A was seen making a big entrance at Heathrow last week—completely rocking a Gucci dress and a blunt bob. Love her or hate her, but the girl's got style! Is it really any wonder, though? A little birdy told me she's been a busy bee on the art scene for the past decade. That's not all she's been up to. Recently rock god Kenzo tagged Miss Atherton on his personal Instagram account with the simple caption: "It's criminal how good this woman makes me look." No wonder London's favorite bad girl has been so quiet lately.

Has the boarding school party girl grown up? Or are we just one step away from major socialite drama? Cast your vote in the comments.

TTFN
Wendy

CHAPTER EIGHT

Ladies Who Lunch

NICOLETTE

A waiter sets down another plate of treats fit for a doll. Why is everything so damn tiny? Did tea portions get smaller? Or have I been living in America too long?

"Vivienne, it must be nice to have your granddaughter back home. It was so gracious of you to support her adventuring."

Well, the people are just as small as I remember.

I quickly lift my teacup to my lips to stop the caustic words from flowing out. The porcelain is smooth against my skin, the liquid warmth floods my mouth with bitterness. A welcome change from the saccharine manners of the well-to-do around me.

The crisp white linens, gold gilded mirrors, and polished silver trays scream elegance. Even the desserts feature gold leaf to remind you of the surrounding opulence. It is the Ritz, after all. Dozens of equally decadent women scatter about the room wearing Chanel, Burberry, or McQueen. All of them congratulating themselves for raising money for the hospital. All of them completely ignoring the fact they spent a hundred times more than they raised.

"Nicolette is an accomplished photographer, Birdie. She recently completed a major piece for Time Magazine. Now she's back to take a more active role in the family." Grandmother Dearest is in her element. Regal in a belted powder blue ensemble with matching hat and purse. She's even wearing ridiculous tan loafers with a slight heel. Even at eighty, Grandmama refuses to defy fashion for comfort. She's discreetly leaning on her umbrella for support, so maybe she's not immune to pinchy shoes after all.

Serves her right.

For the hundredth time, I tense to keep myself from fidgeting. The tulle petticoat under this ghastly pea green frock is digging into my thighs and the Peter Pan collar is choking me. If my friends could see me now, they'd die laughing. The dress has a fucking A-line skirt! I can't wait to strip out of this monstrosity.

"Nicolette, you haven't looked at the auction items yet. Aren't those some of your old schoolmates over there? I'm sure you want to catch up with the younger ladies, anyway."

So much for my peace. I've survived the last hour with minimal socializing as Grandmama's companions would rather talk about me than to me. Pushing down a sigh, I delicately lower the petit four back on my plate and blot my crumb-less lips. Polite smile bolted back in place, I excuse myself to weave between the tables to the edge of the room.

A small group of women my age gather at the far end of the table. I recognize two from my boarding school days, but the other is a stranger. Goes to show how long I've avoided this glittering world.

Taking my time, I study each offering. Ok, I'm stalling in the hopes the girls flit back to their seats before I reach them. The first few aren't too bad, spa packages at the Ritz, a meal at the Savoy. The further I wander, the more outlandish the prizes become. A personal reading by a famous children's author. A signed jersey from the hottest footballer.

"Nicolette, I heard you were back. You look well. How long has it been?" The group has opened towards me.

Dammit.

"Lovely to see you, Aubrey. Eloise. Oh, must be a decade, at least." I lift my lips in a long practiced, friendly but reserved line. "I'm sorry, but I don't think we've been introduced. Nicolette Kato-Atherton." I extend my hand to the stranger in a bright pink flowered dress.

"Serena Wentworth." Her palm is limp in mine in an awkward shake. Does she expect me to kiss her hand? Honey blond hair falls to her elbows in perfect waves. Pink-painted lips smile widely, but her blue eyes hold ice.

As I pull back, Eloise catches my eye. "Are you back to stay? John and I absolutely must have you over for dinner." A large diamond twinkles on her hand as she rests it on her swollen belly.

I swallow a twinge of homesickness. Brianna is in her third trimester, herself. If I miss the birth of my goddaughter, I'm going to shank someone. "Back more regularly, anyway. Business keeps me busy traveling."

"Business? You work?" Afternoon Tea Barbie steps back as if working is contagious.

Sarcastic barbs bubble up my throat, threatening to cut Miss Wentworth to bits.

"Oh, Nicolette is a big-time photographer." Turning to me, Aubrey continues, "I follow you on Instagram. It must be amazing wandering all over the world and taking pictures. Even in school, you always had the most dazzling life."

Her tone seems sincere, but a cold sweat drips down my neck all the same.

I may have been infamous at boarding school—missing curfew, photographed with French bad boys—but nothing about my life was dazzling. It was rather lonely. The truth is, I wasn't close with any of the girls. Some, like Aubrey and Eloise, were friendly in passing, providing pleasant but superficial relationships. Most, though, were cruel. Refused to accept a sad girl who was too different. Too American. Too weird. Too scandalous.

"You can't be traveling all the time. Where have you been hiding for your home base?" Eloise's eyes are bright, her smile genuine.

"The states, mostly. New York and Florida."

The prissy blond opens her mouth, but I'm saved by the committee chair calling for everyone to take their seats for the auction winners to be called. Serena glides off to a table with two middle-aged women seated with heads angled close, watching her approach. Aubrey and Eloise say their goodbyes with air kisses and promises of plans soon.

I glance down at the last item, a one-week stay in a private Swedish villa. The current high bid is none other than Miss Serena Wentworth for a thousand pounds. I quickly scrawl my name and double her price.

Am I that petty?

Fuck, yeah, I am.

Gliding back to my seat, the first genuine smile of the day stretch my cheeks. Not even Grandmama's calculating gaze as they call the winners can dim it.

CHAPTER NINE

Pride and Appetites

REGINALD

The amber liquor in my crystal glass sparkles in the low light as I hold back another sigh at the older man's story. Another dull evening with my parent's circle. A circle that feels increasingly like a noose. Would this be less painful with my bride-to-be here? The smokey liquid coats my tongue and my lips smirk against the rim as I think of Nic.

I've always found society a bit too much. Too loud, too tiring, and well, too people-y.

It's all a big game. There are set rules and expectations. Standard moves and strategies for success. Everyone generally agrees on the end goal—money and power. But at what price?

What good is money and titles if you are trapped in a life you didn't choose?

What if your definition of success doesn't comply with standard conventions?

"I say, Ravenscourt. You are quite the spitting image of your grandfather." Mr. Ashcroft would know, they grew up together.

I shake the reflections from my head and try to pick up the threads of the conversation. No sooner do I grasp what Mr. Ashcroft is saying than the trill of a smoky laugh distracts me, bringing my thoughts back to Nic.

There's something effortless about her. As a rule, I don't engage people, but on that plane I couldn't help myself. After that first unexpected laugh she wrestled from me, I wanted more.

Making small talk, even with my family, has always been difficult for me. My palms sweat, my heart beats a little too fast. With Nic though, the words come easy. On the flight and over coffee, the conversation flowed effortlessly. In the time since, I've even found myself texting with her, a meaningless stream of quips and observations.

I may have spoken with her more in the last few days than Daniel.

The butler calls us to the dining room to sit for our meal. Throwing back my scotch, I repress a sigh and follow behind the crowd into the antique room.

A table of dark wood the size of a small swimming pool dominates the room with six chairs on each side. Candlelight flickers across the crystal and china. Intricate white molding twines across powder blue walls and ceiling. A massive modern painting hangs over a marble mantle, providing a much needed pop of this century in the room.

I take the spot with my name scrawled in elegant font and stare down at my setting. Mentally amping up for the verbal dancing ahead. The hair on the back of my neck stands up as I feel eyes on me. From the corner of my eye, pink frothy skirts flutter as a woman takes a seat to my left. No, she's not it, the feeling is coming from further down the table. I search and find sharp green eyes staring at me under even sharper brows.

The woman is a stranger to me, yet there is something familiar in the set of her mouth and angle of her jaw. White hair is artfully curled to frame her face. She must be near Mr. Ashcroft's age, and although her face is lined, she is still quite beautiful. Or she would be if she wasn't sneering at me. Well, as close to sneering as one gets at a social function.

What did I do to earn that sneer?

A huff draws my attention back and I happily shift my focus away from the dragon in silk. My neighbor struggles to control her voluminous skirts as she attempts to pull closer to the table. Decades of conditioning kick in. I rise to my feet and step behind her chair. "Allow me."

She grabs the material and performs some complicated fold movement to shove them under her thighs as I push the chair in further. "Thanks." The lady turns to me with a grateful smile before dropping her rich voice. "I thought this damn dress was going to swallow me whole there for a minute."

Choking on a laugh, I take another look at her face, hazel eyes filled with mirth meet mine. "Nic? What the hell are you wearing?" I try to keep my expression neutral as I scan her more closely. Her striking hair has been pinned into some plaited twist deal. The dress is layers and layers of pink tulle, from her shoulders to her ankles. It's frilly and poofy and completely hides her gorgeous figure. Nothing like her usual style of bold colors and straight lines.

Ok, I may have Googled her.

What? If we're going to sell this marriage, I need to be thorough.

Soft pink lips smile wider. God, even her makeup looks off. "It's really that bad, isn't it? Grandmama Dearest picked it out. I don't think I'll ever be able to look at cotton candy the same way."

I chuckle as a server fills our wine glasses. "Not bad, just not you." Her eyes widen and so does her smile. Leaning in, I continue, "I've never been happier to see someone at one of these things before."

This time she chuckles. "Me, too. Further proof we made the right choice. It is odd that we haven't run into each other before, though."

"My parents usually attend dinner parties, or my brother."

"So anyone but you." There's amusement in her voice, but it doesn't feel like she's laughing at me.

"Most people prefer it that way. You seem to be an exception."

"Aren't I always, though?" She wets her lips and I find myself staring.

"Nicolette." We straighten with a start. I hadn't realized how close we'd drifted together. It mustn't have been too unseemly, because Mrs. Ashcroft continues, all smiles. "So lovely to have you back, dear. You must join us for dinner soon. My grandson is an art collector, and I'm sure you'd hit it off."

A swift flare of jealousy lights through me. Which is completely ridiculous. True, she is my fiancée, but no one knows that yet. There's no ring on her finger and it's not a love match.

I can't seem to help it. Even on the plane, when Nic had joked about picking another candidate, some residual Neanderthal DNA screamed *mine* and wanted to maim men she'd never met.

"Your dinners are always lovely, Mrs. Ashcroft." Nic's smile is polite and the older woman glows under the compliment. My damn male ego happily notes her reply wasn't a yes.

"What a beautiful name," a middle-aged woman across the table speaks up, "and what a beautiful dress."

Nic stiffens slightly next to me, but her expression doesn't change as she politely thanks the woman. Ever the hostess, Mrs. Ashcroft rushes to make introductions. "Oh, Laura, have you not been introduced? Nicolette is Vivienne's granddaughter. She's been abroad for a while, but is back to stay."

"I do so love spending time abroad," the other woman enthuses. "Were you in France? Italy?"

Servers set down the starters.

"America, mostly. Though I do travel much of the time."

"Ah, I was wondering about your accent."

"Nicolette grew up in America, until she came to live with Vivienne," Mrs. Ashcroft explains.

Next to me, Nic's already rigid posture radiates tension. The two matrons don't notice as they continue this obviously sensitive conversation. Without thinking, I shift my hand under the table to grip Nic's fisted hand. It trembles slightly in my grasp before turning to hold my own.

"I'm afraid what little accent I picked up has dulled. That's the price for being a world traveler, I suppose." Nic adopts an innocent expression and both women twitter as if she made a joke. She pats her lips with her napkin, though I haven't seen her lift her fork.

Mrs. Ashcroft is the first to recover. "Nicolette takes the most darling pictures, Laura. You simply must see one."

Laura nods sagely. "It is so important for one to have a hobby."

"It's much more than a hobby." Heads turn towards me at my sharp tone. I swallow and try again. "Nic is an extremely talented photographer. She recently spent a month in New York completing a piece for Time Magazine. Celebrities beg her to take their portraits." Our end of the table is silent, not even a fork can be heard. Slim fingers squeeze my hand.

"Well," Mrs. Ashcroft's smile is a little strained, "it certainly sounds as if you have a fan. Laura, dear, how are the children doing?"

"Thank you," Nic whispers towards me as she pushes the appetizer around her plate, "but you didn't have to do that."

I don't bother to hide that I'm speaking to her, but match her volume. "It's true. Diminishing your career is completely unacceptable. You are very talented, Nic."

An inky brow lifts. "Where have you seen my work?"

"Your website, after we met." And her entire Instagram account, not that I'll admit to it. "What made you choose photography?"

"My father was an artist, so I grew up surrounded by it. We explored every medium together." Her throat flexes and her eyes dim, lost to memory. "When I went off to boarding school, there wasn't much room for paints or easels, but I had a camera."

"And how did you settle on magazine work?"

"There's a truth in photography that other mediums are lacking. A subjectiveness to paint or clay the camera removes. Sure, you can still manipulate the image with software after the fact, but that original will always tell the truth." She finally takes a bite of the appetizer.

"You don't edit your photos?"

She shakes her head slightly as she sips her wine. "I'll do some lighting tweaks. At most, I'll remove something from the background, but my subject remains unaltered."

Her words roll around my head as the starters are whisked away. Our main course arrives and Nic's other dinner partner draws her into a discussion, leaving me to my thoughts.

The truth.

My life is filled with half-truths at best. Polite, meaningless conversations. Image over substance. Every move I make under a magnifying glass, so every move must be carefully made. So much so I must arrange a fake marriage.

The flaky fish turns to rubber in my mouth.

To my left, Nic's smoky laugh sounds, and like a good scotch, it warms my gut.

No, not a fake marriage. Certainly not a love match, but a true partnership built on shared goals and ideals. That has to be a stronger foundation than the fleeting feelings of lust.

Although, I'd challenge you to find someone who didn't desire Nic—even in that ghastly dress.

I breathe a sigh of relief as the final course is served. Having Nic by me has made the dinner infinitely easier, but I'm still looking forward to getting back to my flat. I manage to draw no more unwanted attention. Everyone happily ignores me until the party breaks up.

The guests stand to leave. I pull Nic's chair back for her, then drop my hand to the small of her back. She gives me a wide smile as her candy-colored dress puffs around her, free once more from it's confines. My pulse beats erratically. Unlike the polite expressions of earlier, this smile is real, and just for me. I lead her to the entry for her coat, when Mr. Ashcroft stops us.

"Ravenscourt, my boy, I have some business I'd like to discuss over a scotch."

When I finally arrive home, I'm struck by how silent it is. Normally, the quiet is comforting, but tonight something is missing. I roughly tug at my tie as I stare out the window at the city. Like every night lately, my thoughts turn to Nic. She didn't eat much at dinner—probably too worried about the dress. Without consciously thinking about it, I pull out my phone.

Me

Fancy a burger? I could go for some real food.

Nic

Yes! I know the perfect pub. I'll drop a pin.

My lips curl into a smile as I pad into my closet to change.

CHAPTER TEN

Black Swan

NICOLETTE

I check the time on my phone yet again. She's cutting it a bit close, isn't she? We really must be heading into town for the ballet.

Despite the ice pick width of my heels, my steps eat up the distance of the entryway. The white kitchen doors swing open as I push through to find our housekeeper and cook, Gloria, kneading dough. How many times did I rush in here after school to the same sight?

"Hey Glo, where is Grandmama? We're going to be late."

The older woman smiles as she wipes her brow with the back of her hand. Her wiry curls are more gray than black these days, and her apron is looking tattered. The smile on her face is exactly how I remember, though perhaps also a bit worn. "Oh, honey, she didn't tell you? Madam's taken to bed. I think she overdid it a tad this week. You should go on without her."

My brows pinch as I frown. "Is she alright?" Grandmama has always been a force of nature. When did she start slowing down? "Maybe I should stay and call for a doctor?"

Gloria waves me off. "Don't you dare. She'd want you to still go. You've always loved the ballet."

"Well, if you're certain." I had been looking forward to this all week. The tickets are paid for, it would be a shame to waste them. Leaning in, I plant a kiss on her pillow-soft cheek, the skin softer than velvet. My fingers lash out and steal a piece of pie dough as I dance back towards the door and away from her weak censure. "Make sure you bring her up dinner and some tea. Thanks, Glo."

As I fold myself into the waiting town car, I replay our arrival home last night in my mind. Was Grandmama off even then?

The ride back had been silent, other than a muttered comment about letting anyone out in society these days. In the foyer, Grandmama had stopped, one pump resting on the bottom stair and her gem encrusted hand on the railing. Her eyes were clouded as she turned back to me over her shoulder. "Thank you for attending tonight. I hope the company wasn't overly rude," she'd said.

It had struck me as odd. In the nearly two decades I've danced to my grandmother's tune, I've never heard her apologize for her friends. Not when they cast aspersions on my father's background. Or when they told her to ship me off to boarding school while calling her a saint for taking responsibility for my mother's mistakes.

No, I'm much more used to being humiliated by her circle and then lectured for not apologizing for existing.

A warmth spread in my chest as I noted true concern in the lines of her face. "It was quite alright, Grandmama," I'd said. "Only a couple of uncomfortable moments. Nothing I couldn't handle." I smiled, and she gave a start. Shaking her head, Grandmama made her way gingerly up the stairs.

Was it too slowly? Maybe it's time she slowed down, did less of these events. God help whoever tells Vivienne Atherton that!

Before I can worry too much, the car stops and I alight outside the Royal Opera House. A crowd still mills in the lobby, so I mustn't be overly late. Thank god.

I was only ten when I came to live with my grandmother. In a moment, my entire life changed. I was suddenly thrown into a strange new world of expectations and rules. Grandmama threw me into different activities to mold me into a young lady of her design. The dance lessons were the only ones I didn't hate. I was much too tall and started much too late to have a serious chance at professional ballet, but I still love the art form.

A hard impact hits my shoulder, knocking me off balance. I pitch forward and my heel slips. Why did I have to insist on wearing these toothpicks? Just as I'm convinced I'm about to eat it on the Royal Opera House floor, strong fingers grip my elbow and pull me back upright. Sandalwood tickles my nose and my heart rate, which had slowed, kicks up again.

"Careful there. Someone might think you're stalking me." Gray eyes twinkle in an otherwise placid face.

"Three times in one week? Seriously, how had we never met before?"

Reginald leans in and lowers his voice conspiratorially. "Probably because we both avoid these things."

"Speak for yourself. I never avoid the ballet."

He briefly scans the surrounding area. "Flying solo, today? Or is someone going to smack me for monopolizing your time?"

"No, you are safe from smacking. Grandmama stood me up." A pang of worry twists my stomach.

"You should come sit in my family's box, then."

"Truly, it's alright." I go to step away, but my arm is still firmly in his grasp.

"You just told me you are all by yourself. What kind of gentleman would I be if I abandoned you as well?" His hand releases my elbow and I feel cold. The warmth of his hand returns to my back as he herds me towards the stairs.

The idea of sitting with him is preferable to sitting alone, but the whispers around me are rising. I so do not need a scandal right now. "Bancroft, thank you, but I don't need rescuing."

"Then you can rescue me from a boring evening with my family." His hand caresses my back and I realize I've tensed. "They don't bite, but they're certainly not as amusing as you." His breath tickles my ear as he leans in. "You were going to have to meet them, eventually."

Despite the murmurs that follow us, I relax in Reginald's company. He's looking especially handsome in a black tux. It must be the confidence. Head held high, he navigates the crowds without a care.

In the box, a stately blond woman I can only assume is his mother, already sits. "Reginald, it's about time. What kept you?"

His hand presses more firmly into my back and I lean into it. "Mother, may I introduce Nicolette Kato-Atherton?" She turns with a gasp as she eyes me from head to toe. "Nic, my mother, Penelope Bancroft, the Countess of Silverbrook." There is something familiar about her, but I can't quite put my finger on what. I've probably seen her before at one of the countless events I've attended with Grandmama over the years.

A younger man stands from the seat next to her. His blue eyes perform a similar perusal of my body. "Well, she's certainly not your usual type."

"Monty. People are watching." Countess Silverbrook's tone is lacking any real censure, and Monty's smile grows.

Reginald's hand turns to steel at my back. "Please excuse my brother."

Brother?

I study the man again. He's slightly taller than Reginald, but narrower in the shoulders. Sandy hair sweeps in a perfect wave from his face. There is something similar about the clean-shaven jaw, but where Reginald is sharp lines, his brother is soft edges.

I much prefer the Bancroft brother I got.

The house lights dim, saving me from any further discussion. Reginald guides me to the chair by his mother and sits on my other side. The curtain rises and I am immediately transfixed as the dancers weave their tale. Meddling guardians forcing a marriage. Maidens compelled to transform themselves at the whim of a man. The prince throws down his crossbow and the lovers embrace before the swan princess is drawn away by her curse.

I am still applauding when Reginald leans into me. "You truly do love this, don't you?"

I glance around to realize his mother and brother have slipped out already for intermission. "Yes. There was a lot I hated when I moved here, but the ballet was something new I loved."

"The glitter used to delight me. It felt like a portal to a world from my books. Too late, I learned shards of glass glitter just as well as diamonds." His hand clenches into a fist on the thigh by me. "I'm sorry there wasn't more you loved about this world."

There's something haunted about his eyes as he stares at the curtain. Touched that he let me see this facet of him, unsure if he even realizes it, I rest my hand on his and squeeze slightly. His hand unfurls and twists in mine, entwining our fingers as our eyes meet.

"I was a grieving child, Ren. It was always going to be a big adjustment." I lean forward and he mirrors my motion, meeting me halfway. "Boarding school brought its own fun. As does access to top designers. It's not all bad. The money has its perks, but it comes with…"

"Strings," he finishes for me. His eyes are so clear in that moment, a swirl of hope and frustration passes through them. "Nic, I…"

"Come now, Reginald, are you going to hog the lady all night? You haven't even introduced us properly." My future brother-in-law claims his mother's chair, grabbing my free hand in a farce of good manners. "Montague, but you can call me Monty, Nicolette. Might I say, beauty like yours is wasted on my brother." His lips brush my knuckles, making my skin crawl.

I know Monty's type a mile away. Entitled, spoiled snots who never worked a day in their life or heard the word no. He thinks he's a gift to women and they should line up for the honor of sucking his dick.

Basically, exactly the sort I asked Reginald to weed out of my matches.

My lips tilt up in a sensual smile. It's practiced, but he's too dumb to see the artifice as his eyes darken with interest. "I don't know about that, Mr. Bancroft. I find Reginald's darker coloring more suited to my own. We make quite the pair, don't we, darling?" The back of my hand glides over my chiffon skirts, removing any traces of Monty's touch. My face and body shift closer to Reginald, effectively cutting his brother out.

Satisfaction burns in his eyes as he captures the hand I ripped from his brother's clasp. Reginald's thumb wipes over the offended spot, sending tingles rippling up my arm. He lifts the hand and my breath catches, inspiring a wolfish smile on his lips just before they brush my skin. The entire interaction is wholly different from the similar one mere moments ago.

"I trust your judgment, darling. You are the professional."

"Professional?" Montague butts in.

"As a sought-after photographer, Nic's eye for composition and color is unrivaled." My eyes dip to his lips as he speaks, Monty all but forgotten beside me. Their mother slips back into the box as the lights dim for act three. Reginald's fingers remain wrapped around mine.

On the stage, the ballroom scene plays out. The black swan enters and like the young prince of the tale, I have eyes only for her. The character Odile is painted as a villain, but I've always pitied her.

When your father is an evil, power-hungry sorcerer, what choices do you actually have in life? Better to just go with the flow.

The curtain sets again as the hero rushes off, realizing he proposed to the wrong girl.

"I've never liked this story. So depressing." Monty leans back in his chair.

"I think the lot of them are stupid." My eyes snap to Reginald as he speaks. "What idiot can't tell his own supposed love apart from a stranger?"

"Well," I start, "I think there was a magic spell involved. Plus, the black swan seduces him with her dance."

Dark brows furl over Reginald's eyes. "I don't care if they were identical. If his feelings were so true, he should have known instantly that poor scared girl wasn't Odette."

"Scared girl?" Monty scoffs. "Odile is the original femme fatale, brother."

"You don't see Odile as the villain?" I ask Reginald, ignoring his brother.

"No, Rothbart is the only villain. Odile is another victim, denied a full life just like Odette but without even a Prince Charming for hope."

I smile, his words so like my own thoughts.

"How well can you get to know someone in a day, though?" Monty shatters the moment, continuing as if our side-bar didn't occur. "That should be the moral. Don't marry a man you just met."

Reginald stiffens, perhaps the remarks hitting a little too close to home with our own situation.

I squeeze his hand, still holding mine. "You'd be surprised. You can see an entire person in a moment if you really look." Monty turns to his mother to start a conversation, and Reginald and I sit silently, smiling at each other until the final act begins.

CHAPTER ELEVEN

Mother Has Spoken

REGINALD

As the curtain rises, I try to view the ballet as Nic does. The movement, the symbolism. It is beautiful. The lovers dive into the lake together, preferring to forsake life as they know it rather than be apart.

Marrying someone you just met isn't the folly. It's giving them the power to destroy you.

Or maybe I'm reading too much into things. After all, the couple reunited; the swans are maidens once more, and the sorcerer defeated.

Happy ending, right?

The theater empties and I use the crowd as an excuse to place my hand on Nic's back again. She looks stunning in the black cocktail dress and her long legs are drawing eyes as she walks. The high neck and knee-length skirt shouldn't be this sexy. Everything about the look is modest.

Maybe not everything.

My eyes dip to the black stilettos that glitter with each step. Already tall, the heels put her a couple inches over my height. I don't understand why men complain about tall women. It is fantastic to not have to stoop down to be heard in this crowd.

The outside brings the relief of fresh air, and also a line of waiting town cars. I open the rear door for her, but almost wish she didn't have to go.

She must feel the same way because she pauses and rests her hand on my arm. "Thank you. For tonight."

"You rescued me, remember?" She smiles and I bend to kiss her cheek, then take her hand in mine to help her into the car.

"Reginald. We really need to go." Leave it to my mother to bring me back to reality.

I repress a sigh as I step back, watching Nic drive off. My hand still tingles from hers, my fist clenches and releases at my side. "Ride with us."

This time, the puff of exasperation escapes. Probably would be best not to mention my flat is in the opposite direction of the manor. Mother is clearly uppity about something and it would be better to get the lecture over with.

That's my primary strategy with my parents. Avoid conflict. Just go along with it and do my duty.

I'm forced to sit in the middle, between my mother and brother. Luckily, the luxury automobile is spacious enough that I'm not completely squashed, but it's not a comfortable fit. Foster shoots me a sympathetic wince in the rearview mirror as he pulls away from the curb. The seconds tick on my wristwatch as I wait for my mother to fill the silence. It doesn't take long.

"Honestly, Reginald. That's who you thought was appropriate for this family?" Mother's blue eyes glitter with disappointment.

"She meets all the requirements Father gave to the matchmaker. What do you find so objectionable about Nic?"

An unladylike snort sounds as her coral lips curl. "That mutt is unworthy of being a countess."

"Excuse me?" I grit out between my teeth. A rushing sound rises in my ears.

"Why, Mummy, I never took you for a racist." Monty sounds bored as he stares out the window.

Mother's eyes widen as they dart between my brother and me. "Racist? No. I'm talking about her social pedigree. Genevieve Atherton may have been a respected debutante in our society, but that was before she ran off to America with some penniless artist. It was quite the scandal. Abigail filled me in on the whole thing at intermission."

I try to calm my stilted breaths. At least Mother is just a run-of-the-mill snob.

"Genevieve didn't even marry the man! They lived some bohemian lifestyle before they got themselves killed, leaving poor Vivienne to care for a child, and so soon after her husband passed, too. The girl was wild, by all accounts. Quite the reputation at boarding school—always breaking curfew and flitting around with a fast crowd."

"Come now, Mummy, you can't believe every piece of gossip Lady Wentworth tells you." Montague is the last person I expected to provide aid. "Give the girl a chance. She seemed lovely when I spoke to her. Intelligent and cultured. She's also very beautiful."

"I never said she wasn't." Mother pouts sullenly and lifts her chin. "Abigail may occasionally exaggerate, but it still stands that she doesn't have the finest lineage. I still don't understand why you can't marry Serena."

"Enough, Mother. Your concerns are noted. Father said I can choose my bride, and I choose Nic. End of discussion."

The rest of the car ride is tense but thankfully short. I shuffle across the seat and hold the door open for my mother. She glides up the front steps of my childhood home without a farewell or even a backwards glance. I wish I could say it was only because she's miffed at me, but this is fairly standard with my family. Montague is already long gone.

I collapse back in the car with a groan and rake my fingers through my hair, completely upending the careful styling.

"It'll be ok, sir." Foster darts concerned looks back at me in the mirror.

"How can you know that? You haven't met her."

"Maybe not, but I know you. If you feel strongly enough to push back on your mother, the girl must be pretty special." I merely grunt and sink further into the leather seats. "That matchmaker had excellent credentials and a thorough vetting process. More importantly, if the lady survived everything your mother described, she's a formidable woman indeed. Sounds like the perfect partner for you."

"Thanks, Foster." I slip into a tense silence. Too burdened with my own thoughts to enjoy our usual banter.

My mind is still clouded as I walk aimlessly around my flat. Am I making a mistake? Would it be simpler to find another bride? It would certainly be easier if my mother approved of my wife.

I immediately shake the thought away as I pour a scotch and stare out over the city lights. A deal is a deal. I gave Nic my word, and I'm not going back on that now. It wouldn't be right.

Besides, the only person Mother would approve of is Serena, and that isn't happening. She doesn't meet Father's only requirement.

The Wentworths are a respectable family, to be sure—titled, connected, but no liquid capital to be spoken of. Serena was always looking for me to bankroll the lifestyle she felt entitled to, and I, the naïve idiot, was only too happy to comply.

A vibration in my pocket breaks my unhappy reminiscence. My pulse leaps at the name on the screen, but when I read the message, my entire focus shifts.

Nic

> Can I come over? Looks like I need a rescue after all.

Where is she? Who is she with? I can't imagine a situation Nic would need rescuing. Well, besides our marriage deal.

Me

> Are you ok? Do you want me to get you?

My heart pounds as those three dots appear and disappear. Moments feel like hours and the scotch turns to lead in my stomach. My knuckles whiten around the phone.

Nic

> I can't stay here tonight. Already in a cab. Be there in 30 min.

She's safe. My pulse slows, but gives a strange blip when her words sink in. She's staying over. I wouldn't call my flat messy, but it's not exactly company ready. The exhaustion of a minute ago dissolves, and I use the sudden spurt of adrenaline to speed clean while I wait for her arrival.

CHAPTER TWELVE

The Devil Doesn't Bargain

NICOLETTE

I'm lightly humming the ballet with a smile as I let myself into my grandmother's house and start up the sweeping staircase. It was a nice surprise sitting with Reginald. His family, not so much, but the view from their box more than made up for any chilliness. It'll be fine. None of us were prepared for the meet-the-family type situation. The undercurrent was certainly strange, though. What was with his mother interrupting our goodbye?

There's some tea there I'd love to hear.

Reginald will have to tell me before the wedding. The last thing we need is for me to step in some drama with his mother if we want this to be successful. I'm surprised they were all together. Nothing he's said ever gave the impression they were close. I'd actually gotten the feeling he was a bit of a black sheep. Like me.

"Nicolette."

I start, then spot the lone figure standing on the landing dressed in a satin bathrobe, a silk wrap over her thick hair, looking every inch the queen of this house.

"Grandmama, are you feeling better? Gloria mentioned you were ill."

"What were you thinking?"

"Pardon?"

"At the ballet tonight."

My mind blanks. What did I do? What could I possibly have done this time? My heel glitters in the low light as I ascend the stairs. Is that it? Did my outfit offend her? My stomach dips. Was I not supposed to go to the ballet alone? "I thought you wanted me to go without you? Did you want me to stay? I'm sorry."

"What were you thinking sitting with that man?"

What man? I was only with... "Bancroft?"

"Don't say his name." All color drains from her already pale cheeks, and I climb the steps faster.

"What?" I can't have heard her correctly.

"Never speak that name. He is a cad and you are not to associate with him."

A cad? First, who uses that word anymore? Second, Bancroft? Reginald Bancroft? The same man who ignored a thirsty flight attendant? The one who was so outraged on my behalf by a thoughtless hostess? We can't be talking about the same Bancroft.

That's it.

"It was unfortunate Montague was there, but I assure you, I was only there for Reginald. I told you I met someone, it was Reginald."

"No. We'll find you a more appropriate match."

More appropriate? What does that mean? Then it hits me. She doesn't think I'm worthy of him. All these years she's pushed for me to marry someone of good social standing. Some part of me thought it was out of misguided concern for me, but that wasn't it at all. Oh no, she doesn't want to be embarrassed by me marrying low, but she doesn't think I'm good enough to be a countess.

"I'm not interested in another match. Reginald has asked me to marry him and I've agreed."

"End it."

My heart drops to my stomach like a stone. I gave Reginald my word. My father always said a person of honor sticks to a promise once made. I've let this woman take everything from me. My home, my style, my freedom—and yet it's not enough, she wants to take my honor, too.

"No, a deal is a deal. Reginald meets all my requirements for a husband. He satisfies all the provisions you set for my trust. We will wed before my birthday."

"So it's all about the money. I guess you are a perfect match, then, if that's all you care about."

My foot falls heavily on the step below as I falter, her words striking a physical blow. My eyes burn, but I refuse to let the tears fall. "I care about integrity. We made a deal, and I will hold up my end."

"The Devil doesn't bargain, Nicolette. You'll regret this, and I won't be here to save you when you do." Her threat still echoes through the foyer as she sweeps off to her bedroom.

A loud crack shakes me. I'm not entirely sure if it's her door or my heart, but I know something is irrevocably broken.

I need to get out of here.

My stilettos carry me to my room. I throw my suitcase on the bed. One hand pulls up the car service app while the other wildly struggles with the bag zipper as I rush to open it. Drawers squeak and hangers squeal as I blindly grab clothes to pack.

"Letty, stop." My childhood nickname brings me to a halt. Soft hand cups my arm, turning me towards Gloria. "Shh. Hush now, love. It'll be ok." Her fingers caress my cheek, tears glistening on the tips. When did I start crying? I never cry.

"I don't think it will this time," I whisper.

Her eyes hold so much emotion as I slip past the older woman into the bathroom. Bottles clack against the marble sink as I sweep products into a waiting bag. Shoving my usual clothes in my smallest case, I leave the glittering silks and chiffon dresses scattered across the room. A nauseating cloud of pastels that reminds me I don't fit the mold here. "I'm sorry about the mess, Glo."

She pulls me in for a hug. I might not be able to rest my head on her ample chest anymore, but the gesture is still comforting. "Don't worry about it. Let me know where you are and I'll send you whatever's left behind."

Her soft cheek tickles my lips as I give her a kiss before leaving in silence. The black car is already waiting in the circular drive as I walk down the stairs. I collapse onto the back seat, my camera bag beside me. The driver's eyebrow lifts in the mirror. He probably rarely sees women in rhinestone stilettos carrying backpacks.

Time has been blowing up my phone asking me to come back to New York for another shoot. I'll stay at the Savoy tonight and fly out tomorrow. Suddenly, the thought of a night alone in a hotel doesn't excite me. It's not like that hasn't been my norm for years.

Tonight, though, I don't want to be alone. Debating for only a second, I text Reginald and then update my destination in the app.

We pull up in front of a modern apartment building in a trendy part of town. The doorman rushes to grab my bag, but I wave him off, making my own way to the elevator and up to Reginald's unit. The door opens as I raise my hand to knock.

"Nic? I was heading down to meet you. Come on in." He grabs the suitcase handle from me and wheels it further into the space, allowing me to look my fill.

The residence is sparse but well-furnished in dark woods and leather. The London skyline glitters through the floor-length windows. I lower my camera bag to the sofa as I admire the view.

"Drink?" Reginald gestures towards the kitchen-dining combo. He's still dressed for the ballet, minus the jacket. A loosened tie and unbuttoned collar expose the planes of his throat. His bare feet softly pad across the polished floor. A sexy, strangely intimate look on the man.

He really is handsome. A girl could do a lot worse in a husband.

Two crystal glasses and a decanter appear on the dining table as I approach. He places one before an empty chair, sinking into the space beside it with his own amber liquid. I grip the cold glass, but remain standing, fitfully running my finger across the raised design.

For once, I'm out of things to say. It was my idea to come here, but now I don't know what I want.

"Everything ok?" The concern in his voice sounds sincere. I merely shrug a single shoulder—I'm not sure anything will be ok. "You want to talk about it?"

That is the last thing I want right now. My hair grazes my cheek as I shake my head. "No. Tonight, I don't want to think about anything at all." My untouched tumbler clacks against the wooden table.

In two long strides, I reach Reginald and straddle him in the chair. His hands close around my waist, but he doesn't move. Neither to pull me closer or push me away.

CHAPTER THIRTEEN

Cold Feet

NICOLETTE

His gray eyes reveal nothing as I lean in. Mine drop to his mouth and then return to his steely gaze. Slowly, I press into him until my lips are a whisper away from his.

Reginald's fingers squeeze my waist gently as his head leans back. "What are you doing, Nic?"

I play with the ends of his hair by his nape, the dark strands are soft as I run my nails through them. "I told you. I don't want to think right now. Who better to lose myself in than my fiancé?" I let go, and move as if to stand. "Or should I find someone else?"

With a growl, his hands slide to my ass and his fingers dig in with bruising strength. The darkening of his eyes is the only warning before his lips descend—firm, unrelenting, as they mold mine as he wishes.

My grip returns to his soft hair, and my head tilts to match his kiss. Tongues dance and teeth gnash as we fight for dominance. His cock hardens, pressing my core through his slacks. I rock my hips, teasing us both with the friction.

With a single fluid motion, Reginald stands, still gripping my ass, and lays me down on the nearby table. Thick fingers trail up my legs, finding the hem of my dress and pushing it to my waist, revealing my black thong. "I think I can manage." His words rumble against my stomach as he peppers kisses along my skin.

His teeth catch on the thin strap of silk. The sharp contact warring with the gentle touch. The rough material scrapes down my thighs and calves until finally it comes free from my heels. Reginald stares down at me like a man studying a painting, still fully dressed.

Now that won't do.

Sitting up, I reach for his bow tie, still draped at his open collar. One large hand grips both of mine. "Not so fast." The scrap of cloth is deftly tied around my wrists which he pin above my head on the table as lays across me.

I pout, lifting my head and trying to catch his lips again. "But I want to see too." My hips tilt to press against him.

Without moving his lower body, Reginald quickly unbuttons his crisp white shirt. He shrugs it off and tosses it carelessly to the floor. The low lights from the kitchen cast his bare chest in a warm glow. Dark hair peppers his trunk, thinning to a line that disappears into his slacks. His eyes burn as he lowers his mouth to my thigh. The faintest of stubble grazes my sensitive skin as his lips blaze a trail to my hip.

Reginald kneels, putting himself at eye level with my weeping center. It's been months since I've experienced an orgasm that didn't require batteries. If I have an itch, I scratch it, but the Time shoot has kept me too busy to prowl the nightlife scene.

His tongue laps me from crack to clit in a torturous lick, causing all thoughts to still. Perfect.

This is exactly what I needed.

My back arches and I moan as he settles between my thighs. He grips my legs, spreading them wider apart for better access. His broad thumbs stroke the sides of my mound, simultaneously massaging and opening me further. Teasing licks leave me panting. My tied hands arc down as I reach for his silky hair, only to whimper as he lifts his head.

Reginald lays along my length as he pins my wrists back to the table above my head. "Stay." His fingers take their time, trailing over my body as he reclaims his spot. Without warning, he thrusts his tongue fully into my pussy. It takes all of my concentration to keep still. Once again, his fingers dig into my thighs as he pushes them impossibly wider. Just as I grow used to the rhythm, his lips surround my clit, sucking gently, before fucking me again with his tongue.

"Please. Oh, god, Ren." My head thrashes against the table, begging for release. One hand releases my thigh so he can rub my sensitive nub as his tongue continues its assault. Within moments, light bursts behind my eyes as my body spasms in ecstasy with a guttural moan.

His low voice rumbles in my ear, "Good girl."

I never thought I had a praise kink, but fuck me, I orgasm again at the words. The crinkle of foil is the only sound besides our ragged breaths. The blunt end of his crown butts my sensitive pussy, making me cry out.

"Ready, Princess?" Reginald stands over me, one hand cupping my hip, the other gripping his girth.

Licking my lips, I nod my head.

"Say the words," he commands, rubbing the thick head against my clit, teasing me.

"Fuck me, Reginald. Now." I wiggle my hips, trying to guide him where I need him.

"As you wish." He slams into me. We both groan as we adjust. My pussy quivers around his length as it gently stretches me. His lips skirt my neck and nibble on my pulse point as he thrusts in quick bursts.

I'm lost to the sensations as another orgasm builds. He stands, his fingers dig into my ass and he pulls me to the edge of the table. He grips my ankles and places them by his shoulders, my stilettos glitter by his ears. His stormy eyes hold me hostage as his hips snap against mine.

"So good, Princess." His fingers find my clit and circle the sensitive nub. The clap of our bodies and the rumble of our moans echo through the cavernous room. He grips my ankle, eyes closed, turns his head, kissing the tender skin on the inner bone.

A spasm ripples through me. My breathing quickens. "I'm close. Oh, god. Reginald." My third orgasm rockets through me. A second later, he joins me, thrusting deep as he swells and empties himself.

My eyes shut on a contented sigh. I lay completely still as he leaves me to take care of the condom. Gentle tugs urge me to a seated position. The tie falls from my wrists as firm hands lift me from the table and set me on my feet.

Reginald pads across the floor, then stops in the opening of a hallway. Looking over his shoulder, he only says, "Coming?"

I follow him into a large bedroom. More dark wood furniture fills the space. Reginald pulls a T-shirt from a drawer and lays it on the navy blue duvet, then heads into the adjoining bathroom. I slip out of my dress, carefully laying it over the back of a chair before slipping the shirt on. The cotton is soft, obviously well-worn, and carries the faintest hint of sandalwood.

"I left a toothbrush for you by the sink." Reginald leans against the doorframe, his hands buried deep in his trouser pockets. His eyes burn as they sweep over my bare legs.

"Thanks," I say as I pass him, with a little extra sway to my hips. He's already under the covers when I return; the opposite side turned down. The sheets are smooth and cool as I slip under the heavy blanket.

He clicks off his bedside lamp, plunging the room into darkness.

"Goodnight." It comes out in a whisper, but I know he hears me. A warm arm snakes around my waist, dragging my body against his. "Oh," I start, "I wasn't expecting cuddling. It's fine."

The arm turns to steel around me. "Shut up, Nic." I'm somehow pulled deeper into him as his warmer body engulfs mine. My feet brush his shins, shocking a hissing breath from him.

"Sorry." I quickly pull my legs away. "My feet are always cold. Circulation issues."

His foot hooks my ankle and sandwiches my icy toes between his legs. "Did I tell you to move them?" I smile into the dark. Bossy Reginald is kind of fun. "Admit I was right."

I turn to look over my shoulder, our mouths inches apart in the darkness. "Right about what?"

"Sex isn't an issue." His voice rumbles deeper. "Or do I need to prove my point again?" His cock twitches where it nestles along the curve of my ass.

"Tempting, but I need to fly back to New York in the morning. Time has been calling and I can't put it off any longer."

"How long are you going to be there?" Is that a slight whine?

"A week, but then I need to be back in Florida. I'm going to be an auntie any day now."

He grunts behind me. "When am I going to see you again?"

I flick through my schedule in my mind. There's no hurry to come back to London as long as I'm on the outs with Grandmama. Would Reginald come to Florida?

Oh god, the girls! I have to tell them first.

My stomach twists. For some reason, the idea of sharing Reginald with others bothers me. I like this bubble we're in. The romance may be fake, but enjoying his company is not. If only we could get away together. Then it hits me.

"Fancy a mini-break to Sweden?"

September

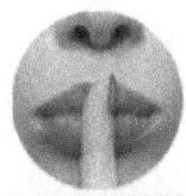

Whisper Wire

There may be an alliance afoot! Although historically, the tall, dark, and delicious earl-in-waiting has been the gloomy foil to his charismatic little brother, Viscount Ravenscourt and Miss Nicolette Atherton were seen at multiple events together—including the London Opera where Miss A sat in the Silverbrook family box. She was even introduced to the countess.

Faithful readers have shared a number of candid photos of the two around town—there's even a shot of Miss A leaving Lord R's flat quite EARLY in the morning. She quickly flittered back to New York, leaving our most eligible bachelor all alone. If the pictures of him on Bond Street with a little De Beer shopping bag are any indication, she certainly made an impression!

Whatever could be next for these two? Hurry back to London, Miss A, life in town is so much more lively when you are here!
Keep sending in your tips and photos!

TTFN
Wendy

CHAPTER FOURTEEN

Market Research

REGINALD

Daniel drones on about sales projections and running expenses on the screen in front of me. I try my best to pay attention, but I'll confess my mind is elsewhere. The velvet box on the desk by my monitor might as well be blinking for how easily it draws my eye back to it again and again.

"The website placeholder is up and I've secured coordinating social accounts across the major platforms. Following is slowly growing but we might need some help there. I finally understand why marketing is a full-time job."

"Yeah. Well, if we need it." My thumb strokes the soft plush covering before popping the box open, revealing the three-carat diamond ring nestled within. One look at the pear-shaped solitaire and I knew I'd found the right one. Funny, I'd always expected when the day had come, I'd either feel sick with nerves or a heavy sense of duty. Browsing the ring counter, I'd felt neither—simply a sureness of purpose—and maybe a mild excitement to see Nic's reaction.

Nic.

"I was thinking we could hire strippers for the marketing," Daniel says.

It's been two weeks since Nic flew back to New York for work. The agreement was to stay out of each other's way when we're apart, but I'm finding that term harder to uphold than I'd expected.

She'd looked so sad that last night.

"We can spray paint our website on them and let them pole dance."

My cheeks tighten as a grin lifts my lip. Well, she wasn't sad when she left. I had definitely been right about our sexual compatibility. I've never had a first time be that natural and easy. And so damn hot. That night has provided sufficient inspiration for weeks.

"Of course, I'm talking about male strippers, so we have the most real estate to work with. Our slogan can go right on their cocks."

"Wait, what?" My head jerks up and a grinning Daniel regains my attention. "What the hell are you on about?"

"I knew you weren't really listening. So are you finally going to tell me what's up? The gossip columns are going crazy, saying you're getting engaged." With a sigh, I sink in my chair. Without a word, I hold up the open ring box to the camera. "Holy shit, so it's true? Weren't you very much single when we went to the bar a month ago? Why the rush?"

"The earl has declared it is time."

"Bancroft..."

"It was always going to happen, Dan. I'm actually pretty lucky as far as society matches go—I genuinely like Nic. Plus she fully supports us launching 'Elysium' and giving me all the time and space needed to see this through. Not sure many earl-approved brides could say the same."

"Ok, so the earl approves. What about your Mother?" I wince. "That bad, huh? Is that why you bought a new ring instead of using the Silverbrook diamond?"

"How the hell do you know what the family ring looks like? Or that it exists at all?"

His ears redden on the screen. "Whisper Wire may have posted about it."

"Dammit, Dan. Whisper Wire? Seriously?"

"I follow them for market research—they are the biggest competitor if we want to launch a social magazine. The fact her current posts are about my friend just makes me read them closer." I grunt at him as I toss back the rest of my now cold tea. "So when are you planning to pop the question?"

"Technically speaking, we're already engaged, but I'm going to give her the ring this weekend. We're taking a holiday in Sweden." Daniel chokes on his pop. "What now?"

"You're taking a holiday?" His eyes are wide as he dabs at his shirt.

"Yes. Why is that so shocking?"

"Not sure I've ever seen you take a holiday. Business or family trips, sure, but not one for fun. I can't wait to meet this woman." My best friend grins at me like an idiot.

I grit my teeth, picturing the two of them together. "I'll have the laptop with me if you need me, but you won't."

"Just make sure you draft that editorial first."

I nod as I end the call. Dan's making something out of nothing. In a lot of ways, this is also a family trip—she is going to be my wife after all. I can't be changing because of Nic. That's ridiculous.

The sun is setting when the villa finally comes into view. It's a picturesque cabin dusted by snow—like something from a storybook. Cheery lights glitter in the windows telling me Nic has already arrived, and from the steady puffs of smoke from the chimney, lit a fire. My phone buzzes, lighting up with a text from the woman herself.

Nic

Front door's open, just come in.

I shake my head. What is she thinking, leaving the door unlocked while staying there all alone? Though, I will admit there are no other houses as far as the eye can see and the cab hasn't passed another car for miles.

The air outside sends a chill through me. I shrug deeper into my coat, happy I'd thought to pull my winter jacket from storage.

This week has been brutal. My mother has summoned me every day. When lectures didn't change my mind, she tried tears, and then a parade of young women at various luncheons, teas, and dinners. I haven't had a single meal in peace since Nic left.

My heart skips a beat as I climb the porch steps. I don't want to admit how much I've been looking forward to this holiday together. Not only because I want to bury myself between her thighs again—which I most certainly do—but because I can't forget the sadness in her that night. She'd slipped out the next morning before I woke. I was half convinced it was all a dream until I found her heels and dress in my closet.

I still don't know what happened that drove her into my arms that night. We've texted, but between her photoshoot and my mother's hysterics, it's been stilted. She's hiding something from me. Then again, I haven't been fully upfront with her either.

Nic doesn't know I agreed to marry her for the money.

That's not quite right. I agreed to marry Nic because I genuinely like her. My father is letting me marry her specifically for the money.

This weekend alone will be the perfect opportunity to talk without interruptions or distractions. I'll lay it all on the table. She'll understand, I know it. Then we can have a nice dinner. I'll surprise her with the ring, and then we can announce the proposal publicly.

What if she's offended?

Maybe, I'll soften her up with the ring first. It'll all be fine.

CHAPTER FIFTEEN

Two Truths and a Lie

NICOLETTE

The occasional pop of the fire is the only sound as I lounge on the couch with my book. After two weeks in the city, the silence almost makes me think I'm going deaf. The auction had listed this place as a villa, but it's more like a cabin. Not that it isn't completely charming.

The A-frame house is fully surrounded by a wooden porch and set up on stilts in a small glen. A coal stove provides needed warmth against the chill northern air. Blond wood planks on the floors, walls, and ceiling complete the rustic look. Large glass windows with delightful green trim and gorgeous fabric sashes offset any ruggedness and give a very fairy tale ambiance. A modest but well-stocked kitchen shares the first floor with a narrow dining table and the built-in couch I'm currently lying on. Above sits a loft, divided into two bedrooms which look out over the living space. The only closing door is the postage stamp sized bathroom. Everywhere, lanterns and strings of fairy lights are sprinkled, providing low mood light.

Headlights flash, sending shadows dancing across the wall. He's here. Footsteps echo off the wooden steps moments before the doorknob turns. Reginald walks in, dropping a leather duffle and shrugging out of a thick peacoat. I place my bookmark and tuck my feet under my ass to make room for him.

He sinks into the cushion with a slight sigh, his head falling back.

"Long flight?"

"More like a long week."

His gray cable-knit sweater hugs his torso and highlights his coloring. This might be the most informal I've seen my husband-to-be. He toes off his loafers and props his argyle covered feet on the coffee table. My lips quirk at the pattern and the dress slacks. So much for casual. How the man can stand to fly in those restricting clothes, I can't understand.

"Business or family drama?" I ask.

Reginald's hand scrubs down his face before his elbow falls to the arm of the couch. He braces his temple on his upturned fist and turns tired eyes in my direction. Smudges darken the skin under those steely eyes. His straight lips look extra firm.

I find myself wishing I could do something to lighten his load. Which is a very off-brand thought.

This world doesn't value softness or kindness. It is not designed to reward the timid. Nice is seen as weak. No one will go out of their way for you. Everyone is out only for themselves. They may seem to be your friend, but only as long as your goals are aligned. As soon as it's you or them, they'll choose them every time.

Don't get me wrong. I'd do anything for Bree or Anna. Kidney, liver—just not the whole heart. Even from them there are pieces of myself I keep locked away and safe. If they needed something, they only need to ask. Even that damn leprechaun and lumbering marine they've decided to marry. A shock reverberates through me at the realization that Reginald has joined that list of people I'd go to war for. And in only a month of knowing each other.

"The business is going fine, at least for now. My mother, however..." He lets out another sigh.

Creases form at the sides of his eyes. There's something he doesn't want to say. The unspoken truth hangs like a weight in the air.

Anna once asked me how I pick apart people. I don't actually know how to explain it. There's this current around people which shifts with their mood. I guess the mystics would call it your aura. It's not literal colors radiating around a person, more a vibe or resonance. Something felt rather than seen—like the wind. It can tell you a lot about a person's motivations, their character in general, but by watching for the shifts, you can tell if someone is holding back or full-out lying. I sort through the strings until I find the right one to tug.

Why would his mother be unhappy? Is it the business? There's this double standard in our circles about working. Men are expected to continue growing the family's wealth for future generations, but not with their own hands. They're supposed to delegate, invest, sponsor. Then use their leisure time, sprinkling their time and money on the less fortunate like benevolent figures. It's supposed to show how generous they are, but unquestionably it's about proving how rich they are. They have so much they can give swaths of it away, no problem.

Something tells me it's not the business though. I would bet Countess Silverbrook doesn't even know about it. Which is its own tantalizing puzzle to pick apart. So if it's not Reginald's work, that only leaves...

"She doesn't approve of me, does she?"

His hand drops as he jerks upright and winces. Bingo. "It's not really you, Nic. She had her own vision of my future and is having trouble letting go."

I nod absently. "I get it."

"I'm sorry." He rests his hand on my thigh. The warmth seeping through my thick leggings and spreading through me.

Sitting up, I rest my hand on his. "Actually, in some ways, I'm relieved."

"However so?" His brows pinch in genuine confusion.

"My grandmother isn't exactly a fan of yours, either." I wrinkle my nose in sympathy at his shocked look.

"Does she know about my title? I thought that's what every grandmother wanted?"

I chuckle and pat his hand. "Not this one. In fact, she disapproves so much that we can count on one less seat at the wedding."

"I'm sorry, Nic. This isn't what you signed up for. If you want to end this now, I'll completely understand," he says, his expression guarded.

Is that what I want? It would make things easier with my grandmother, but then what? How would I find someone else who meets her impossible and apparently changing standards? No. My word is good for something. I made a deal and I'm going to stick to it.

"You're not getting rid of me that easily. I'm still in this."

His lips lift in the barest hint of a grin. I wonder, again, what a full smile would look like on this handsome, broody man. "In that case, I have something for you." Still holding my hand, he reaches with the other to grab a box out of his messenger bag. With the push of a button and a slight snick, the velvet parts to reveal a stunning ring. "It reminded me of you. Classic but unique. I hope you like it."

"It's beautiful." Lifting my hand, he gently slips the ring on my finger. It fits perfectly. "Wow." This feels real now. How does a hunk of metal and carbon change so much?

"I guess we should start planning the wedding, only a couple of months to go. Have you thought of a location yet?"

"Not really. I might like to throw a good party, but a society event of the year isn't exactly my thing. Honestly, I was going to let my grandmother plan it, but that was before…" I slump down, nibbling at some dry skin on my lip.

Reginald squeezes my thigh. "I'd ask my mother to arrange it, but…"

"Yea… Don't you wish we could just elope? Skip right over all the pomp and ceremony?"

A gleam appears in his eye. "Well, why can't we?"

"Are you serious?"

He grabs his phone from his pocket and starts typing away. "There's a national park nearby that has an elopement package. We only need to get a license in town tomorrow. It's completely legal."

I slump back against the cushions. "Well, it would certainly make things easier. I'd have full access to my trust fund."

His face falls. "Dammit. We haven't signed the prenup yet."

The oh-so-dramatic prenuptial agreement, if anything, is a reminder that marriages started as business deals, a literal contract detailing out the aftermath of a divorce. I'm an heiress, of course I've always known I'd need one. Thank god this isn't an actual love match, and that Reginald is from a similar background or this could have been awkward.

Wait, that's it, he's from a similar background.

"We don't need it." I wave him off.

"What?" Reginald's eyes widen.

"You're going to be a fucking earl. Half of our combined can't be that much off."

"Nic…" he looks pained. "About that…"

"Look, I'm not planning on a divorce anyway, are you?"

"Well, no…"

"Then it doesn't matter. Come on, show me the options."

Ok, yeah, maybe I was looking forward to shopping for some haute couture wedding gown. How often do you have the excuse for a dress that costs as much as a car if not to marry a peer of the realm? Overall, this marriage is a means to an end. No need to drag it out. Especially when the biggest advantage the both of us are getting is maintaining our freedom.

"Nic, I really think you should reconsider."

When he doesn't move to show me his phone, I continue. "Divorce happens because of hurt feelings and too much emotion. We're going into this with open eyes and a solid basis for an alliance. I'm not worried. Plus, didn't you need to find a place in New York? This will make paperwork so much easier."

"Are you sure this is what you want?"

"Absolutely." A sense of calmness comes over me as I realize I honestly mean it.

CHAPTER SIXTEEN

Dancing Lights

REGINALD

The sky is bright as the lights dance overhead. The air is crisp but the blankets and mulled wine stave off the cold as I sit out on the deck of the cottage with my wife.

My wife.

Strange how those two words fill me with a sense of satisfaction. It must be knowing that I did something my own way. Getting married wasn't my choice, but I got to decide exactly who, exactly when, exactly where.

When I was a boy, I imagined my wedding—odd as it may seem. I was dragged to so many society weddings with my parents, like an accessory, rather than their son. They were all precisely the same. Extravagant trappings, pretentious food, free-flowing alcohol. It was about the clothes, the display, the spectacle, not about the actual couple.

I hated it, swore when it was my time, it would be different—I was nine and didn't know any better.

The ceremony was brief—very no nonsense, like my bride. But the setting was ethereal, surrounded by the natural beauty of the park. Not a single piece of tulle or silk in sight. It was like something from Tolkien. I felt as if I were the heroic knight. That I'd come to this magical glen for a secret marriage to the fair princess before riding off to war.

Fantastical thoughts. Silly even. But our wedding was as close to my childhood dream as possible.

Nic splays across the Adirondack chair next to mine. Wrapped in a blanket, knees slung over the wooden arm, she looks deep in thought but happy. Her diamond catches the fairy lights outside the cabin as she cups her mug of wine.

A flash of guilt sinks in my gut. I should have told her about the money first, like I'd planned. I could say I tried, but I certainly could have tried harder. When Nic got excited, I let myself be swept up in it.

Divorce isn't an option for me. I mean, legally, sure, but I made a vow to Nic and I plan to hold to it.

I'd be an idiot to let her walk away. Her charm and easy nature perfectly balance my lack of personality. She is a much more strategic choice for me and the Bancroft line than any title-hungry social climber my parents would have chosen.

Someday my mother will see that.

What I mean to say, is that I do not expect a situation where the prenup would have been necessary, but I still wish I'd given Nic all the information before she made her choice. Starting a marriage with a lie, even a lie of omission, is an ominous beginning.

"So, my lord. How's married life so far?" My lower stomach clenches. I've always hated it, but I could get used to hearing her say it.

"No complaints so far. But maybe give it a couple more hours."

"Rude!" She flails one long limb to kick my shin.

I chuckle. "You knew that about me. Buyer's remorse, already, Lady Ravenscourt?"

She shakes her head. "Is that what I am now? Lady Ravenscourt?"

"Technically, the Viscountess Ravenscourt, or informally simply Lady Ravenscourt. When my father dies, it'll be Countess Silverbrook. Does it really matter to you?"

"No." Her cheeks darken in the dim light. "Actually, I was thinking about keeping my maiden name if it's all the same."

"Because of your business?"

"That, but mostly for my father. His last name is all I have left of him. I've recovered some of my mother's childhood items from my grandmother's house, but everything of my father's was lost."

"I'm so sorry. You were young when they died, right?" She nods. "What was it like with them?"

"It was amazing as a kid. I told you my father was an artist. He worked on these incredibly detailed animations for a studio in America. Mom stayed home with me and taught the neighborhood kids piano lessons for some extra money. I remember the house was always full of laughter and music. And so much color."

That sounds amazing. What would it be like to grow up in a family like that? With warmth and shared interest? "That must have been quite the shock after you moved in with your grandmother."

She gives a dry snort. "You could say that. She wasted no time shipping me off to boarding school. Boy, was I a regular fish out of water! It was Paris, though, so I found an artist community like back home. I made it work."

"I can see that. You're incredibly strong, Nic. It's one of the first things I noticed about you."

She looks away, her shoulders hunching. I have no idea what I said to upset her, but I find myself wishing I could take the hurt in her eyes away. I scan our surroundings as I search for something to say to restore the lighter mood. Overhead, the *aurora borealis* dances, giving me inspiration.

"Aren't the lights beautiful? There are many legends about them. Some say they are a bad omen, others the tails of giant arctic foxes. Most say they are souls. My favorite myth is Norse in origin. King Oden sent his Valkyries to lead fallen warriors to Valhalla. The lights are reflections off the armor of these fierce women."

"Why is that your favorite?" I glance at her, but her eyes focus on the flowing colors above.

"It's a story about your worth being defined by your actions, not by the clothes you wear or the things you buy. Rushing headfirst into battle wasn't enough, you had to earn it with your honor. Every man had an equal chance of being found worthy."

"That does sound nice." With a slight gasp, she springs to her feet and runs towards the door.

"Nic? What is it?" Carefully putting down my mug, I rise to follow her, only for her to appear again in the doorway. "Everything alright?"

"You inspired me to take a picture. Stand right there by the railing." She fusses with the back of the camera. Wadding up her blanket, she sets it as a cushion on the chair and balances the camera with the lens pointing up at me. With the click of a button, she rushes over to me, grabbing my shoulders and positioning me how she wants. "Hold still, it's only a ten-second timer."

Her eyes reflect the green lights above as I stare into them. Steam rises between us from our breath in the cool night air. She's so beautiful. I lean forward... CLICK.

Rocking back, she dives for the camera and checks the screen, tsking. "Not quite right. Your jacket is too bulky. Take it off." She's pulling her chunky sweater off as well.

"Pardon? Do you realize how cold it is out here? Do you want me to freeze my bits off? It is technically our wedding night—and you want me to spend it with frozen balls."

"Oh, shut up," she laughs, "I'll warm up your balls when we get inside." Her sultry voice is enough to ensure blood flow stays squarely in my groin, avoiding any further danger of sperm-cicles. "This one is going to capture longer. You need to hold completely still."

She squints at me, then up at the sky. Her eyes widen and she rushes back inside, reappearing with a tiny stool which she places in front of me. Flitting back to her camera, she double-checks the angle, clicks the button, then rushes to step up.

I look up at her, waiting for directions.

She bends at the waist until her lips are a whisper's breath away. Her hands hover just beyond my shoulders, like she's frozen, reaching for me.

I stare into her eyes. Everything else fades away as emotions dance like the lights overhead. My breaths come faster, the steam rising again. We don't move, don't say a word. Simply stand inches apart, staring into each other's eyes as the seconds drone on. I've never felt something so intimate before. No parts of our bodies are touching, but I can sense her within me. A feeling in my chest builds, one I have no name for.

CLICK.

Nic blinks, then dives for the camera to check the shot. She's beaming as she looks up at me. "There, that wasn't so bad, was it?" She slinks up to me all sex and confidence. "Come on, hubby, a promise is a promise. Let's go defrost the family jewels."

Breaking the News

NICOLETTE

The air is oppressive as I wait for the yellow door to open. My hair sticks to my forehead, but my arms are too full to fix it. How is it still this hot in September? The muggy Florida climate is a harsh contrast to the crisp autumn in New York and downright chilly nights in Sweden.

Where the fuck is everyone?

I juggle the packages as I fumble for my phone to text for help, the door finally opens to reveal Bree's husband, Colin. "About time, Irish. Where's my niece? I was ready to lean on the buzzer." Blessed air conditioning caresses my face as I push past the man and into the cool interior of the stylish home.

"I need to have the damn thing deactivated. The doorbell sets off the dog. When he barks, the baby cries, and when she cries, I think I might too." He wipes a hand down his face, his typical dimples notably absent. Dark circles accentuate his green eyes and brown hair. Still stupidly handsome, but obviously tired.

"Here." I shove a package full of Toblerone, English biscuits, and strong tea into his hands. As he studies the contents of the box, his signature dimples finally make an appearance.

Though I'll never admit it to Colin or the girls, I like the Irishman who earned my best friend's heart. When he first showed up, I'd been suspicious, but he's proven himself since then.

Not waiting for a reply—I have a reputation to maintain after all—I sweep down the hall to the living room. On the sofa, Bree sits in a pair of yoga pants and tank top, her wavy, chestnut hair loosely secured in a bun on her head. In her lap rests an open Tupperware container, and she's shoveling forkfuls of pasta into her mouth and moaning between bites.

After depositing the other gifts on the floor, I turn to my friend. "Christ, Bree, careful of the white couch!" I lean down, kiss her cheek, and squeeze her shoulder.

Waving a fork at my words, Bree answers around another mouthful. "Kid's already puked on it twice. Not to mention the blowout diapers." She shudders, then returns to her food. "White couches and babies don't mix."

I flop onto the cushion next to her, leaning in to steal a hunk of sausage, only to have my hand stabbed. Laughing, I retreat. "How's it going?"

"Good." She chews and looks thoughtful. Like her husband, Bree sports dark circles under her eyes, but where Colin looked stressed, she radiates serenity. "She nurses every two hours like clockwork, so I spend most of my day right here."

"So if you're here, and Colin got the door, where's the baby?"

"Anna's changing her diaper so I can eat. While Riley supervises, of course."

I glance around, only now realizing that Bree's typical shadow, her Yorkie-mix dog, Riley, is absent. "How's Riley taking the change? I know you were nervous since he's so attached."

She chuckles as she finishes another bite. "I think he's more loyal to her than me at this point. He watches her sleep, even tried to climb into the bassinet with her!" Bree huffs and spears another sausage.

"All clean." Anna emerges from the hallway, a wriggling pink blanket clutched to her chest. Bree moves to put her food down but Anna walks right past her to the recliner. "You, eat. I'll cuddle baby Nora for a bit and give you a rest."

I walk over for a better view. Nestled in the soft blush fabric rests a head haloed in rusty curls. Giant eyes, still a newborn blue, gaze up at Anna—who is making the most ridiculous faces. Nora's little face scrunches up and her lips spread open, showing a gummy smile and a single divot on her chubby cheek.

"Look, she's smiling!" Anna says between silly expressions.

"Pretty sure that's just gas. Don't you have a million little brothers? Why don't you know that?" At my voice, the baby rolls her head and gives me a wide-eyed, open mouth stare. Sooty lashes blink slowly. Oh, this girl is going to be a heartbreaker.

Watching Irish lose his shit is going to be fantastic.

As if my thoughts summon him, Colin moves to stand behind his wife, resting a hand on her shoulder.

"Nice work, Irish."

"Don't look at me, it was all Bree."

"Oh, I know. I meant good job not fucking it up."

Bree squeezes her husband's hand and looks up at him adoringly. "I think she's our best product launch yet."

As the Chief Product Officer and Chief Technology Officer for a top research and development firm, they'd know all about launches. They met when she was a project manager and he was an engineer exec working to launch a groundbreaking new device. Now they practically run the entire innovation branch of the company.

"Tell that to the gray hair coming in." He shudders. "What can I get you, *a ghrá*?"

"I'm good. Go get some rest." She holds her hand up as he opens his mouth. "The girls are here if I need anything. I'm taking a well-earned break between feedings. You should take one too."

"Well, if you're sure. I could go for a shower and a nap. Love you." He drops a kiss to his wife's head.

"Love you, too," Anna and I say in unison as Colin heads towards the master bedroom shaking his head.

I flop back onto the couch next to Bree and grip her leg affectionately. "You did it. Look at you, mom. How are you doing, honestly?"

She takes a deep breath, sinking further into the cushions. "It's the hardest, most exhausting thing I've ever done, but I just love her so much." Her large cobalt eyes shimmer with tears. With a sniff and hard blink, Bree visibly pushes back the emotion. "So, what's new with the two of you? How were your trips?"

"Oh my gracious," Anna says, she slowly rocks in the recliner with Nora tucked against her chest, "baby cuddles are so addictive. Wait until you smell her head, Nic." She buries her nose in the soft russet curls.

"You look like a crack addict, Anna."

"You know what, if they could bottle this scent, we could solve the drug crisis."

This is normally when I'd throw a pillow at her, but she's saved by the precious shield.

"So Anna, how was your brother's wedding? You said you had news in the group chat—I assume you and David made up? Was I right about the makeup sex?" I arch a brow at her.

At the beginning of the summer, Anna's childhood sweetheart showed up out of the blue. It was a shock for everyone—especially us, since she'd never mentioned him before—but he seemed determined to win her back. The two were pretty cute together until he broke up with her a few weeks ago. Anna figured out he did it in some misguided assumption her life was better off without him and stormed back home to Georgia to knock some sense into him over Labor Day weekend.

Bree laughs as she swaps her empty Tupperware for a giant water bottle.

A slight blush colors Anna's cheeks. "Everything worked out, the wedding was beautiful, and..." she holds up her left hand where a diamond solitaire glitters in the sunlight streaming through the glass windows. "We're engaged!"

"Engaged? Isn't it a little soon?" Bree's brows pinch in concern.

"Says the woman who moved her boyfriend in with her on day one," I snark at Bree before turning back to Anna. "You have to admit, broken up to engaged in a weekend sounds a bit fast."

"Bree married Colin less than a year after meeting, and you agreed to marry some guy you met on an airplane. Seems to be going pretty swell for the both of you." Anna whisper-yells as she holds the sleeping baby, but sarcasm drips heavily from her tone.

My eyes ping back and forth between my friends as my gut sinks. The ring on my own finger, so far unnoticed, weighs a thousand pounds. "About that. We eloped in Sweden."

The air is oppressive as I wait for the yellow door to open. My hair sticks to my forehead, but my arms are too full to fix it. How is it still this hot in September? The muggy Florida climate is a harsh contrast to the crisp autumn in New York and downright chilly nights in Sweden.

Where the fuck is everyone?

I juggle the packages as I fumble for my phone to text for help, the door finally opens to reveal Bree's husband, Colin. "About time, Irish. Where's my niece? I was ready to lean on the buzzer." Blessed air conditioning caresses my face as I push past the man and into the cool interior of the stylish home.

"I need to have the damn thing deactivated. The doorbell sets off the dog. When he barks, the baby cries, and when she cries, I think I might too." He wipes a hand down his face, his typical dimples notably absent. Dark circles accentuate his green eyes and brown hair. Still stupidly handsome, but obviously tired.

"Here." I shove a package full of Toblerone, English biscuits, and strong tea into his hands. As he studies the contents of the box, his signature dimples finally make an appearance.

Though I'll never admit it to Colin or the girls, I like the Irishman who earned my best friend's heart. When he first showed up, I'd been suspicious, but he's proven himself since then.

Not waiting for a reply—I have a reputation to maintain after all—I sweep down the hall to the living room. On the sofa, Bree sits in a pair of yoga pants and tank top, her wavy, chestnut hair loosely secured in a bun on her head. In her lap rests an open Tupperware container, and she's shoveling forkfuls of pasta into her mouth and moaning between bites.

After depositing the other gifts on the floor, I turn to my friend. "Christ, Bree, careful of the white couch!" I lean down, kiss her cheek, and squeeze her shoulder.

Waving a fork at my words, Bree answers around another mouthful. "Kid's already puked on it twice. Not to mention the blowout diapers." She shudders, then returns to her food. "White couches and babies don't mix."

I flop onto the cushion next to her, leaning in to steal a hunk of sausage, only to have my hand stabbed. Laughing, I retreat. "How's it going?"

"Good." She chews and looks thoughtful. Like her husband, Bree sports dark circles under her eyes, but where Colin looked stressed, she radiates serenity. "She nurses every two hours like clockwork, so I spend most of my day right here."

"So if you're here, and Colin got the door, where's the baby?"

"Anna's changing her diaper so I can eat. While Riley supervises, of course."

I glance around, only now realizing that Bree's typical shadow, her Yorkie-mix dog, Riley, is absent. "How's Riley taking the change? I know you were nervous since he's so attached."

She chuckles as she finishes another bite. "I think he's more loyal to her than me at this point. He watches her sleep, even tried to climb into the bassinet with her!" Bree huffs and spears another sausage.

"All clean." Anna emerges from the hallway, a wriggling pink blanket clutched to her chest. Bree moves to put her food down but Anna walks right past her to the recliner. "You, eat. I'll cuddle baby Nora for a bit and give you a rest."

I walk over for a better view. Nestled in the soft blush fabric rests a head haloed in rusty curls. Giant eyes, still a newborn blue, gaze up at Anna—who is making the most ridiculous faces. Nora's little face scrunches up and her lips spread open, showing a gummy smile and a single divot on her chubby cheek.

"Look, she's smiling!" Anna says between silly expressions.

"Pretty sure that's just gas. Don't you have a million little brothers? Why don't you know that?" At my voice, the baby rolls her head and gives me a wide-eyed, open mouth stare. Sooty lashes blink slowly. Oh, this girl is going to be a heartbreaker.

Watching Irish lose his shit is going to be fantastic.

As if my thoughts summon him, Colin moves to stand behind his wife, resting a hand on her shoulder.

"Nice work, Irish."

"Don't look at me, it was all Bree."

"Oh, I know. I meant good job not fucking it up."

Bree squeezes her husband's hand and looks up at him adoringly. "I think she's our best product launch yet."

As the Chief Product Officer and Chief Technology Officer for a top research and development firm, they'd know all about launches. They met when she was a project manager and he was an engineer exec working to launch a groundbreaking new device. Now they practically run the entire innovation branch of the company.

"Tell that to the gray hair coming in." He shudders. "What can I get you, *a ghrá*?"

"I'm good. Go get some rest." She holds her hand up as he opens his mouth. "The girls are here if I need anything. I'm taking a well-earned break between feedings. You should take one too."

"Well, if you're sure. I could go for a shower and a nap. Love you." He drops a kiss to his wife's head.

"Love you, too," Anna and I say in unison as Colin heads towards the master bedroom shaking his head.

I flop back onto the couch next to Bree and grip her leg affectionately. "You did it. Look at you, mom. How are you doing, honestly?"

She takes a deep breath, sinking further into the cushions. "It's the hardest, most exhausting thing I've ever done, but I just love her so much." Her large cobalt eyes shimmer with tears. With a sniff and hard blink, Bree visibly pushes back the emotion. "So, what's new with the two of you? How were your trips?"

"Oh my gracious," Anna says, she slowly rocks in the recliner with Nora tucked against her chest, "baby cuddles are so addictive. Wait until you smell her head, Nic." She buries her nose in the soft russet curls.

"You look like a crack addict, Anna."

"You know what, if they could bottle this scent, we could solve the drug crisis."

This is normally when I'd throw a pillow at her, but she's saved by the precious shield.

"So Anna, how was your brother's wedding? You said you had news in the group chat—I assume you and David made up? Was I right about the makeup sex?" I arch a brow at her.

At the beginning of the summer, Anna's childhood sweetheart showed up out of the blue. It was a shock for everyone—especially us, since she'd never mentioned him before—but he seemed determined to win her back. The two were pretty cute together until he broke up with her a few weeks ago. Anna figured out he did it in some misguided assumption her life was better off without him and stormed back home to Georgia to knock some sense into him over Labor Day weekend.

Bree laughs as she swaps her empty Tupperware for a giant water bottle.

A slight blush colors Anna's cheeks. "Everything worked out, the wedding was beautiful, and..." she holds up her left hand where a diamond solitaire glitters in the sunlight streaming through the glass windows. "We're engaged!"

"Engaged? Isn't it a little soon?" Bree's brows pinch in concern.

"Says the woman who moved her boyfriend in with her on day one," I snark at Bree before turning back to Anna. "You have to admit, broken up to engaged in a weekend sounds a bit fast."

"Bree married Colin less than a year after meeting, and you agreed to marry some guy you met on an airplane. Seems to be going pretty swell for the both of you." Anna whisper-yells as she holds the sleeping baby, but sarcasm drips heavily from her tone.

My eyes ping back and forth between my friends as my gut sinks. The ring on my own finger, so far unnoticed, weighs a thousand pounds. "About that. We eloped in Sweden."

CHAPTER EIGHTEEN

Lord Grumpypants

NICOLETTE

"What the actual fuck?" Bree shouts.

Simultaneously, Anna yells, "You did what?"

The baby startles awake with a wail, disturbing the tiny dog standing sentry by the recliner. Riley barks at Anna like she's not the same woman who's snuck him treats for years, and a crashing sound from the bedroom rounds out the chaos.

With skilled hands, Bree takes Nora and soothes her as she settles in to nurse while Riley jumps onto the couch between us. The screeching has thankfully ended, but both of my best friends are glaring at me as if they'd like to continue the yelling.

A very wet Colin comes flying down the hall in only a very small towel. "What happened? Is everyone ok?"

Bree keeps her glare on me as she dryly answers her husband. "Shocking news. Anna's engaged and Nic's married."

He tenses, resembling one of the marble statues I used to sketch at the Louvre—all the way down to the killer abs. His eyes dart around the room, confirming his family is safe and trying to process his wife's words. The confusion is too delightful to resist.

"I see you haven't developed a dad bod yet, Irish."

Green eyes widen before dropping down. His hand flexes on the edge of the towel, holding it more securely. "I need pants for this." He retreats back down the hall, still muttering, "and a coffee—with some whiskey in it."

"Aren't you the kettle calling the pot black? Giving me grief over getting engaged to a man I've known twenty years when you up and married a man you've known five minutes."

"More like seven weeks," I correct. Anna glares at me. "My situation is completely different."

"Oh, because you're a socialite and I'm a country bumpkin?"

Ouch.

The money has always been this weight around my neck. Sure, it opened doors, and I never worried about paying my bills, but it also made it hard to trust people. I always thought Anna and Bree were different, that they saw me and not my bank balance. Sure, they teased me about my pretentious name and galas, but at the end of the day I thought we were friends. Maybe it was about the money.

"No, Annabel, because we both went through extensive background checks and a matchmaker." I swallow back a lump in my throat and the heat in Anna's eyes simmers a bit. "I'm happy you and David worked it out. Truly, I didn't mean anything by it. Just don't rush the fun part."

Bree snorts. "Says the woman who's been married—what?—a week?"

"We were going to be married in a couple months, anyway. Neither of us wanted to go through the big society event."

"Oh, I bet your grandmother loved that." Bree's words send a pang through my chest. I still haven't spoken to her since I left England almost a month ago."

"I'm sorry, Nic." Anna sighs. "Maybe I'm sad we weren't there for your big day, and another part of me is sad you don't get a love story like us."

"A platonic partnership was always the plan, Anna, and that's ok. I don't want some epic love story like those books. What Reginald and I have is a partnership built on mutual needs and goals. In families like ours, that is what you need to survive."

"Sounds so cold when you say it like that."

"Marriage has been business a lot longer than it's been emotion. I may not be madly in love with him, but I enjoy our time together," both in and out of the bedroom. "Seriously, these matchmakers know what they are doing."

"Well, ok then. Where is this ideal husband of yours tonight? When do we meet him?" Bree shifts Nora to her shoulder for a burping.

"He's in New York for work and looking for an apartment for us."

Anna's brows pinch in confusion. "I thought you already had a place in the city?"

I force a smile as I answer. "Technically, my grandmother owns it. Figured we should buy our own home."

We've shared everything since we met in college, but we've all had secrets buried from before. My family has always been a topic I've avoided with the girls. When I escaped to college, I threw my all into living as normal a life as possible. When you're running on borrowed time, you make every second count. My friends didn't even know about the trust fund until long after we'd met.

"Where does a future earl buy property in New York, anyway?"

The front door opening saves me from having to reply. "Who's that?" I ask.

Colin appears, now fully dressed. "I called in reinforcements. Sounded like we needed to celebrate."

A giant bearded man enters the room, his biceps bulge as he carries five boxes of pizza and six-pack of beer. He stops in the living room doorway, eyes darting around the women staring at him. "What? You said not to ring the doorbell." He lowers the bundles to the coffee table, then sits on the floor at Anna's feet, leaning back against her as they smile at each other.

Scooping his daughter up to his chest, Colin rocks the baby as he stands by his wife. Bree grins up at them as her dog crawls into her lap.

My friends are so happy and settled in their lives here.

I've never felt more like a fifth wheel in my life. My heart aches as I watch them all together. "I'll go grab some plates and napkins." Without waiting for a reply, I dart into the kitchen to settle myself.

A vibration in my pocket breaks my self-pity.

Reginald

Hey what do you think of this one?

I click the link he sent, finding a three-bedroom residence in Chelsea. It's an older apartment building renovated into townhouses. A pretty perfect blending of classic and modern.

That looks perfect. Book a showing. If it's half this nice, put in an offer. Cash. Fast close.

Reginald

Will do. How's it going with your friends?

Great.

Reginald

I'm glad. :)

The three dots dance at the bottom of the phone and I gnaw my lip.

Reginald

So what's your schedule like in October? Will you be in New York?

The truth is, I'm free as a bird. I'd planned to stay in Friendship Springs for the next few weeks—help out with the baby, hang out with Anna. But everyone's fallen into a routine while I've been gone. Laughter floats to me from the living room, making me wonder if they'd even miss me.

I could be… what do you have in mind?

Reginald

There's going to be a new flat to decorate, and I'm rubbish at that stuff

Do you forget I've seen your place?

Reginald

> I paid someone to do that. Why pay money when I married an artist?

My stomach gives a little flip.

Reginald

> Do I need to remind you of points 3 and 4 of our deal? Joint space means joint work and you owe me a week here, anyway.

Me

> I'll be there as fast as you find us a place.

Reginald

> Deal. Don't bother unpacking, Princess.

My teeth dig into my lip and I can't stop the smile at the last line. I shouldn't like the nickname, a delicate flower in a fluffy gown is the farthest thing from who I am, but there's just something about it.

"Princess, huh?"

With a half gasp, I whirl, smacking Colin squarely in the jaw.

"Ow!"

"Don't sneak up on a city girl!"

He rubs his face, but the damn leprechaun grins at me, mischief clear in his green eyes. "That the new husband? If he calls you *Princess* what do you call him? My Lord?" His eyes narrow at my silence. "No, that's too simple. It's gotta be something more specific. Lord Grumpypants? Discount Darcy? Am I close?"

I glare at him. "I usually call him by his name: Reginald. Occasionally, Ren."

Colin's face slackens. "I don't get it. You have nicknames for everyone. Irish, Soldier Boy, Deputy-Do-Right, Pretty Boy…"

My cheeks heat. He's not wrong. The truth is, I haven't been able to think of one—though that Lord Grumpypants isn't half bad. Flippant nicknames feel wrong with Reginald. "Well, he hates his name, so there's that."

His intelligent green eyes study my face, seeing too fucking much, because that cocky grin slowly spreads on his tired face. Damn dimple and all. "Sure. This'll be grand." He grabs a stack of plates and leaves.

Fuck.

October

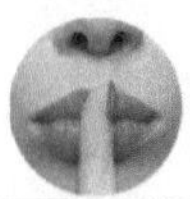 **Whisper Wire**   ○ ○ ○

In a twist even I didn't see coming, our most eligible bachelor and bachelorette are now married… to each other! Completely unfair to the rest of us, but hats off to finding a loophole.

The couple eloped in a picturesque ceremony during a mini-holiday in Sweden some time last month. The event was photographed by the bride herself who posted the selfies this week. Public records show the purchase of a Manhattan townhouse in the couple's names. Whatever could be the reason for this speedy union? And why the need to move so far away? The new Lady Ravenscourt has multiple properties in America, but surely a peer of the realm needs to stay within his earldom.

The representatives for the Bancroft and Atherton families declined to comment.

Here's hoping we have ex-pats in New York who can report back! No way this is the end of the story.

TTFN
Wendy

CHAPTER NINETEEN

Unpacking

NICOLETTE

I glance up at the white brick exterior of my new townhouse. Adjusting my camera bag higher on my shoulder, and take a last deep breath before stepping up to the front door. A pang echoes through me at the thought of leaving my old apartment behind. It's been my home-away-from-home for so long. And yeah, the doorman and million dollar view were fantastic. This will be fine. Good, even. The property belonged to my grandmother, I'm married now and need my own place.

If my life has taught me anything, it's that you have to move forward. The world is going to keep moving around you, if you are ready or not. So hold the fuck on and try to enjoy the ride.

My shiny new key slips into the lock and the door opens silently. "Honey, I'm home," I call. The strains of classical music float faintly from somewhere above. Exposed brick along the exterior walls gives the space an old-world feel that strangely fits with the gray walls and dark wood floors.

I drop my bag on the gray leather sofa, which dominates the main area. It's also the only furniture in the room. Floor to ceiling built-in bookcases already filled with books flank the long wall of the room and large windows overlook a rear terrace.

There are no other furnishings on the main floor. Where has Reginald been eating? The kitchen, if you can call a handful of cabinets and miniature appliances a kitchen, would make Anna cry. Good thing neither Reginald nor I actually cook.

At least I don't think he does. Probably something I should learn about my new husband.

Where the fuck is my new husband?

I follow the strains of the piano back to the front and climb the staircase. Two rooms open from the landing and the sound gets louder. I approach the larger room, pausing in the doorway. Where the first floor was sparse, this room is fully furnished with a small table, file cabinets, and hanging TV.

Reginald sits scowling at his laptop. He's dressed formally but has undone the top button of his shirt. His hair is tousled like he's been pulling on it.

"Knock, knock."

His head jerks up, eyes widening before he looks down at his watch. "Dammit, I was going to meet you downstairs. What do you think?"

"I think we need to go furniture shopping."

His lips quiver like he might smile. "I told you I wasn't shopping without you."

"Great find, hubby. It's even better than the video tour you gave me. I like it. Work giving you trouble?"

"Yes. No." He sighs and leans back in his chair, massaging his brow. "Work is going well. Social media response is promising. The team works really hard, and it's paying off."

"But?"

"I want to build morale a bit. Show my appreciation for everyone's dedication. I've been searching for ideas for hours." He scoffs and shifts the laptop slightly. On the screen are lists of tourist locations and group tours.

"Why don't we throw a party here? Halloween is only a couple of weeks away."

"Halloween party?"

"Yeah, I know it's not as big in England, but it's a whole thing here. It'll be fun. I'll help. What are society wives for?" I flutter my eyelashes at him, which gets a chuckle. "Now go change. We have unpacking to do."

I walk over to the other bedroom to inspect my new studio. The space is smaller, but has a built-in bookshelf by the windows. Moving boxes stack neatly along the long wall.

Cracking my neck, I stand in the center when I feel Reginald approach. I turn to see him better and my breath catches at the sight. He is wearing a white T-shirt and plain gray sweatpants, loose enough to skim his hips and thighs, but tight enough to hint at what lies beneath. Honestly, he'd make a remarkable Christian Gray. My fingers itch for a camera.

Ducking his head slightly, he runs a hand through his hair, leaving it more disheveled, the motion as out of place for him as the casual clothes. "What?"

"I was starting to wonder if you owned anything other than a suit."

"Very funny. I wasn't sure how you'd like the room set up, and perhaps a little afraid to touch any of your equipment."

"It's fine. I'm pretty particular about my organization, anyway. I'll open and point, and you carry."

Together, we work through the boxes. Props, lenses, and light gels go in labeled bins in the walk-in closet. Backdrops pile neatly along the wall, and I make a mental note to add a rack to my shopping list. Lights, tripods, bouncers, and defusers similarly stack against the far wall. My table abuts the windows to take advantage of the natural light.

It is smaller than my old space, but it's cozy. I could see myself working here.

"What's in these?" Reginald asks as he steps up to the wooden crates I've left untouched.

"Oh no, that's..." Too late. He already has the top off and has pulled out a framed print from the box. The photo shows a vivid sunset of pink, purple, and blue reflected over a river with white lightning cracking overhead. "Nothing," I finish lamely.

"Is this yours?"

I nod, but he ignores me as he pulls out the next. This one is an ocean pier in forced perspective that seems to travel on for miles, with a citrine and cerulean sky above. A black-and-white photograph of a gargoyle statue emerges next, followed by brightly painted buildings with a street musician framed by a wrought-iron gate. The final is a high contrast black-and-white photograph of the Royal Opera House, the bright lights reflecting on the wet cobblestones.

"These are beautiful." He turns to me with awe in his eyes. "Are they for a show?"

"No." I shift uncomfortably and flick my nail with my finger. "They were up at Pop when we first opened to fill the space. Soon after, I started curating local artists to display and sell their pieces as another revenue stream for the restaurant, and these have sat here since."

My art has always been something of a touchy topic.

For years, my grandmother told me it was only a hobby and wouldn't amount to anything. I know I'm good at capturing the essence of a person or object for a magazine. That's not art though. I simply capture what is already there, not create something formative. Something emotional. My camera lets other people shine, but it's not for me to shine.

The girls have never understood. But they're not really artists.

Sure, Anna is a culinary genius and creates the most delectable and visually appealing treats. Brianna can appreciate the mathematical side of ratios and balance. But neither of them understands color and composition.

Reginald reverently replaces all except the last back into the crate. The opera house he lifts and strides out of the room carrying it.

"Where are you going with that?" Even with my long legs, I have to struggle to catch up as he climbs the stairs two at a time to the third floor. The entire level is a master bedroom. A king-sized bed sits center, a small lounge area tucked in the corner, but the main attraction is the glass slider leading out to a private rooftop terrace.

Undeterred, Reginald places the frame on the mattress and then walks to what is presumably a closet.

"Hey, Joseph Pulitzer, what the fuck are you doing?"

"Looking for a hammer."

"Why?"

"I'm hanging your picture up."

A burst of warmth shocks through my system. He actually likes them. Enough to want to hang them in our bedroom. He wasn't saying it to be nice. Then again, have I ever seen Reginald do something just to be nice since I met him?

"First, you need special hardware for that." His shoulders deflate. "Second, it's after eleven. Let's order a pizza and put on a show. We can pick up the wire hangers when we go furniture shopping tomorrow."

At the word "pizza," his stomach growls. An adorable blush stains his cheeks and a small smile tugs at his firm lips. I launch the delivery app and reorder my go-to pizza while he hops in the shower, then we settle in on the couch with my laptop to watch one of my favorite sitcoms and debate furniture placement. The clock strikes one as we crawl into the massive bed side by side, too tired to do anything but drift off.

It's a completely uneventful night full of a normalcy I've never known before. So different from my typical NYC nights chasing excitement. Maybe I was actually trying to escape loneliness, because this simple night at home with my husband is the best I've had in a long time. And that thought is terrifying. One best left alone. Tonight I've done enough unpacking.

CHAPTER TWENTY

Dark Knight

REGINALD

My fingers fly over the keyboard as I try to type the last few sentences of the article. It's silly. We don't have a publication date. Hell, we don't even have a theme for the magazine, but I feel behind. There's this driving need within me to do something, write something down, but this frustrating blockage of words and ideas has me in a choke hold.

The door to my office opens and Nic floats in. She's covered in skin-tight leather from neck to stiletto boot. She glares at me with one black tipped hand on her hip. "Why aren't you dressed yet? They'll be here any minute!"

I look down at my black suit, crisp white shirt, and gray tie. "I am dressed."

She throws up her hands and stalks closer to my desk until she can sweep those gorgeous hazel eyes over my body. My cock twitches at the attention. Down, boy. There isn't time, and a quickie is never enough with this woman.

"That is not a costume."

"I didn't agree to wear one."

"It's Halloween, for fuck's sake! It's assumed." We square off, matching scowls warring with each other. The doorbell rings downstairs, and Nic gives in with a frustrated screech. She stomps around to lean over me and shuffle through my desk. She's practically laying across my lap, her firm ass perfectly positioned for me to admire in the form-fitting outfit. My hand clenches and releases in an attempt to hold back from grabbing the tasty treat laid out before me.

Nic leans further into the drawer, her breasts grazing my arm. Another flash of desire rushes to my cock, now at half mast. Just as I'm about to give in and grab her, guests be damned, she stands up with a triumphant cry. Spinning back to the table, she scrawls something onto a piece of paper. Before I can catch a peek, she grabs my hand and hauls me downstairs to meet our guests.

In the entryway, Nic grips my lapels, tugging me closer. My eyes drop to her ruby red lips and I lean in. A sharp smack on my chest stops me short, and I realize she's smoothing my jacket, not pulling me in for a kiss.

The last couple of weeks have been comfortable living with Nic. Shockingly so.

We've fallen into an easy routine. I learned early that she's not a morning person, so I slip from our room and head to the gym. On my way back, I grab breakfast and coffee from her favorite cafe. The smell usually draws her to the kitchen, sleepy and adorably rumpled. We'll both spend the day working on our own things, but always let the other know if we have a meeting. A late dinner and some TV before settling into bed.

It's downright domestic. Unlike anything I've experienced. And so much like those sitcoms she likes that I often forget it's a business arrangement. At best, we're friendly roommates who happen to have sex. Fucking hot sex. Probably the best sex of my life. But I can't forget there are boundaries.

Shaking myself, I open the door to reveal Daniel in a red and white striped shirt, jeans, and a beanie with his usual black-framed glasses. "What the fuck are you wearing?"

"A costume, asshole. It's a Halloween party!"

"Told you." Nic steps up next to me and taps me with her shoulder.

Daniel quirks a dark brow at me as he scans my outfit. "What are you supposed to be?" he asks.

I move to reply, but Nic interrupts me. "He's batman." She points to my chest.

"I'm not batman," I start, then follow her finger to find a label which reads, "My name is Bruce Wayne." I chuckle as I shut the door behind Daniel. She got me.

Quickly, more of our staff arrives, and the party moves into full swing. There's laughter and chatter. This is exactly what I was hoping for, and it's all thanks to Nic.

I scan the crowd and see her by the fireplace, speaking with our marketing director, Tyra Milligan. The younger woman is talking animatedly, her dark hands sweeping towards the photograph hanging over the mantle.

It took some convincing, but Nic's work is displayed in every room of the apartment. After a number of glasses of champagne, and orgasms, I even got her to show me more of her portfolio and agree to make additional prints. That first week here we spent hours combing the city for furnishings. I thought it would be torture, but I'm quickly learning anything with Nic is going to be fun.

I slowly approach the pair, picking up the strains of the conversation.

"This photo is stunning—I've seen a lot of nature shots, but this is so unique."

"That's one of Nic's," I proudly share.

"You took this?"

Nic is strangely still next to me, as if the charming hostess I always see has frozen. She did the same thing when I first brought up the prints as well. "All the photographs are hers."

Daniel slides up next to me, following our eyes to the image silently.

Tyra's eyes widen. "The perspective you've chosen is genius. I feel like I've been transported to some secret world."

"Thank you. I photograph for magazines, portraits mostly. These are a little hobby. Bancroft found them in my studio and insisted we hang them up."

"All the photographs are yours?" Daniel asks. Nic nods curtly. "I've seen your catalog work, especially the Kenzo shots. You're good, but Tyra's right, these are special. If you are interested in showing them, my friend owns a gallery in SoHo. I'd be happy to make an introduction."

"I'll think about it." That Colgate smile appears on her lips. The same one she used at the awkward dinner party. What is it about her photographs that make Nic so uncomfortable? They're fucking amazing.

I've grown up surrounded by art. From Picasso to Monet, I've seen them, studied them. Museum galas, gallery events. None of them ever affected me the way her work does. It's raw, emotional, personal. I will get to the bottom of this, but for now, I'll cut her a break and lead the subject away.

"Have you seen the view from the terrace? Let me grab you a drink on the way."

"I'd kill to have access to a photographer like you for the magazine."

Dammit, Tyra didn't take the bait.

"I'd be happy to help out when you prepare the first edition. Sign a waiver or something." Nic excuses herself before Tyra can launch into another enthusiastic monologue.

The rest of the party continues without further incident. Daniel even manages to coax a real smile and chuckle from Nic as he helps clean up the abandoned bottles and cups. Not for the first time, I envy his easy air. Blue blood not withstanding, charming is not a word anyone would use to describe me. Broody and cold are more likely. No, we are as opposite as can be. I'll never know why he decided to adopt me in university, but I'll always be grateful.

When it's just the two of us, I follow Nic up the stairs to our bedroom. My eyes are glued to the rounded swell of her ass as her hips sway in front of me with each step. Perfectly at eye level. Watching her in that damn cat suit has been torture all night.

She strides across the room towards her walk-in closet. Hand already reaching for the zipper at her chest.

"What do you think you're doing?"

She twirls on one ice pick heel. "Changing."

I stare into her eyes as I prowl forward and a deep sense of satisfaction rises as the hazel orbs darken with desire. We may not have been a love match, but there is no denying this mutual attraction.

My hand lashes out, branding her hips and pulling her against me. She gasps as my rock-hard cock digs into her front. "I've been picturing all the nasty, depraved things I would do to you in this outfit for hours. You will not be changing out of it that quickly."

She bites her lip and purrs like the goddamn sex kitten she's dressed as. "Well, it's too bad you're Bruce Wayne. Catwoman only fucked Batman."

"Woman. I will show you the fucking dark knight."

Lightening fast, I grip her hips, turning her and pushing her towards the bed until she stands hovering over the covers on her hands. Leaning forward, I drape my body over hers, rubbing my aching cock up and down the crest of her ass until she moans.

"I'm going to peel this off of you and taste every inch I expose."

"Yes, please."

"Not so fast. First, I'm going to make you writhe and scream. Make you beg for it, desperate, like I've been for hours."

Her head arches back, exposing her neck for my teeth as her ass grinds against me. Seeking friction. Seeking relief. Relief I refuse to give.

With a dark chuckle, I retreat. One arm bands her hips, holding them still, while the other whispers over the material, up her torso. Her breasts heave with her great breaths as I touch and tease her.

"How badly do you want it, Princess?"

A deep moan vibrates through her body, making my cock twitch. "Reg-Reginald. Please, I need you to fuck me."

Suddenly the game isn't worth it. I could drag this out more, truly have her mewling on the bed, lost to her passion. But I'd much rather be buried in her sweet cunt.

The zipper gives a sharp snick as I tug it all the way down, past her pussy radiating with heat, and down her leg. My hand scorches a trail up her smooth skin and finds her center dripping and bare. "It's a good thing I didn't know you were naked under here. I would have given our guests a show when I bent you over my desk."

I make quick work of my own trousers and thrust into her. Seating myself in one stroke. We both groan together at the feeling. "Such a good girl." I hold her still as I pound into her, the only sound our ragged pants and the slap of skin.

"Tell me you only drip like this for me. That no one else makes you wet like this."

Her breaths come faster and I can tell she's almost there. So am I. My hand pushes her back further down so I can adjust the angle. With a pinch of her clit, I send her over the edge seconds before I join her. I ease up on the pressure on her back, but hold her hips still as the final tremors rush through us both.

I pull out and immediately miss the feel of her hot pussy on my cock. Her knees wobble as she tries to stand, so I steady her. With her hand on my shoulder, I kneel down and remove her knee-high boots one at a time, then peel the costume off her.

She shoots me a saucy wink as she saunters into the bath, naked and confident. Quickly stripping my suit, I join her in the shower for another round before we fall exhausted into bed. A lifetime of incredible sex with this woman—I don't know how I got this lucky, but I'm not going to waste it.

November

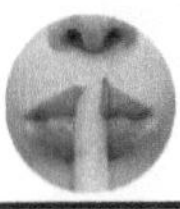 **Whisper Wire** ○ ○ ○

Curiouser and curiouser. Our current favorite couple was spotted around NYC last month out and about town. Buying furniture, late night dinners, and taking in a show. They even threw a fancy dress party at their new apartment—the Instagram photos are delish! MEOW. But now it seems the new Lady Ravenscourt has run off to Florida and left her husband high and dry in NYC. Trouble in paradise already?

I'm sure there are plenty of young women who'd be willing to let the dashing Lord Ravenscourt cry on their shoulders. Americans go nuts for an accent after all. Whatever is Lady R thinking?

In other news, drama on tour. Kenzo's leaving a string of broken hearts as he jet sets across Europe—and rioting husbands. Has the rock star Romeo gone too far? Find out next issue.

TTFN
Wendy

Birthday Girls' Night

NICOLETTE

I look around my kitchen at the canvas tote bags on the counter, taking a mental check I've got everything ready.

Comfy clothes, check.

Snacks, check.

Booze, double check.

Did I seriously make a mental list and check it off? Goddamn it. A decade with Bree is rubbing off on me.

A knock at the door has my feet moving even as I shake my head with a rueful grin. I open the door, expecting to find my ride for the evening. Instead of warm chocolate eyes, steel gray ones are gazing at me intensely. The smile disappears from my face as I take in the severe features of my husband on my doorstep.

The furrow between his brows deepens as I step back. His hands are shoved deeply into his pockets as he stands there awkwardly in my doorway, a messenger bag and a small rolling suitcase at his feet.

"R-Reginald, what are you doing here?" I wince at the sharp words.

His head ducks and cheeks redden slightly. "Can I come in?"

My own face heats with embarrassment as I realize we're both still standing in the doorway, facing each other like strangers. "Of course. Sorry, you surprised me. Did you fly in from New York or London?"

"London." He follows me through the open penthouse apartment to the kitchen area. His fingers finally leave his pockets to flip one of the straps of the bag on the counter. "You have plans tonight." It's a statement, not a question.

Desperate for something to do with my hands, I flit about the kitchen, grabbing glasses to fill with water. "Yeah. Just tonight, though, I'm free the rest of the weekend."

His hand drops from the fabric. His features are still tense, a muscle spasms in his jaw. Storm clouds dance in his gray eyes. Suddenly he looks so lost, so sad, I'm filled with the desire to cheer him up.

Sidling up to him, I lay my hand on his arm. "I am happy to see you." I catch his gaze with my own and some of the tension relaxes around his eyes. His hand reaches for me and lightly circles my waist. "I kind of suck at surprises." I grin at him and his lips twitch into a slight smile.

The hand squeezes my side briefly, then leaves me. I instantly miss the contact and try not to show it.

Reginald digs into his carry-on and hands me two small boxes covered in newspaper with an envelope tucked into the twine. It's obvious he wrapped them himself; the realization fills me with warmth. My eyes dart between the gifts to the man in front of me.

"Happy birthday." The flush returns to his cheeks and I'm surprised at how sexy I find it.

"How did you know?" I carefully place the packages on the counter and eye him over my shoulder.

His face tips down, one palm grips the back of his neck while the other dives back into his pants pocket. "The profile from the matchmaker."

I chuckle slightly and pull out the card. It is a simple piece of folded card stock with his confident handwriting slashed across the crisp white paper.

To my wife,

Like the swans, may you soar free

Happiest of birthdays

RB

In the envelope, I also find tickets to the New York Ballet's production of Cinderella. I shoot him a grateful smile as I move on to the first box. Inside an acrylic case sit a pair of black pointe shoes. A feminine signature scrawls across the bottom of one.

"Those are from the production of Swan Lake we saw together." His voice rumbles by my shoulder, where he's stepped closer to see me unwrap my gifts.

I set the box on the counter where I can see the shoes easily, and move on to the next surprise. Inside is a novel and a pair of socks. Brows pinching, I flip over the book to read the back. It is a retelling of Swan Lake from Odette's perspective by Mercedes Lackey. The dove gray socks are a thick knit, small black swans embroidered at the cuff of each.

Reginald clears his throat. I glance over to find him rocking back on his heels, both hands firmly in his pockets. "You seemed to appreciate Odette at the ballet, and I've seen you with a novel when you travel. I thought you might like this interpretation. The socks are a winter-grade thermal fleece. Figured they could keep your feet warm..." His voice trails off like he was going to add something else but had second thoughts.

"When you're not there to?" I chuckle, remembering our first night together. He ducks his head slightly, making me smile. "Thank you." I turn into him, planting a kiss on his warm cheek and snaking one arm around his neck. "I love it."

As I'm about to pull away, his arms close around my waist, holding me tight. My breath escapes me in a sigh as I relax into his warm embrace. The tension slowly leaves my shoulders as I lean into him. I'm quickly getting addicted to Reginald's hugs.

The sound of a key in the lock echoes through the quiet room. We both stiffen as the front door flies open.

"I hope you're ready to go, suga', but first I'm seriously about to pee..." Anna comes to a sudden stop. Her eyes are comically huge as she stares at us. "...Myself."

"Uh, Anna, you want to shut the door?" Reluctantly, I step back from the hug. Reginald keeps one arm firmly around my back, so I rest my palm on his chest.

She remains frozen, her eyes darting back and forth between us. Suddenly regaining control of her body, a dazzling smile lights up her face and she whirls into action, shutting the door and striding forward. "Hello, you must be the husband." Her eyes drop to our intimate pose. "Or at least I hope you are." She sticks her hand out towards him.

A slight smile lifts his lips as he relaxes next to me. "I am. Reginald Bancroft, at your service. And you would be Anna?"

"Oh, so she's told you about me? Funny, she's been very tight-lipped about you." Her eyes flare with fire as she shoots me a pointed look.

"I thought you had to pee." Crossing my arms, I glare at her.

The irony is not lost on me. I cross-examined both Bree and Anna's partners when they first showed up. Not so enjoyable being on the receiving end. I tell myself that's the only reason I've continued to keep the two sides of my life separate.

Anna waves me off with her hand. "I can hold it a little longer. So, Reginald, how long have you been in town for?"

"Flew in today to surprise Nic for her birthday for a few days before heading back to New York for some meetings. I'm assuming you are her plans for the night?" The tension leaves his shoulders.

"Yup, for our birthday girls' night tradition. You should come." I stiffen and Reginald strokes my hip soothingly.

"I'd hate to interrupt a tradition. Plus, it was a long flight from London. I'll rest here and leave you ladies to it."

I grab his hand and the carry-on bag. "Come on, I'll get you settled in while Anna pees." Shooting daggers over my shoulder at my friend, I tug Reginald to my bedroom. I point out the area in the closet and three drawers I'd cleared out in case he ever came by, and sit awkwardly on the edge of the bed as he looks around.

He walks over and tugs me to my feet. "Are you staying over?"

"Probably not with the baby there. I'll let you know either way, though."

He nods slightly and drops a kiss to my temple. Some of the tension reduces. "Ok, have fun with your friends. Tomorrow we can celebrate your birthday together."

The kitchen is empty when I return. A flush sounds from the powder room off the living room. Quick as a snake, I grab the socks and put them in my bag. My fingers itch to pick up the book and shoes. The water is still running in the bathroom, so I clutch them both and move them to the mantle over the electric fireplace before darting back to my bags in the entryway.

When Anna reappears, I usher her to the door, anxious to leave the apartment as quickly as possible. The ride to Brianna's house is quiet, Anna growing tired of my one-word answers to her probing questions about Reginald. She's practically vibrating by the time we enter the house.

I wonder how long it will take her to take the first shot.

Turns out it's exactly 3.5 seconds.

"Nicolette forgot to mention how handsome her husband is," Anna calls out as we walk into Brianna and Colin's living room.

"She didn't have to. A simple google search will show you that." Bree looks drained as she sways with a fussy Nora in her arms. Her faithful dog, Riley, tracking her motion intently from his perch on the couch.

"You looked him up?" I set my bags down and plop onto my normal spot on the love seat.

She adds a little knee bend to the swaying. "Well, you've been annoyingly secretive about the whole thing. Gorgeous wedding pictures, by the way. I told Colin we need to go to Sweden for a bit the next time we fly out to the Dublin office." She turns back to Anna with sharp eyes. "What happened?"

Dammit. I really should find dumber friends.

"He's at the penthouse. I walked in on the two of them all wrapped up together."

Two sets of eyes turn to me. One set, cobalt blue, wide with surprise. The other, chocolate brown, burning with victory.

"That's a tad dramatic. I was thanking him for my present and hugging him."

Brianna jerks back. "Since when are you a hugger?" Nora's fussing escalates into full yells as her mother stops rocking. Riley starts barking, clearly giving Bree an earful on his opinion of her parenting style.

"Is Nora ok?" Colin, Bree's husband, rushes in from their bedroom, looking equally haggard.

Oh, for Christ's sake. This is the last thing I need. Blindly, I grab the wine from my bag, twisting off the cap, and taking a swig directly from the bottle. Yes, even heiresses drink twist tops.

His eyes dart around the room, finding no immediate danger, he gently takes his daughter from his wife. His large hand engulfs the baby's back as he holds her. Nora gives a fitful breath and squirms against his chest before settling slightly. "What's going on?"

"Nic's husband is in town." Bree's gaze softens as she watches her family together.

A ping of longing unfurls in my stomach. I quickly drown it in wine.

Colin turns to me, eyes widening in shock. "Right now? And you left him at your apartment?"

"It was a surprise visit." Three hard sets of eyes stare me down. I block them out of view with the end of the bottle as another guzzle tickles down my throat. "Besides, he's jet-lagged, anyway." The excuse sounds lame even to my own ears.

The truth is, I'm still not entirely sure why I've been so adamant about keeping Reginald separate. It's probably tied to old habits.

I've been keeping my London life and personal life separate for half a lifetime. Part of it probably stems from noticing that Reginald doesn't particularly enjoy socializing. There's some other reason that lurks just at the edge of my mind. I'm reticent to dive too deeply, though, afraid of what I might discover.

Nora lets out another whimper, saving me from further questioning. Bree sighs and goes to take the baby back, but Colin stops her. "I got her, *a ghrá.*"

"Are you sure?" She looks conflicted.

Colin pulls her close and kisses her much shorter head. "That nap did me wonders. You haven't had a night with the girls since she was born. I'll drive her around for a bit. Maybe see if David wants to grab some coffee." With one more thoughtful look at me, he heads towards the door, a giant diaper bag on his arm.

Anna and Bree follow him out. In the case of the former, presumably to prepare snacks, and to watch her family leave for the latter.

With another sigh, I lean back and take another sip of wine. I hiss as my bare toes connect with the leather sofa, chilled by the constant air conditioning. Setting the bottle on the side table, I reach for the nearby blanket and spot the socks at the top of my bag. Pausing for only a moment, I grab them and slip them over my icy feet. I wriggle my toes inside the luxuriously soft fleece and soon warmth flows to them.

Who knew that socks could be a thoughtful gift?

By the time the girls reappear, I've finished the first bottle by myself. Mistakes have been made. Mistakes very much not like me.

"So, that's Reginald, huh?" Anna asks from her seat in the recliner.

"Yea." I keep my eyes on my gray covered toes as I wiggle them.

"You seemed...friendly."

"We are friends." My mind is getting fuzzy from the wine.

"So you said he got you a gift?" Bree asks hesitantly.

"Signed pointe shoes and a novel retelling Swan Lake." Didn't Anna go for snacks? Where's the salty good stuff?

"Swan Lake?" Anna's voice raises at the end, making it a question.

"Yeah, it's my favorite ballet. We saw it together in London." I'd even go for a fruit plate about now. Why didn't I bring a charcuterie board?

"You like ballet?"

"Yeah, since I was a kid." Sitting up, I dramatically turn to my friends. "Where are the snacks, sister?"

They share a confused look. Anna pushes the popcorn bowl closer to me. I grab it and happily start munching away.

Bree perches on the couch closest to me. Head cocked, she peers at me like a puzzle she's trying to figure out. "So if you're friends, is this one of those platonic marriage of convenience things?"

Flashbacks to Halloween send heat pooling in my stomach. "More like a husband with benefits."

"Well, that was a gamble," Bree says.

"I knew you were sleeping together!" Anna crows. "Is he any good?"

"Wouldn't you test drive a car before purchasing?" I scoff. "We have an understanding."

"Nic..."

"Bree."

"That never ends well. I've seen that plotline a thousand times. Someone always catches feelings."

"This isn't one of your rom-coms, Brianna." She opens her mouth, but I hold up a hand to stall her. "I know this comes from a caring place, but just stop. This is my life. Trust that I know what I'm doing and drop it."

Her big blue eyes glisten with tears, and her chin trembles slightly. "I'm sorry, Nic. You're right. I worry about you. This all happened so fast and you've hardly said anything about him. You have the best sense of people of anyone I know. I'm sure you picked a good one."

"Ok, but how good in bed is he?" We both turn slack-jawed to our sweet southern friend, who has gotten more sassy since reuniting with David. "What? Just because I don't swear doesn't mean I'm a prude."

"What do you want? A score out of ten? Or a rank?" Chuckling, I rifle through my tote for another bottle of wine. "I am very satisfied with my arrangement."

"That's it? No details?"

"Come now, Anna. A lady never tells."

"That's right! Do we need to call you 'your grace' now or some nonsense?"

"Grace is for dukes. He's only a viscount," Bree explains.

I groan around a mouthful of wine. "Would you both please drop it and put the fucking movie on already?"

We agree on a single film rather than our typical three movie marathon. I push back a pang of sadness. What a change two years makes. It'd be easy to blame Colin for it all, but as much as I like to give the guy shit, it would also be unfair. Not once has Colin ever stood in the way of girls' night. In fact, he always offers to drive us, fetch snacks, or leave us alone. He was only the first of many changes for us.

Time keeps moving. It doesn't care if we want a moment to last a lifetime, or a season to race by. She has her own pace and we are simply trying to keep up. I cannot picture a time where these girls won't be my family, but as our individual worlds change, so will our friendship. Girls' night will turn into couple's game night. Happy hour will morph into brunch—when the kids don't have an activity.

Maybe it's the Malbec, but the thought doesn't scare me as much as it used to.

CHAPTER TWENTY-TWO

Impromptu Boys' Night

REGINALD

The door closes behind Nic and I'm dropped into silence. Not exactly how I saw the evening going in my head. I wouldn't say I was expecting her to jump into my arms when I showed up at her door, but her slack-jawed expression was like a punch to the gut.

I don't know what I was thinking when I booked that ticket to Florida instead of New York. It just felt like the right thing to do. Of course, she had plans already.

At least it's not a date. That's what I first assumed when I saw her with a packed bag by the door. Jealousy had flared, hot and violent. A new feeling, but one I'm experiencing more often in my marriage. Why did I agree to that stupid open relationship clause?

Because, for once in my life, I was totally sure about what I wanted in life. I grabbed it with both hands and I'd be damned if I'd let it go.

With a sigh, I set about canceling the dinner reservations I'd made earlier that day. Then unpack my meager belongings into the spaces she'd indicated. With nothing better to do, I try out her luxury shower, claiming part of the shelf for myself.

Clean and with no other distractions, I face the silent apartment. What time will she be back? My stomach growls, reminding me it's been hours since I last ate. The fridge is bare, and the pantry shows an array of microwave ready soups and pastas. As I'm debating between white cheddar mac and cheese and chicken noodle soup, a knock at the door draws my attention.

Did Nic take pity on me and send food?

Instead of a delivery man, the door reveals a man with a giant bag and—is that a baby strapped to his chest? He grins at me, revealing a long dimple. "Ah, so you would be the husband?"

I try to conceal my surprise at the blunt non-greeting. Who the bloody hell is this? The jealousy and doubt from earlier comes rushing back. Maybe she does have a local boyfriend after all.

But who brings his baby on dates?

"Colin, can you wait to interrogate the guy until we get inside? This shit is hot." A taller man steps closer, heavily muscled arms bulging as he holds two aluminum trays.

"After all the shite Nic gave me when I first came to town? Don't I deserve to enjoy this a bit more?" With a dramatic sigh, he turns back to me. "Right. Well, are you going to let us in? We brought food, and knowing Nic, the pantry is empty."

Numbly, I step back, and follow them to the kitchen. Silently, they work in tandem, obviously familiar with the apartment. Dimples puts a case of beer in the fridge. The big one uncovers trays, revealing tantalizing scents, then grabs three plates from the cabinet. I still have no idea who the fuck they are.

Undeterred, the big one loads a plate up with wings, sliders, onion rings, and something that looks like an egg roll. He holds the plate out to me, then builds a second for himself.

I take a tentative bite of the egg roll, finding it filled with spicy chicken, tangy ranch, and crisp, shredded carrots. The wings are in various flavors: garlic Parmesan, Korean BBQ, and one that's both sweet and tangy. I groan slightly with each new flavor. "This is delicious."

The giant smiles proudly. "My Bella's a hell of a cook. We stopped by the restaurant on the way here."

My eyes dart to the paper takeout bag next to the trays of food. Pop. The restaurant Nic owns with her friends. Suddenly it clicks. "You must be David then. Which would make you Bree's husband?"

"The baby didn't give it away?" He sways to the side, and I catch a glimpse of copper curls and rosy cheeks. "Figured we could have a little boys' night to welcome you to the crazy."

"Not that the girls know we're here," David adds. "They think this one is driving around to lull the baby to sleep. Instead, he grabbed me and convinced Asher to pack up food. He would have joined us, but he's in charge when Annabel isn't in the kitchen."

"Hey now, I told my wife I'd see if you wanted to grab some coffee. Didn't mention it would be at Nic's apartment, or that it would include Nic's secret husband." He turns to me and his green eyes sparkle with intelligence and interest. "So, how did you manage to tie down that one?" With practiced motions, he unclips the carrier and starts feeding the baby from a nearby bottle.

"How much do you know?" I'm stalling.

"Not much. Bree made the story sound like something out of a rom-com. The whole situation is so out of character for Nic."

"How so?" I try for casual but I'm dying of curiosity.

"Nic doesn't do relationships." Colin shrugs casually as he continues to feed the baby.

I grit my teeth, "Friend of hers or not, careful how you speak about my wife."

"Colin, that was a bit harsh," the big one adds.

"It's true though. She's always seemed happiest in a crowded room or completely alone. No boyfriends—serious, casual, or otherwise. So why now? Why you?"

"Is this the part where you threaten me?" I stare him down as I take another bite of the egg roll.

He laughs. "The first time I met Nic, she threatened to bury me where no one would find the body. No, the girl doesn't need protecting."

"Maybe you don't know her as well as you think." I'm not sure where the words come from, or why I feel so strongly defensive. Deep down, I know he's mistaken. Nic is in need of protection. The attitude, the clothing, it's all armor to protect her delicate core. In her I see another lost soul just as desperate for human connection and as alone in a crowd of people like me.

"If you keep trying to scare him away, Col, I'm going to start thinking you miss having the girls all to yourself."

"Oh, aye, I miss having Anna's cooking all to myself." He shoots a dimpled grin at the taller man, before his thoughtful look returns to me. "I'm an engineer. It's my nature to take things apart and see how they work. And this relationship is fascinating."

"Well, leave the guy alone. I'm looking forward to a third player for cards. Damn tired of Go Fish."

We sit around the dining room table and David shuffles a deck from his jacket pocket. "So y'all met on a plane? Or through a matchmaker? Damned confusing putting together the info through the girls."

I open my mouth to respond, but then pause. This is all unfamiliar to me. Besides Daniel, I never had many friends. Definitely no new ones as an adult. They seem nice enough, but anyone can sell you out to the tabloids these days, and that Wendy has been relentless with her obsession with us.

David's eyes pinch momentarily, then smooth with understanding. "Sorry, I grew up in a small town, so I'm used to everyone being in each other's business. And this one," he jerks his thumb at Colin who is patting a wide-eyed baby on the back, "he's practically been one of the girls for two years now and doesn't remember how overwhelming it can be at first."

"Appreciate it, mate. So how did you all..." I trail off unsure of the right word.

"Join the circus?" David supplies, drawing chuckles from us. "I grew up with Anna—childhood sweethearts. But I fucked it up and went off to join the Marines before finally getting my head out of my ass earlier this year."

"How did you manage that?"

Colin snickers. "A lot of begging." David flicks a card at him. Colin ducks to the side, his hand protectively covering his daughter's head. "Careful! Precious cargo here."

"Pretty sure there's video evidence of your begging," David dryly adds.

I lift a brow at Colin, waiting for the story. He doesn't disappoint.

"Bree and I met at work on a project. Things were going well until there was a slight misunderstanding..."

David snorts, interrupting Colin, who glares at him in return. "A naked woman in your hotel room is a misunderstanding?"

"I wasn't in the room, now was I, eejit? Anyway, then Anna helped me make a grand gesture and win back my girl."

"He's skipping the part where he proposed and she said no. The whole thing is up on social media. I'll send it to you."

"She said yes eventually," Colin grumbles.

We play a few hands of poker. It's not a serious game, repeatedly interrupted by Nora's cries.

After the tenth time, David scoops the baby out of Colin's hold. The infant looking incredibly small in his thick arms. "Does she cry like this often?"

Colin runs his hands through his ruddy hair, the slight curls standing up. "All the time lately. Poor thing just screams all night long."

David lays a burp cloth on the table and then settles the baby on her back. He pumps her little legs and makes silly faces at her.

"Isn't she a little young for leg day, Dave?" Colin quips.

He only rolls his eyes and keeps up the little leg pumps. Suddenly, a deep gurgling noise, like an old-fashioned coffee percolator, vibrates against the table. A series of wet squelches and an unholy odor comes from the tiny baby. All three of us yell and gag.

"There you go, daddy. I think Nora needs a change."

Nora looks up at the three of us, a tiny dimple on her cheek as she wiggles.

Colin looks down at the now happy baby with wide eyes, his grin absent for the first time. "I hope I brought enough wipes. That sounded like a blowout." He gets to work pulling out supplies and changing the baby like she's a ticking bomb. David chats away about gripe water and football holds the whole time. Unsure how I fit in, I search the kitchen for disinfectant for the table. And a candle.

"David, you know what you're doing. Do you have kids?" I ask as I wipe down the surface.

"No," he shakes his head, "and not fixing to any time soon. Bella and I spent a lot of time taking care of her little brothers growing up. Kids are great, but we need time just the two of us for once."

"You planning on getting yourself one of these?" Colin cuddles the now clean, happy, and sleepy baby to his chest. I will admit they make quite the picture.

"Eventually. An earl's first priority is to secure the family legacy, after all." The words taste sour.

"That's right. Do we have to call you 'my lord' or some shit? What's that like?" David leans forward with interest. Colin simply relaxes, grin firmly back in place. It's always the Americans who are intrigued by the title thing.

"Please don't. It's nice escaping all that when I'm in America." I take a deep breath, considering my next words. "It's actually a difficult question. Being the heir is all I know. It'd rather be like asking what it's like to be Southern, or Irish. I have no basis of comparison." The cold glass of the empty bottle between my hands lulls by the sense of familiarity I go on, "I will say, it's not as glamorous as the novels and movies make it look."

"You mean *Bridgerton* is fake?" David pushes a fresh beer towards me, and I take it with a grateful nod.

"You do realize that's set hundreds of years ago, right?" Colin drolls.

"Wait, you watch it too?"

"Um yeah, I prefer *Gilded Age* currently. Though nothing compares to *Downton Abbey*." We both turn to Colin slack-jawed. "What? TV happens to help keep me awake while I'm rocking a screaming baby all night and I happen to like cuddling with my wife and watching her shows makes her happy."

I chuckle into the mouth of my beer. These two are obviously close, they banter more like friends of years rather than months. What would it be like to be part of this circle? To have couple friends to see movies or play games with. Little kids running around on holidays. It sounds idyllic, and so different from the life I grew up living.

"Sorry, you were saying, Bancroft? So no fancy schools and parties?"

"Oh, there are tons of fancy schools and parties, but none that a child wants to be at. I learned which of the silver spoons to use at the age of five—by a nanny, of course, because my parents were too busy managing charities and traveling. The parties aren't for fun. They're for networking, and showing status, and bolstering your family name through archaic traditions that won't die out. Believe me, it can be more dystopian than romance novel."

"Wow, that sucks, man," David says. They both look grim. "I guess the grass really isn't greener. We struggled growing up. My mom was always working after my dad left, but she never let that impact my childhood. We had a community full of love and support ready to pitch in. I'm sorry."

"I probably shouldn't complain. The perks are nice—usually. I'm not into the social games like my family. Nic helps a lot. She's much better at the politics and charming a room than me. Still, if I could, I'd leave it all behind for a normal life. Like Nic tried to do." They both give me quizzical looks as I sip my beer. "She's from one of the richest families in London. She grew up with all the same glitz and glam I did. You didn't know?"

"We knew she had a trust fund and family in England, but she's very tight-lipped about her past."

Nodding, I grip the cool glass in my hand. "Well, I suspect we both saw something of a kindred spirit in the other. Pressure from family for an acceptable match in a sea of wholly undesirable partners. I jumped at the chance of a spouse as disillusioned with the glitter as I am."

David clinks his beer to mine, startling me. "Welcome to the family, brother. Here's to more time here and less at the Ritz."

"Thank you." My cheeks ache slightly, and I realize I'm smiling, the feeling completely foreign on my face.

"The girls are crazy, but they're our crazy." Colin glances down at the dozing baby. "Speaking of girls, I should take this one home. We're all meeting up at the restaurant tomorrow to paint. You should join us. Meet some of the other guys."

"That sounds nice," I say, and I mean it.

CHAPTER TWENTY-THREE

Down the Rabbit Hole

REGINALD

I clean up the bottles and take-away containers, mulling over the surprising evening. I like them. To be welcomed so wholly to their group based on Nic's stamp of approval is amazing.

The door opens with a thud. Nic stands in the entrance, swatting away an amused David who is following closely, hands out as if she's about to fall.

As she takes two wobbly steps inside, I understand why. "Hands off, soldier boy, I'm perfectly fine."

I meet her in the entryway. She stumbles into my side, but doesn't resist my steadying arm. In fact, she flashes a drunken smile. "You're proper drunk, aren't you?"

"Pssh." She tries to wave her hand but loses her balance. "It was only two wines."

My eyebrows pinch in confusion. I've seen Nic drink, but never drunk. "Two glasses of wine got you this drunk?"

"It was bottles." David shakes his head. "If you got this one, I'll get back to that one." He jerks his thumb to where Anna is leaning against the hall, mumbling to a sconce.

"Is girls' night always like this?"

"Nope," Nic answers, "they were being douchecocks. It was the damn Spanish Inquisition, and I needed ammo."

David and I share a look and a shrug, before he lifts his fiancée up and throws her over his shoulder like a sack of flour. It sounds like she's muttering about ghost peppers as they disappear to the elevator.

"Come on, Princess. Off to bed you go."

She doesn't fight me as I lead her to the bedroom. She sits on the edge of the mattress and flops back, arms spread wide.

"Don't fall asleep yet. You still need to get undressed." I kneel as Nic groans, tossing around. I reach for her foot and smile when I see she's wearing the socks I got her.

A scrap of cloth hits me in the head. I peel it off my face, holding it out. It's Nic's bra. My eyes dart to her and she's still fully covered in her T-shirt. How the hell did she wriggle out of that contraption while laying on the bed?

Tossing the garment aside, I return my attention to her feet. As the first fuzzy length clears her heel, she sits up. Eyes wide. "No, not my socks. I like my socks."

I hold in a chuckle. "You don't need the socks in bed, Princess."

"Sure I do! Sometimes my toes touch my other leg and wake me up. They're fucking icicles, Reginald!"

"Well, when I'm here, you can thaw the icicles on my legs."

"Mmmm, 'kay." She still looks unconvinced, but slips under the sheets that I pull back for her.

I turn off the lights and climb into the massive bed next to her. Only debating for a minute, I scoot my pillow closer and reach my foot out to check her temperature.

She's already mostly asleep, but with a stuttering breath, she rolls towards me. "This is nice," she murmurs.

It certainly is.

I slide my arm under her head in invitation, and she immediately burrows closer to my warm body. Before Nic, I wouldn't have imagined I was a cuddler, but with each night of her in my arms, that dark hole in my chest closes bit by bit. Maybe someday, it can fully heal.

The toaster bings as the bedroom door opens. Nic stumbles out, looking adorably mussed in last night's shirt and her short hair standing up. I pour a cup of coffee and add her almond creamer exactly the way she likes. It joins the plated toast on the kitchen island. Nic is a bit of a beast on typical mornings, even without two bottles of wine.

Nic grunts as she sits on the stool. Her fingers grip the mug like it's a magic elixir to cure her hangover. Eh, maybe it is.

"Morning." Another grunt. "I wasn't sure where the aspirin was. Shower should help, then we better head over to Pop."

A deep V appears between her brows. "What? Why are we doing that?"

"The walls aren't going to paint themselves."

"How do you even know about that?"

"David mentioned it last night."

"Oh." She hunches over her drink. A determined pout crosses her face. She throws back the rest of her coffee and then sets the mug down with a clatter. "Fine, I'll go hop in the shower. But Anna better have a hangover breakfast ready at the restaurant!"

I chuckle as she stomps off to her bedroom.

With nothing better to do, I eat the toast and tidy up the neat kitchen. Last night was fun, but Nic's girlfriends won't have as warm a welcome. If Colin and David's stories are to be believed, the girls are fiercely protective of each other. We may already be married, but this feels like the 'meet the family' moment.

The ride to Friendship Springs is quiet. I rely on GPS to guide me as Nic dozes in her seat. We leave the highway behind and drive through narrow roads with angled parking on both sides. Quaint buildings with large windows line the streets boasting cafes, boutiques, and services. Young families push strollers while sipping coffee. Old men play chess at bistro tables. Everything is colorful and cheerful.

"You've arrived at your destination," the electronic voices says, breaking the peaceful silence.

As Nic rouses, I pull into a spot out front and study the building. It's very much like it's neighbors, exposed brick with white trimmed, tinted glass. Above the door hangs an unlit neon sign shaped like a champagne bottle with overflowing bubbles and the word "POP". I'm utterly charmed.

I follow Nic out of the car, instead of the double doors in front of us, she keeps walking down the sidewalk to a papered up entrance next door. Inside, is an open area clearly under construction—the new event space. Round tables stack in the middle of the floor. Two women sit at the single table set up—the blond from last night, and a brunette holding Nora. This must be Colin's wife, Brianna.

Nic collapses into an empty seat, folding herself onto the table with a moan. "More coffee. Breakfast. Now."

It's a struggle not to chuckle as I pat her back. The two women eye me. Anna is smirking, but Brianna's dark blue eyes hold an intelligent spark as she studies me. Looks like I'm going to have to make my own introductions. "Hello. Anna and I met briefly last night, but you must be Brianna. I've heard a lot about you." I extend my hand, she takes it in her smaller one with a surprisingly firm grip.

"And you must be Reginald. I wish I could say the same."

"Most people call me Bancroft. There's honestly not much to tell, I'm afraid. Aristocrats are only interesting in books or movies."

"So it's not all galas and nights at the opera?"

"There's a lot of that, especially if my mother has a say. Never developed much of a taste for them myself." I look down at my disgruntled wife, currently blowing her hair out of her face in loud raspberries. Taking pity on her, I remove the offending piece and receive another grunt in thanks. "Though the ballet does have its appeal."

"Food," Nic groans.

"Breakfast is in the kitchen, suga'." Anna chuckles. "Go on and help yourself."

Nic grunts. "Too tired. Why the fuck are you so chipper?"

"Some of us didn't drink two bottles of wine."

"Goddamn it, Daisy-Mae, it's too early for your shit." Nic makes a show of dramatically pushing her hands against the table like the weight of the world is on her shoulders.

Giving in to the growing chuckle, I squeeze her shoulder. "I'll go make you a plate." I turn to Anna. "Is David in the kitchen?"

She shakes her head, her brows raising in surprise. "No, he's still out picking up the paint with Colin. Asher and Johnson are in there, though."

I push down the disappointment. The idea of meeting more people is overwhelming, but both Colin and David spoke highly of these two. The double doors open into a tidy industrial kitchen with gleaming countertops and stainless steel appliances. Two men stand in an aisle in front of a spread of hearty breakfast foods. French toast, scrambled eggs, bacon, biscuits, gravy, and...fried chicken?...laid out like a monstrous feast.

The blond man spots me first. He's a little taller, an obvious gym fanatic. With his striking blue eyes and hair pulled up into a bun on his head, he resembles a modern Viking. He hands me an empty plate as I approach. "You must be the husband. Colin mentioned you'd be joining us. I'm Asher, this is Johnson."

The other man nods at me. He's more lanky, dark hair with a clean-shaven square jaw and dimpled chin. "Hey, man, good to meet ya."

"Same, call me Bancroft." I fill a plate for Nic, then take a second for myself. "How did you two get pulled into this? Nic's only talked about Bree and Anna. Is there a fourth one I should know about?"

"Hell no. The three of them are trouble enough." Asher laughs. "If they pull out a bottle of Fireball, run. I'm the head bartender here."

"Don't forget about being part owner." Johnson waggles his eyebrows as he chomps on a piece of crispy bacon.

"Do you work here too?" I ask him. These people's lives are more complicated than a Greek tragedy. My head spins, trying to keep it all straight.

"Bree is my boss, but at an engineering firm nearby. Colin and I are friends, and he introduced me to this asshole."

Oh! It suddenly makes sense. "Oh, so how long have you two been together?"

They both laugh. "Just friends," Asher says. "He's too pretty for me. My ego couldn't handle it."

"Come now, Ash. Don't be so hard on yourself—you're totally in my league." His cheeks crease as he turns to me. "We're the token bachelors around here. We buddy up so we don't feel left out. Well, us and David's business partner, Ronnie. Where is he, anyway?"

Asher shrugs and grabs a flaky biscuit. "Dunno. He told David he was busy. So how's married life?"

Before I can answer, the double doors fly open as Nic storms through. "I see you met Tweedledee and Tweedledumb." She slides up beside me.

"Gee, Nic, which one of us is which?" Asher quips.

"She's just hungover. Here, I made you a plate."

Her eyes light up as I hand it over. "You are forgiven." Arms protectively holding the food, she turns and plants a loud kiss on my lips, then shoves a sausage link into her mouth with a happy sigh. Her hips regain a bit of their swagger as she heads back to the event space. "Coffee, please, and make it Irish!"

"Only if I can be Tweedledee," Asher calls back.

Nic holds a piece of bacon aloft as her only acknowledgement of Asher's statement. I like this side of Nic. Here in Friendship Springs, she is more relaxed. Yeah, she's a cranky, hungover mess this morning, but she's more genuine than I've seen her. Freer. More like when it's only the two of us.

CHAPTER TWENTY-FOUR

Painting the Walls Pink

NICOLETTE

Grease and hair of the dog helped, but after a few hours, I'm dragging again. There's still so much to do to transform the new space into an event hall. Bree handed out tasks to everyone—crazy bitch even has an itemized to-do list and clipboard. I got stuck with unpacking the cases of party supplies. It's a monotonous chore, opening plastic packets and pulling out the fabric within.

Anna walks up beside me. "Hey, how are the linens going?" We opened Pop almost six years ago, and it's been a very profitable restaurant ever since, but this expansion is her brainchild.

The boxes of napkins I'm currently sorting don't get any emptier. It may be because I've been quite distracted this whole time. I sneak another peak at the scene unfolding on the other side of the room. "Ok. Why did we need so many napkins, anyway? What about the ones from the restaurant?"

"Double the space means double the linens. Get to counting."

I groan as I toss one of the cream napkins onto the pile. "I keep losing track."

"Can't imagine why." Anna plants a fist on her cocked hip.

Bree steps up on my other side, baby Nora strapped to her chest. "Oh, I can."

Across the room, five sets of bare shoulders bunch and bulge as the men in our lives paint a wall flamingo-pink. Besides our three significant others, Asher and Johnson have joined in on the painting party.

"Why are they all shirtless?" Anna asks.

"Beats me," Bree quips, sounding not at all concerned.

"Are you really complaining?" I ask.

Anna's chocolate eyes turn molten as she scans her fiancé's tattoo covered torso. He is an arguably impressive specimen, the tallest of the group with heavy muscle from years in the Marines.

There's not an unfortunate one in the pack, and a man for every preference. Asher's icy looks, man-bun, and gym-hardened muscles. Or Johnson's superman pretty boy style. Even Irish is handsome with his toned body and dimples.

My eyes keep wandering back to the same set of pink-splattered shoulders. Unmarked skin stretches across a broad back. Dark hair sprinkles his chest and arms. Somehow there is not a hair out of place on his dark head.

The bass pumps with some rock music. The volume is turned way the fuck up but you can still hear the good-natured ribbing of the men echoing through the cavernous room. When Reginald turns, I see a grin on his face. He looks completely at ease with my friends. More so than even with his own brother.

The door to the restaurant opens behind us. "Chef, table five is...holy shit." Vicky, one of the servers, joins us on Anna's other side. "Are we now doing thirst traps for TikTok?" We laugh at her wide-eyed expression as a blush stains her cheeks. "Please tell me the dark-haired one is single."

A flash of unexpected possessiveness flares through me. Not an emotion I can say I've experienced much, and definitely not one I wish to repeat. Or dig too deeply into. Reginald chooses that moment to turn. He pulls his T-shirt from the back of his waistband and mops at his glistening brow, ignoring the beads of sweat trailing across his bare chest. Catching me staring, his lips spread into a grin and he shoots a wink my way before turning back to the wall.

"Unless you mean the one in jeans, you're out of luck. Now what did you need, Vicky?" Anna looks amused as she talks to the younger girl.

"Huh?" Vicky turns glassy eyes to Anna, then shakes her head. "Oh. Table five is asking for you, Chef."

"Problem?" Bree asks. Trust her to be business minded.

"Don't think so. It's a pretty big group and they've eaten pretty much everything on the menu." Her eyes keep wandering back to the men.

"I better go see what's up." With a last look at her fiancé, Anna heads back to the kitchen doors. Pausing at the doorway, she turns back to the still frozen server. "Come on, Vicky."

Bree shifts her weight from foot to foot, gently swaying as her daughter sleeps contentedly. "I will admit, I was worried when you said you got married, expecting some uptight peer of the realm, but I like the guy."

"Oh, yea?"

"He's different, not like one of your usual puppies."

I turn to her, keeping my face carefully blank. "What's that supposed to mean?"

She turns to me, brow raised as she continues her sway. "Come on, Nic. You collect men in every city like postcards. Each one absolutely mesmerized by you as they let you walk all over them."

A pang goes through me. "Wow, did you seriously just call me a slut?"

"No. That's not what I mean at all." Bree sighs. "You have this gift of attracting people to you. You see through them and change yourself to best blend in or influence them to do what you want—like a chameleon. It's not a bad thing, Nic, it's what makes you so good at your job. But sometimes I think you use it to keep people from seeing the real you."

I do tend to take the easier path. If I give them what they want, they'll leave me alone. If I distract someone with some glitter, they can't get close enough to hurt me.

Bree absently kisses Nora's head as she studies me. "What I'm trying to say, badly, is that I see why you picked him. He lets you be you without all the extra stuff. The fact he came to help today tells me he cares." She holds up her hand as I open my mouth. "As a partner and friend. I like him." She grabs a bottle of water and walks off to the corner where her husband is studying his handiwork. As she comes abreast of him, his face splits into the same goofy smile he gets every time he sees her. Colin drops a kiss to the sleeping baby, then wraps his arm around his wife as they talk.

Napkins forgotten, I continue to watch the guys as my mind wanders. So much of my time is spent alone in hotel rooms or flitting from party to party. These in-between moments are rare, and I miss them more and more. It wasn't even two years ago that Bree introduced Colin to our lives. He, in turn, brought Johnson around more often. Then David showed up at the beginning of the summer, and now Reginald has rounded out the group.

I love my girl-time, but the guys bring a different dynamic. Laughter. Banter. Competition. Both of my best friends are lighter now. Happy. Confident. Chasing their dreams, all while cheered on by men who adore them.

Reginald approaches me, smiling. I hand him my water bottle and he guzzles half of it down in one go. "Thanks. Who knew painting was such good exercise?" My eyes sweep his glistening body again as I make a noncommittal noise. "When are you opening?"

"New Year's Eve. We're throwing a big party as our official opening."

He nods and scans the room. "We'll have to fly in right after Christmas. That gives a few days for final preparations."

"We?"

"Of course. You need to be here, and I'm not spending New Year's without my wife."

A warmth spreads through my chest at the word wife. It still feels so foreign. I know it's on paper only, but I can't help it when his voice rumbles over the term.

My eyes lift to a shock of pink in his dark hair. Unthinking, my hand lifts as I finger the hard lump in the otherwise silky strands. His grin heats as a firm arm bands around my back, pulling me closer to his naked chest.

"You have paint in your hair," I explain.

"You'll have to wash it out for me. That shower of yours is big enough for two."

"Oh, is that so?" I strive for aloof, but my lady bits are definitely not opposed to the suggestion.

"Do you have any idea how amazing your ass looks in those pants? I've been hard for hours watching you bend over that box." His fingers glide down, grabbing a handful and pulling me to him.

I gasp as the proof of his statement presses against my clit. My thighs press together, trying to ease the ache, but only squeeze his cock harder into me.

Reginald groans in my ear. "Keep that up, Princess, and you'll end up dragged into the supply closet. I'll fuck you hard and leave my handprint on your ass as a reminder not to tease me."

Heat floods my body at his words. No one's talked to me before the way he does. Bree's right, I easily dominate every man I meet. It's thrilling to be on the other side for once—not that I'll admit it to him.

Mistaking my stillness for compliance, he chuckles darkly. "That's my good girl." I struggle not to shudder as my core clenches. "Hurry up and finish this. Then I'll take you home, rip these pants off you, and make you cum until you beg me to stop."

With one last squeeze, he heads over to where Asher and Johnson are hanging glass shelves, as if nothing happened. As I catch my breath, I enjoy the confident swagger of his hips.

The remaining three boxes of napkins are sorted and counted in record time. Which has absolutely nothing to do with the dark promises of my husband.

Nope, nothing at all.

December

 **Whisper Wire**   ○○○

Well, love appears to be back in the air. After weeks apart, our viscount charming flew off to Florida to reunite with his blushing bride. Am I the only one disappointed at not seeing a steamy reunion at the airport? Lord Ravenscourt arrived alone and took a cab to his wife's penthouse apartment in central Florida. Sources spotted the newlyweds out and about, dining at the popular restaurant, Pop, owned by the former Miss A's longtime friend.

Just when we thought Florida might be their main home, Lord R ran back to New York alone. Since returning to the Big Apple, he's been his usual antisocial self, only seen in the company of university friend, Daniel Gooding. A quick search turned up some interesting bread crumbs. Business loans, licenses, and web addresses have been all recently formed under his name. What are you boys up to? And what is Elysium?

I smell a story.

TTFN
Wendy

CHAPTER TWENTY-FIVE

Ghosts of Christmas Past

REGINALD

The evergreen garlands and white lights fail to cast a cheery glow on the ever frosty front steps of Silverbrook Hall. I glance over at Nic beside me as her eyes dart over the monstrous facade of my parents' house. There is no shock or awe—after all, Nic grew up in this world for half her life—but there is a glint of appreciation.

I guess it's pretty, though I've always found it constricting rather than beautiful. The architects aren't to blame as much as the occupants.

Nic's hazel eyes are still on the carved details of the exterior when she speaks. "This is where you grew up? It's lovely, but a bit cold."

I take her gloved hands in mine and squeeze them. When she parrots my inner thoughts back to me, it is like the sun coming out of the clouds. Like she absolutely sees me like no one else.

The grand front doors open and Foster opens the door with a smile. "Good to see you, sir."

I clap him on the shoulder with a genuine smile as he takes my coat. "Happy Christmas, Foster. This is my wife, Nic." I slip her red wool coat off her slim arms and hand it over.

Up to now, Nic has been studying the foyer with her artist's eye, but at the introduction she turns to us, slipping under my arm and wrapping hers around my waist. In an instant, she smiles at Foster, not her social one, her real one. I find I can easily differentiate between all her smiles.

Foster's eyes crinkle as he beams at her. "It's a pleasure to finally meet you, ma'am."

"You as well. Merry Christmas, Foster." She squeezes his arm with her free hand.

He clears his throat as emotion glistens in his eyes. "The family is in the ballroom with their guests. Your mother has already asked after you." The last is added quietly.

I groan internally. Of course she has. In years past, I've been a most dutiful son and arrived hours early to listen to Mother's lectures on who will be attending and ensure I'm standing by Father's side when the first guest entered. Our original flight from JFK was canceled because of snow and we only landed in London a few hours ago. We'd crashed as soon as we got to my flat and woke in a rush.

The roar of people talking greets us before we enter the ballroom at the rear of the house. Nic falters as we approach the threshold and I squeeze her hip encouragingly.

"Holy shit," she whispers in my ear. "I thought this was a family Christmas party."

"Oh, it is, plus our close family friends. My mother does this every year. Come on, let's get this over with."

We make our way through the crowd, stopped repeatedly by acquaintances of my parents who want to wish us a happy Christmas and congratulations on our recent marriage. Mother shoots pointed looks our way from her spot by the fireplace and storm clouds are practically brewing overhead by the time we reach her.

"Mother." I stoop for the required kiss to the cheek. "Happy Christmas."

"Where have you been?" she seethes through gritted teeth. "I expected you hours ago."

"Weather cancellation. We got out on the first available flight."

The explanation does nothing to quell the anger in her eyes. "Why did you wait until the last moment? You should have been here days ago."

"I'm afraid it's my fault," Nic says. "Radio City Music Hall asked me to do the Christmas photos for the Rockettes this year."

"Oh, hi, Nicolette." Mother gives Nic a once-over, her lips pinched. "Now that you're married, I imagine you'll be giving all that up." Nic stiffens next to me, but her face reveals none of her inner turmoil. She opens her scarlet-painted lips to answer, but Mother cuts her off. "Where is your grandmother? I invited her but didn't hear back. Quite rude, actually."

Of course she did. Vivienne Atherton is a pillar of society. She's headed more charities than anyone else—there are more hospitals, museums, and libraries with the Atherton name than any other. It doesn't matter that my mother is titled and the Athertons are not, having her attend would be a coup.

"Grandmama sends her regrets, she has other obligations for the holidays. We'll have to arrange a tea after the new year." Her best social smile is pasted on her face, but there's a sadness in Nic's eyes. Something is going on there.

"We'd better circulate. I see Lord Firth at the refreshments table and must congratulate him on his recent award." With a nod to my mother, I anchor my hand on the small of Nic's back and guide her away. I pick a few items from the buffet and hand them to her as I sidle up next to the older gentleman.

"Lord Firth, congratulations on your recognition for the conservation efforts at Pemberley. It is wonderful to see such modern advances at a historic estate."

"Ravenscourt, my boy, thank you. Most of it is my grandson's doing, but it is quite exciting. Congratulations to you on your recent marriage. Is this lovely young lady your bride?"

"Yes, let me introduce my wife, Nicolette." I hold her close to my side.

"Of course, Edgar's granddaughter. Good to see you, girl. Your grandfather was a very good friend of mine. Is your grandmother here tonight? I'd like to pay my respects."

Again, at the mention of her grandmother, Nic stiffens. I squeeze her hip, wishing I could do more when she's so obviously in distress. Her smile never falters, though her eyes pinch the slightest bit.

"Unfortunately, no, but I will pass on your wishes."

"Firth, there you are." My father blusters as he stumbles up on Nic's other side, visibly drunk.

"Silverbrook, I was congratulating the happy couple."

"Reginald is the lucky one. The boy has nothing to offer but sour grapes. Don't know how he got this one to agree to marry him." He grabs at Nic in an awkward half-hug with his hand entirely too close to her breast.

My vision tinges red. Tightening my own grip on her, I propel her in front of me and to the other side, far from my father. My chest puffs out as I stand at my full height and glare down at him. Not that he notices.

Lord Firth continues as if nothing happened. "So, Ravenscourt, your mother says you've been spending a lot of your time in New York. What's been keeping you so occupied in America?"

"We bought a flat there. Nic is a gifted photographer with many clients in New York. You probably saw her work in the latest issue of Time magazine."

"So you're a house husband?" Father snorts like he's made a joke.

"Actually, Reginald has been making connections within the publishing world of New York. He's got a great eye for editing."

"Yes, well, hobbies are important, I suppose. There's Winston." Without another word, he stumbles off towards another portly gentleman in the corner.

The night blurs in a string of meaningless conversations, none nearly as pleasant as the interaction with Lord Firth. Empty congratulations. Thinly veiled inquiries as to why we eloped so quickly. Nic handles it all with grace and poise. Redirecting the old biddies and charming the codgers.

It is probably the best Christmas Eve gathering I've ever had.

As the party winds down, my father disappears into his study with a few gentlemen—most likely to play cards. Nic hides a yawn, and I take that as our cue to leave.

I approach Mother where she sits with Lady Wentworth. "We're going to say goodnight now, Mother. Happy Christmas."

She turns briefly to glance at us both. "Yes, yes, dear. Happy Christmas." She returns to the conversation before we've even stepped away.

Foster is waiting with our coats by the door. Nic gives him a quick squeeze as she takes hers. The older man beams as I help her slip the red wool on. Feeling bold, I grab her hand and interlace our fingers.

Without hesitating, she leans her head onto my shoulder. "Come on, let's go home."

CHAPTER TWENTY-SIX

Ghosts of Christmas Future

NICOLETTE

The moon is high, streaming through the windows when we reach Reginald's apartment. Shoes are kicked off at the door and coats tossed on the dining room table to be cleaned up tomorrow.

I stagger to the black leather couch and collapse across the cushions. "I feel as though I've run a marathon."

That rare but sexy laugh rumbles through his chest; rough like it's been rarely used. With one hand, he lifts my feet, moving them to his lap as he joins me on the sofa. "I always feel that way after a session with my parents." His strong hands start kneading the sore muscles of my feet.

"Oh my god, don't stop. I'll give you anything if you keep going. Blow job, butt stuff. Name it, just don't stop. Doing. That." My head falls deeper into the cushion.

His lap shakes under my legs with his laughter. "Why the hell do women wear heels? They look like torture."

"Probably because of a man."

"Fair enough." I soak in the silence, enjoying his hands working the knots out of my feet. Then he breaks it. "Thank you for coming tonight. I always dread those parties."

"Are they always like that?"

I slit open my eyes, studying him. Reginald stares off, looking tired and sad.

"Usually they're worse."

I shudder. "Isn't Christmas supposed to be about family? Did you at least spend Christmas Day the four of you?"

"Never. I spent it in my room with a new book while Father fought a hangover and Mother started planning her next event. How about you?"

"Grandmama would take me to see the Nutcracker, then to midnight mass. There would be presents under the tree when we got back." I swallow back a lump at the thought of my grandmother.

"What's wrong, Princess?" His hands pause and his eyes glint with concern in the moonlight.

I push down the swell of sadness for the dozenth time this evening. "What do you mean?"

"There's this sad look every time someone mentions your grandmother. Do you miss her? Why don't we go see her tomorrow? I can try to find tickets to the ballet."

Slowly, I shake my head, sit up, and hug my knees to my chest. "I called the house earlier, and Gloria said she wouldn't talk to me." I stare at my legs, wanting to share more but not sure how to word it. "She hasn't spoken to me since before the wedding. We've never been exactly close, but nothing like this."

Reginald leans forward and swipes the moisture from under my eye. "I'm sorry, Nic. I had no idea."

I smile at his obvious care. "Thanks." My hand covers his, still cupping my face. "The party wasn't all bad."

"It was rather nice to have someone on my side for once to help navigate the social jungle. An ally."

"You mean a spouse?"

"Better, an ally with benefits."

I kick his thigh with my foot, but we're both laughing.

Reginald checks his watch. "It's well after midnight. Would you like your present?"

"You didn't have to buy me anything."

"I wanted to." He gives my calf a last squeeze and retrieves a large, flat package from behind the tree. I sit up fully as he approaches. There's a vulnerability in his eyes as he holds the gift out. Whatever this is, it's important to him.

Carefully, I balance the flat package on my knees and tear open the brown wrapping to reveal a framed print. Once the image is fully visible, I angle it in the moonlight for a better look. It's a drawing of a little girl, her hair in black pigtails smiling at the viewer with a black cat winding around her legs. It's drawn in clean lines and vibrant colors. The initials HK are scrawled in the corner.

Hashi Kato. My father.

I lift wide eyes to Reginald. "Where did you find this?"

He grips the back of his neck. "Daniel's gallery friend, Henri, helped track it down. There weren't many of your father's works still in circulation, but we were able to buy this one."

"He was a cartoonist mostly—there wouldn't be much out there—but I remember this one. It was one of the last he did before the accident. He was developing a comic series, he said I would be his inspiration and drew this to show me. I never knew what happened to all his art." I place the precious drawing on the couch and approach Reginald. His arms open immediately to hold me as I wrap mine around his shoulders. "Thank you."

He holds me close, a large palm cupping the back of my head, then draws back with a sigh. "There's one more thing. When Henri was at our flat, he saw your photos. He loved them and wanted to offer you a show. I have his card for you." I go to argue, but he holds a finger against my lips. "You know, I think your work is amazing, but I didn't seek this out. You earned it on your own. No pressure, it's up to you."

The twist in my stomach relaxes. Reginald is nothing but honest. If he says no pressure, then he means it. He's providing me with options and letting me decide. This isn't his way of telling me he wants me to be more successful as an artist. There's no hidden agenda.

"Now where's my present? I believe there were offers of blow jobs and...butt stuff?" Reginald waggles his eyebrows at me.

I laugh as I let him pull me towards his bedroom. This has been the best Christmas in a long time.

January

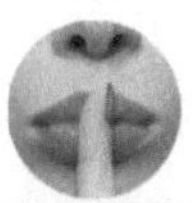

Whisper Wire

The jet-setting couple is at it again. They appeared together at the annual Silverbrook Christmas Party—flying in from JFK in the nick of time. Sources say they were attached at the hip the entire event and made "quite the delightful couple." After spending Christmas Day in Lord Ravenscourt's London flat, they boarded another plane, this time bound for sunny Florida. Rumor has it they're attending the New Year's Eve Party at Pop. They realize they are nobility, right? You would think the couple would invest in a private plane or at least airline stocks for all these excursions! It's not like they're hurting for the money with their combined wealth.

Still unsure what Lord R is up to with this Elysium venture. The website and social media accounts link to feel-good stories about everyday people and celebrities alike. Is this a gossip channel? An internet replay account? Are you boys trying to be me? Flattering, but your angle is all wrong. Come and get me, I'm not scared.

TTFN
Wendy

CHAPTER TWENTY-SEVEN

New Year Hopes

REGINALD

I lean back from the table, wiping a soft linen napkin across my lips. My stomach is borderline overfilled. Nic is leaning towards Colin in a heated debate, as the rest of her friends and their partners surround us. I'm happy to sit back, watch, and eat.

The gifted chef herself sits next to me. Her eyes dart around the room, and her fingers grip David's—just above a shiny new wedding band.

"You have nothing to worry about. I'm not sure I've ever eaten so much delicious food at an event before." She turns to me with wide eyes. "Seriously, not even the Savoy high tea holds a candle to you. This is a triumph."

Anna takes a deep breath, her shoulders relax as she releases it. She rests her hand on my elbow and her voice fills with emotion when she speaks. "Thank you." Her eyes focus on me, brows pinching slightly. "So what are your hopes for the new year?"

I go to push back the typical discomfort in social situations, and find it missing. While I haven't spent much time with Nic's friends, they've been welcoming and easy to talk to. "I'm not sure. I'm content as I am. What about you? With a launch and a wedding, what more could the New Year bring?"

She laughs. "You have a point there, suga'. Maybe some peace and quiet should be the goal. For both of us." She lifts her glass and I clink mine to it.

David stands, resting his hands on his wife's shoulders. "Come on, Hell's Bells, you owe me a dance." He winks at me as he leads her to the crowded dance floor.

Laying my arm on the back of Nic's chair, I survey the other side of the room. The girls have truly made something marvelous here.

The room sparkles with crystal and mood lighting, giving an elegant atmosphere, but the subdued furniture and decor keep it from feeling stiff. Behind the backlit bar, two bartenders flip bottles and pour drinks. The center of the room features a white dance floor with colorful lights and projections. On the nearby stage, Anna's brother, Huck, plays with his band. It's the best parts of a New York club and London ballroom mixed together.

A warm weight lands on my arm as Nic settles back. Her debate evidently finished, she turns to me with a smile, then leans closer. "Having fun?"

"Yes. This is so much better than my parents' last week. Do you think we could convince Anna to cater next year? Then at least we'd be miserable and well-fed."

She laughs and presses into me more. "Your mother might even smile. It's hard to be in a bad mood when Anna's cooking." Her scarlet-painted lips lift as she sips her champagne. "Thank you for being here. It's nice. Sharing this with you, I mean." She turns.

With our noses inches apart, I can see the vulnerability in her eyes. My stomach clenches and my heart pounds. I skirt my fingers along her delicate jaw, her pulse thundering under my hand. I tuck a loose strand of hair behind her ear. "There's nowhere I'd rather be."

Emotions dance across her eyes. Like me, she's learned to school her features in public, but I could watch her expressive eyes forever. Confusion, heat, and something that looks a lot like hope swirl within.

"Ren..." She leans in, her eyes on my mouth. My hand still cradling her jaw. Just before our lips meet, the song ends and the crowd breaks into loud applause, shattering the moment. She blinks the haze from her eyes and pins her social smile back on. "You know what? Huck's band is actually pretty good. I'm going to go grab some footage. You good here?"

I nod and reluctantly remove my hand. My eyes trail her as she darts through the crowd, a vision in a backless silver cocktail dress that clings to her lithe form.

"What a night." Asher plops down into Nic's abandoned seat. "Let's hope this next year is quieter. I could use a break." He tosses back the rest of his drink.

Johnson sits on my other side, the glow of his phone screen lighting his face. I glance at him curiously. "Two weddings, a baby, and an expansion at Pop? This town can't take much more excitement than that." He doesn't even look up, his fingers flying across the screen.

We sit and enjoy the music for a minute. When Johnson still hasn't lifted his head, I turn to Asher with a questioning look. He merely shrugs and shakes his head.

The curiosity finally gets the better of me. "Hey, mate, what are you doing on your phone?"

"My guild has a siege tonight and as the only paladin I couldn't let them down."

Was that supposed to clear anything up? I turn to Asher again, this time for translation, but he looks as lost as me.

Feeling the silence, Johnson finally looks up. "It's an online multiplayer RPG. You don't game either, do you? Dammit, when is this group going to get more gamers?"

"Sorry, I've always been more of a book person."

With a muttered curse, Johnson returns to *sieging*, or whatever he's doing.

Asher leans across me towards his friend. "What a waste having that face on a complete nerd. Don't you even want to get laid? You got enough numbers tonight." In answer, Johnson flips him off without looking up. Asher only shakes his head at his friend and turns back to me. "So you're a reader? What genres?"

I settle into my chair. This is a topic I'm always comfortable with. "Started with the classics in the family library—Shakespeare, Austen, Shelley, Keats, Byron. Then I moved on to the American legends—Hawthorne, Twain, Fitzgerald. Now with my e-reader I'll pick up anything. Suspense, fantasy, space opera, horror, even romance."

"Wow, that's eclectic taste. So is that why you got into publishing? Nic mentioned something about it."

"Sort of, though Elysium is strictly a human interest magazine. We don't do books."

"Well, why not?"

"It's a completely different market. Hard to break in with the big houses dominating the industry and ad space."

Asher shakes his head and leans in further, forearms resting on his knees. "I'm not talking about the trad houses. Self-publishing is an underserved market. If you already have the printing and distribution infrastructure from your magazine, offer services to indie authors. Editing services, copywriting, graphics, special edition runs, hell, even subscription boxes. You have it all there in a magazine. Just expand to partnering with indie authors who pay upfront, so no risk to you if it doesn't sell."

His words bounce around my skull, sparking ideas and thoughts. Books have always been a cornerstone in my life. The one comfort in a life of stricture. Could I actually be part of that?

Pale arms wrap around my shoulders, and I smell Nic's familiar perfume. "Come on, you haven't danced with me and it's almost midnight."

I nod at the guys and follow my wife into the crush on the dance floor. It's too crowded to really dance, so we merely sway to the music. It's too loud to talk, but our eyes are having a conversation all their own.

Ten...

As the countdown begins, I pull her fully against my body.

Nine...

She arches her back slightly, pressing her hips more firmly into mine

Eight...

My hand strokes up her bare spine to bury in her hair, keeping her face close.

Seven...

Her lips part and her fingers grip my shirt.

Six...

My nose glides along hers in a slow, intimate caress.

Five...

A gasp, more felt than heard, leaves her parted lips.

Four...

My fingers trail along her neck to cup her jaw.

Three...

The green flecks in her eye sparkle in the lights, holding both secrets and promises.

Two...

The room fades away. My heart picks up speed as her eyes drop to my lips.

One...

We both lean forward, our closed lips meeting. I tilt my head for a better angle, my tongue seeking access. My hands softly clutch her to me, afraid to hold on too tight, terrified to let go.

Nic melts against me, opening herself as her arms slide further around me.

A cacophony of emotions shakes me—too many to name or properly process—but I do my best to convey them to her with my tongue. This isn't our first kiss, far from it, but until now, we only shared impassioned embraces during sex. Any public displays were chaste and for show.

"Happy New Year!"

The crowd cheers and we break apart—reluctantly on my part. Friends pull us into a heartfelt round of hugs and well-wishes. As we're passed around the circle, we maintain eye contact. I see the same questions reflected in her eyes that are echoing in my mind. What now? What does this mean? Where do we go from here?

The only thing I know is there's no pretending now.

CHAPTER TWENTY-EIGHT

Reality Check

NICOLETTE

It's been a peaceful morning, both of us sharing space but concentrating on our separate tasks. One week in Florida has blended into two—neither of us seeming anxious to return to colder climates when we can work remotely. For me though, work just isn't... well, working today. I drop the tablet onto my lap and pick up my still steaming mug of coffee.

Warm sunlight streams through the floor to ceiling windows, bathing me in it's happy glow. It's why I put the couch in this spot, so I could take catnaps in the sun without going outside. I wriggle my toes, smiling at the swan symbol as the fuzzy material of my fleece socks stretch around my feet.

Without looking up from his laptop, Reginald gives my foot a gentle squeeze where it rests between his hip and the back cushion. As the couch is wide enough for two, we've taken to both sitting on opposite ends with our legs sharing the middle—like a pair of Manolo Blahnik pumps in a box.

Dressed in soft trousers and a henley, Reginald is about as casual as he gets. I need to buy the man some athleisure clothes. His dark brows pinch behind his reading glasses. Slate-gray eyes dart across the laptop screen before him. Each word bringing a more pronounced pout to his lips. I miss the warmth on my foot immediately as he lifts his hand to hit the backspace key repeatedly.

"What's wrong?" I tap him with my toe to gain his attention.

With a sigh, he pinches the bridge of his nose, lifting his glasses. My core clenches. I never had a thing for teachers, but this sexy scholar look is working for me.

"It's this list of articles for the magazine. I'm not sure they're right."

"What do you have so far?"

"Lord Firth's environmental efforts, the book drive at Cambridge, that artist working with orphanages, and an interview with an up-and-coming actress who grew up a war refugee."

All worthy topics of a human interest magazine dedicated to positivity, but I immediately see why he's struggling. "Those all sound good, but it's a bit repetitive."

"What do you mean?" His brows pinch, appearing more confused than angry.

"Well, all those pieces are about public figures. Who is your demographic? Are their stories represented? Most people like reading about themselves."

I see the moment it clicks.

His eyes widen and his lips form an adorable O before spreading into a full grin. "You're right. Brilliant as usual. Thank you." His hand returns to my foot.

I laugh, secretly warmed by his praise, as I glare down at the offending tablet. "Not sure about that."

"Something troubling you at work?"

"It's this photoshoot next month. I can't find the right theme. They gave me full creative control and I'm not sure what to do."

He closes the laptop and removes his glasses. Warmth blooms in my chest at his full attention.

"Don't you typically have full control?"

"Not really. There's usually a brief—something laying out the theme and basic requirements. This magazine keeps saying they trust me after seeing the Time piece. Why did I have to do such a good job?" The buttery leather of the sofa arm cushions my head as I sink lower.

Reginald chuckles as he squeezes my foot again. "Because you're brilliant—like I said. What is the feature about? Who's the client?"

"Playbill," I mumble.

His fingers still. Immediately feeling the loss of his touch, I kick his hand until he resumes his foot rub with another warm chuckle.

"That's amazing, Nic. I'm so proud of you."

My cheeks warm at his praise. "It's not a big deal."

"The hell it isn't. Why do you do that? You always play down your accomplishments. It's like you're allergic to compliments."

"Well, the girls always say I'm allergic to emotions, so it tracks." My lips spread in a smile, though I feel no amusement. Instead of laughing, Reginald's jaw clenches. "What?"

"You deflected. I'm trying to have a real conversation with you, and you have your social face on."

"My what?" My face goes cold and my stomach drops.

Reginald crosses his arms and again, I immediately miss the warmth of his hand on my foot. "You put on a show with people. Tell them what you think they want to hear. Don't do that with me."

"Are you calling me a liar?" My shoulders lift. His comments, so similar to Bree's, putting me on edge.

"No." He rakes his fingers through his hair, leaving it standing up. "You don't lie, but you smile at them and send them off in the wrong direction. You hide behind that mask and everyone eats out of your hand because you're so goddamned beautiful."

I'm not sure if I should be angry or flattered. On the one hand, he's calling me fake, but on the other he thinks I'm beautiful. How does he want me to react? Dark brows lower over stormy gray eyes. Jaw clenched, but lips not pinched. Closed body language with his arms, but still facing me...

"Stop it." I blink dumbly. "You're trying to read me so you can shift your answer. Look, I get it. I grew up in the same shallow world you did. I appreciate your ability to work a crowd... when we are out being Lord and Lady Ravenscourt. But when we're here..."

He propels himself forward until he is sitting before me. Frowning, he looks down at my hands as he holds them in his own. "When it's the two of us. I want you to be yourself. Just say whatever is in that beautiful head of yours."

My heart skips a beat. I search his face and only find sincerity.

He leans his forehead against mine with a groan. "Just be yourself with me, Princess. I promise to be your soft place to land—I won't judge and I won't pull away."

"You think I'm beautiful?" I whisper.

With a bark of laughter, he pulls back, a smirk clear on his lips. "You know you're gorgeous, but I'll make sure to say it more often." With a squeeze of my hands, he stands up. "No more work. I'll go make a snack and we'll binge some of that dating show you've been dying to watch."

I perk up in my seat. "The one where they are in those pod-thingies?"

He nods as he heads to the pantry.

As we sit close on the couch, an empty bowl of popcorn between us, I relax.

Be myself.

That's the scary thing. I do feel myself when I'm with him. It's easy to let go of the filter I constantly run my thoughts through. From the moment we met, I have said exactly what I want with no consideration of the consequences.

Accepting praise is not so easy, partially because of that shallow world he mentioned.

"I'm not used to compliments."

Reginald pauses the show and turns to face me better.

I keep my eyes on my hands in my lap, worrying a cuticle. "At least without a punchline. You know, the ones that include 'but', 'if only', or something similar. So I learned to give people what they want so they don't look too closely and find the 'but'."

He pinches my chin, and raises my eyes to his. I almost expect to see pity, but it's something closer to rage and sadness. "Listen to me. They're just jealous of you, Princess. You've rejected everything their world has handed you and made a fabulously successful new life for yourself. You've proven you don't need them, and it terrifies them."

My eyes burn, tears threatening to spill over at his impassioned words.

Warm fingers tuck a strand of hair behind my ear as he searches my eyes. "Don't make yourself smaller to fit their box. Kick the walls down and make them grow. Yeah?"

I nod once.

Satisfied, Reginald wraps an arm around my shoulders, tucking me into his side. His lips press to the top of my head before he resumes the show.

On the screen, couples talk through a divider, spilling their secrets in the hope they'll find their soulmate based on something deeper than looks. I laugh along, but my mind is still chewing over the last few minutes.

There's another reason his compliment threw me. One I'll never admit out loud.

His praise lit me up like fucking Times Square inside. And that scares me more than anything has in a long time. If being with him can make me feel this good, I don't want to imagine how bad it can feel without him.

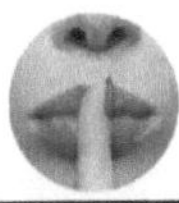 **Whisper Wire** ○ ○ ○

Ok, I'm big enough to admit when I'm wrong. I thought Lady Ravenscourt was slumming it for her choice of New Year's Party, but the footage on her Instagram is amazing. She obviously knows something I don't about Florida.

She and Lord R will be back on English soil soon, though. February means the annual Red Hearts Gala—the ultra posh event is the largest fundraiser for the Bancroft's Red Hearts Foundation, which supports major hospitals and heart disease research. Everyone is dying for an invite, surely Lady R wouldn't pass up the chance to be seen.

Speaking of which, she hasn't been spotted with the honorable Mrs. Atherton for quite some time. I've been so focused on Lord R's side of the match, have I missed family drama on the other? What do you think, readers?

TTFN
Wendy

CHAPTER TWENTY-NINE

Red Hearts Gala

REGINALD

I check my watch for the tenth time in as many minutes. First big Bancroft family gala as a married couple and we're going to be late. Mother is going to have a fit—not that it takes much to get her going these days. My eyes are still on the crystal face as I step into our bedroom. "Nic, are you almost..." I stop in my tracks as my eyes catch the first sight of her in the full-length mirror in the dressing room.

Red silk hugs her body, then pools around her feet. Thin lines of embroidered sequins glitter at the bodice and sleeves, which artfully leave her shoulders bare. A thigh-high slit shows the slightest peek of leg as she stands, one sequined heel pushed forward for inspection. Her ebony hair zigzags in gentle waves. Her ruby-red lips are pinched, and creases form around her smokey eye makeup.

Concerned, I step up behind her and lay a tender hand on her shoulder. "What's wrong, Princess?"

Doubt clouds her eyes as they meet mine in the mirror. "Is it too much?" Before I can comment, she rushes on. "When I bought it, I thought it fit the theme, but now I'm not sure. Everything is covered but... it's still too sexy."

"You look stunning. There is no such thing as too sexy, though as your husband I am arguably biased. I love the red. Certainly different from all those pastels you normally wear to these things."

"I don't want to embarrass your family." She leans her shoulder into me, as if for support. Her eyes glimmer as they hold mine in the mirror.

The vulnerability in her eyes is my undoing. How could this amazing woman be brought so low by self-doubt? Who did this to her? Instantly I want to know, so I can hunt every bully down.

"You could never be an embarrassment. You are my wife. Frankly, you are the only reason I've survived these past few events without scaring off investors."

Her lip trembles in a half-hearted smile. "Grandmama would hate this dress. Are you sure your mother won't be mad?"

Honestly, she might be, but lately my mother has no trouble finding something to be offended by. "Fuck them."

Her eyes widen but a crease of concern still mars her beautiful face.

I'll just have to do something about that.

My left hand grips her hip, pulling her ass against the erection tenting my tuxedo pants. My lips brush the shell of her ear as I whisper, "Can't leave you in your head all night. I'll have to give you something else to think about." My other hand trails along her wrapped bodice, following the swells of her body until it finds the warm flesh of her thigh. Fingers slip beneath the scarlet fabric, searching the hidden depths for the valley of her thighs. Instead of a scrap of cloth, I feel her bare pussy, and groan. "No panties, Princess?"

Her breath increases and her tongue darts out to wet her lips. "I didn't want to worry about lines." Her legs shift ever so slightly, allowing me better access.

"Knowing you are naked under this dress is going to distract me all night." I lightly trace her slit. Soft, teasing strokes highlighting the torture she's about to unleash on me.

Nic rocks her hips, rubbing her ass against my erection and encouraging my fingers to further explore. "I'm sorry."

"I'm not," I growl in her ear. Gathering some of her building arousal, I circle her clit, all the while watching her eyes glaze with lust. Stepping in closer, I curl my hand, slipping into her slick center. She groans and her inner muscles quiver. A second finger joins the first. The heel of my hand presses on her sensitive bud with every stroke.

Her head falls back. A slew of incoherent moans falling from her mouth.

My hand leaves her hip to grip her chin, forcing her to face the mirror again. "Don't you look away. Watch how beautiful you are in your passion. You are a fucking goddess and don't you forget it." I thrust in and out of her pussy with each word.

Her eyes meet mine. "Reginald, please."

My fingers pick up their grueling pace, curling to hit that spot I know she likes best. "I wish I had time to fuck you properly. I want you dripping down your legs all night thinking of all the ways I'll take your body when we get home. Now cum."

Mouth opening in a silent scream, she does. Wetness rushes as her core clenches around my hand. Her weight now rests on my chest more solidly as her breasts heave at the sweetheart neckline in panting breaths. Her eyes stare as I lift my fingers—glistening from her orgasm—to my lips and suck them clean. "That's better."

She smiles. It's small and tentative, but she finally looks more herself.

I drop a kiss to her temple, then head to the door, calling over my shoulder, "Finish up, we're leaving in five minutes."

She steps towards the bed to retrieve her clutch and wrap. I'm satisfied to see a slight wobble to her legs. "Where are you going?"

"To change my tie." With a yank, I pull the black silk from my neck and toss it to her. "Leave that one. We'll be needing it later."

The limo pulls up to the red carpet in a sea of lights. I stand and tug my jacket in a practiced gesture as cameras flash like fireflies in the crowd. Reaching down for her hand, I watch Nic exit the car with her confident smile back in place. She could have been an award-winning actress if she'd wanted to.

We make our way, stopping for photographs in front of the charity banner. Nic looks gorgeous in her dress, and I'm not the only one to admire it. Men and women stare at her as she gracefully moves by my side. I wrap my hand around her ribs, resting just under the swell of her breast.

Is it a possessive gesture? Damn right. Borderline immature and might cause tabloid stories tomorrow? Right again. But at this moment I don't care. Nic is my wife, and everyone else can sod off.

She doesn't move away, if anything, she leans closer to me as we pause for photographs. Halfway down the carpet, she turns her head, leaning in so close that her breath tickles my ear. "Lord Crawford's dates get younger every year—I swear this one could be his granddaughter. Imagine what we'd raise for erectile dysfunction instead."

My lips quiver as I fight a smile.

"We could call it the Little Blue Gala."

Unable to hold back any longer, I let loose a belly laugh. It sounds rusty to my own ears. When was the last time I really laughed? The thought is sobering enough to school my features back into their stoic mask.

We reach the end of the carpet where my family waits. A grim look of displeasure mars my mother's otherwise flawless face. "Where have you been?"

Nic stiffens slightly under my arm as I lean in to give the expected kiss to my mother's cheek. "It's my fault. I had to change my tie."

"Red? The two of you really should clear your outfits with me in the future."

I grit my teeth to moderate my tone. "Relax, Mother, the theme is red hearts. Aren't you overreacting a tad?"

"Whatever has gotten into you lately, Reginald." She shakes her head, every strand of hair staying perfectly in place.

"I, for one, think Nic looks lovely in that gown, Mother," Monty leans in, grasping Nic's hand. "Quite ravishing."

Mother grabs Monty's arm with a hard look. "Well, it's too late now. Go mingle and remember who you are." With one last glare at us, she turns to a couple approaching, summarily dismissing us.

Father is barely paying attention to us as he smiles and nods at the crowd.

Nic slips her hand into the crook of my elbow and we enter the gala itself. We make the rounds, schmoozing donors and family friends alike. My wife is unstoppable. She uses that uncanny ability of hers to draw everyone in.

The band plays the opening refrain of a waltz. "Shall we dance?" I hold my hand out to Nic. Her eyes twinkle as she takes my hand and lets me lead her out onto the floor.

"You're quite the dancer, Lord Ravenscourt." Her cheeks blush beautifully as I swing her through another turn.

"Five years of ballroom lessons. Mother insisted."

"For once, I approve of something your mother did."

I chuckle. "Thank you for coming with me tonight."

"Of course. Wasn't that part of the deal?" Her lips quirk into a sassy smile.

"True, but I appreciate you being here all the same. This one isn't as terrible as they usually are, and I'm positive you're the reason."

"I haven't done anything."

"Tell that to Lord Fairchild! For years, my mother has been trying to convince him to sponsor the foundation, yet in one night you have him writing a check large enough to build a new hospital wing." I couldn't help smiling down at her as she wooed elderly Lord Fairchild, a man who has single-mindedly hated my family for years.

"That big teddy bear?"

I tighten my arm at her waist, pulling her in closer than strictly proper. "You are marvelous. What would I do without you?"

She leans in with catlike grace. "Pray you never find out."

Damn convention. I lean forward to give her a kiss, but before my lips make contact, a hand lands on my shoulder.

"May I cut in? Never got a chance to dance with the bride at the wedding." Monty grins at me, waggling his eyebrows.

I look at Nic. She nods, but I see frustration in her eyes. It's the only solace I have as I let go. My feet take me to the bar, every instinct telling me to go back and drag her away from Monty.

The first scotch goes down like fire. The burn of the second is more welcome, matching my roiling emotions. I set the glass down with a clink as a cloud of pink fabric invades my peripheral vision.

"I've missed you, Reggie-bear. We need to talk."

My stomach drops at her voice. Instead of looking at Serena, I turn and track my wife as she dances across the floor with my brother.

CHAPTER THIRTY

Inconvenient Feelings

NICOLETTE

My earlier enjoyment of the night quickly fades as my dance partner draws me in. Where Reginald is a graceful dancer, Montague is forceful. His insistent hand at my waist pulling me in closer than I want to stand. A little too close for polite society, but not to the point that he's clearly being inappropriate.

"How are you enjoying your first gala?" The scotch is thick on his breath.

"It's hardly my first—I grew up with all this too."

"That's right. It's still your first Bancroft gala, though."

I make a noncommittal noise, counting down the seconds until I can excuse myself. Although I haven't spent much time with Reginald's younger brother I can tell that he's everything I hate about London's upper crust. Entitled and spoiled, to the point he believes he's invincible. Add on his natural good looks and he thinks all women should fall at his feet.

"Well, that certainly didn't take long." Montague's eyes stare at something behind me. As we take the next bend, I scan the crowd for what might have caught his eye. "I must say, you are a lot more calm about this than most brides would be."

As we take a turn, I spot Reginald with a young blond woman in a ghastly pink dress. She smiles up at him. There's something familiar about her, but I can't place the face. Did he really think a random woman would make me jealous? "There are husbands speaking to women who are not their wives all over this room, Monty."

"True, but how many of them are their ex-fiancée?" The air catches in my lungs. I concentrate on maintaining my calm expression, but his eagle eyes catch some of my discomfort. "I'm so sorry. I assumed you knew. Mother was heartbroken it didn't work out. She and Lady Wentworth are childhood friends, and she was so looking forward to having Serena as a daughter."

The orchestra plays on, my feet follow along by pure muscle memory while inside, I'm crumbling. The worst part is I don't even have a right to be jealous. He's never told me he loves me. We even signed a contract saying our time apart was our own. So why does it feel like someone has kicked me in the chest?

"Looks like things might not be as over as I thought. But, hey, you got the ring on your finger. That means you won, right?" The song ends, and he steps back, again gazing towards the bar.

I follow his eyes and see Reginald and Serena there. She's leaning close into him, touching his arm, the skirts of her pink ballgown pressed against his leg. From this angle, I can't see Reginald's face, but he certainly makes no move to push her away.

The crowd presses together, slowing my path to the bar. Absently, I nod as acquaintances call my name, my eyes only on the hideous pink silk ahead.

"I'll be waiting for you, Reggie-bear." The bitch rests her pink tipped claws on Reginald's arm possessively as I approach from behind him. Her eyes sweep over my body, her lip curling. When she meets my gaze, triumph flashes in the cold blue depths.

My husband steps back from her and closer to me, an unreadable look on his chiseled face.

"Serena, may I present my wife, Nicolette? Darling, I believe you met her parents at the Christmas party. Our mothers are old friends." Reginald rests his hand on my spine. Instead of the comforting warmth of earlier, it feels like a lie. He gives me a curious look as I step away.

"We've met." I don't bother turning towards the other woman. "Reginald, your mother was adamant we thank all the donors."

His gray eyes narrow ever so slightly. "Yes, of course. Excuse us, Serena."

As we pass through the ballroom, he grips my elbow, pulling me up short. "What's wrong? Are you alright?"

"Fine. Why ever wouldn't I be?" I don't meet his eyes as I widen my debutante smile.

The rest of the gala is quickly over, though the time drags without the earlier air of lightness and fun. I smile and nod at each donor, asking all the right questions. Outside, I'm the happy society wife. Inside, I'm that same scared little girl, wondering why no one loves me.

Reginald is the only one to notice. He shoots me some concerned looks but doesn't press it further.

The limo ride home is silent. My fingers dig into my arms as I stare out the window. The space between us is less than a few feet, but it might as well be miles. So different from the ride here, full of heated looks, both of us thinking about what his hands did to me in this dress. Was that only a few hours ago?

The wheels barely stop and I'm out the door and across the lobby, boarding the elevator without a backwards glance. I press the button for Reginald's floor, willing the doors to close faster. His hand appears, catching the doors at the last second. Brows pinched over stormy gray eyes.

I hold my breath as he leans in, but he only stabs the button. The tension is so high, I can hardly stand still. The diamonds on my wedding band dig into my fingers as I make a fist, eliciting a fresh wave of pain and confusion. As soon as the elevator opens, I shoot out, my long legs eating up the distance despite the heels.

He follows close behind, like an enormous cat stalking its prey. "Would you like to tell me what the bloody hell is going on?"

I keep walking. Through the living room, and into his bedroom. This dress that once felt like a dream, is now a nightmare of barbed wire, and I'm desperate to be rid of it.

Reginald slams the bedroom door. "Goddamn it, Nic. Tell me what is going on." He grabs my arm and turns me to face him.

Even in his anger, his grip is gentle. That touch shatters me all over again. My heart pounds. I clench my fingers, worried I'll pull him closer instead of pushing him away. I want to hate him, but I can't.

His eyes soften as they search my face. "Did someone say something?"

A harsh bark of a laugh claws my throat. "You could say that."

I tear my arm from his grasp, turning away. Numb fingers grip at the zipper, trying to gain leverage.

"It was Monty, wasn't it? What did he say?"

"Something illuminating." The zipper finally moves in jerky bursts before sticking halfway down. I grit my teeth and contort my body to better grip the closure.

"For Christ's sake, let me help you." He takes two steps towards me, hands outstretched.

My temper flares. With a last tug, the zipper gives way, and the dress falls to the floor. I step out of the red silk puddle and stalk towards him wearing only my heels.

His eyes heat to molten steel as they rake my body before returning to my eyes.

Despite my rage, my inner self purrs in satisfaction at my effect on him. I lift my chin, filling myself with all the haughty air I can muster. "I want the truth. Even if you don't think I'll like the answer. Even if it's uncomfortable. A lie will always be worse than the truth."

He falters, surprised by this turn in conversation. "I agree."

"I'll ask you a series of questions and I only want yes or no answers." He nods briskly. "Were you engaged to Serena Wentworth?"

He blanches and takes a step forward. "Who told you? It's more compli…"

I hold my hand up, halting him mid-word. "Yes or no?"

Reginald's jaw clenches. "Yes." The word drips with ice.

"Is Serena interested in continuing the relationship?"

Emotions flash across his face. I can't tell if it's regret or guilt. "Yes."

I nod. My eyes drop to the cold floors, the closet, anywhere but the man in front of me. "I better wash this hairspray out before bed." My feet numbly walk to the en suite, pausing at the door without looking back. "I have an early flight back to Florida." I slip into the bathroom, falling back against the door as I throw the lock.

He calls my name softly through the wood and tries the handle. "Nic, please, let me explain." It sounds as though his forehead is pressed to the door, right by my own. I cover my mouth, desperate to stifle the sound of my broken breaths.

The moment hangs. Him waiting for me to answer. Me trying to hold myself together.

When his voice comes again, it's the faintest of rasps. "I'll be out here when you're ready, Princess. I'm not going anywhere."

The cold tile stings my feet as I rush to the shower, turning the water on full blast. My skin burns as I slide down the wall to the floor. The ruby heels clatter as I toss them across the bathroom floor. A mocking reminder of my naïve hope at the beginning of the evening.

I let my head fall back against the tile, and finally give in to the overwhelming emotion. Hot tears stream down my face like lava. I haven't cried like this since I was a child.

After my parents died and my grandmother rejected me, I swore I would never let people close again. I've done well until now, but I need to face the truth. At some point, I let that unassuming, broody husband of mine into my heart.

We had a deal. I'm the one who wants to change the rules now. That's not fair to him. Yet as the scalding water washes me clean, I can't quite let go of the hurt. I shouldn't be mad at him. This is a me-problem. So I need a me-solution.

Florida. Everything will be better with some distance.

I just need a new project to distract me from these inconvenient feelings for my husband.

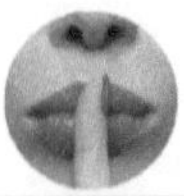

Whisper Wire

●●●

Patience is a virtue, my friends—though not usually one of mine. I was almost growing bored with the idyllic image of Lord and Lady Ravenscourt, but I held strong with my vigilance, and boy have I been rewarded!

The couple made a dramatic entrance at the Gala with coordinated outfits. Lady R turned heads in a shocking red dress, but evidently not shocking enough to hold her husband's attention. While his wife was dancing with his dashing brother, Lord R was seen renewing an old...friendship. Enter Miss Wentworth—Lord R's longtime girlfriend. Rumor has it the young woman and Lord R were on the verge of wedding bells themselves before a mysterious parting. Official sources for Lord R claim they are long-time family friends. If it were so innocent, why is Lady R back in Florida while Lord R attends functions alone? Functions where Miss W is also in attendance?

I just adore a good love triangle, don't you?.

TTFN
Wendy

CHAPTER THIRTY-ONE

Junk Food and Feelings

NICOLETTE

The Florida golden sunset shining through my penthouse window does little to lift my mood. The apartment feels cold and empty in ways I've never noticed before. I toss my phone across the couch, wanting that vile gossip rag to disappear.

If I ever find out who that Wendy is, I'm going to make her life miserable. I can take an unflattering candid and post it all over the internet. How's that for poetic justice for a tabloid bottom feeder!

This marriage of convenience is becoming quite inconvenient.

I don't care that Reginald has a past—we all do. I don't even care that his ex is some heinous society bitch—though it does make me question his taste. It's the insinuations that they are still...something that has me irritated.

It shouldn't.

That was the deal! I'm his wife in name only. When we are apart, he can do whatever, whoever he wants. And so can I—not that I have.

Reginald is the only person I've slept with in a year. Oh, there've been offers. I'd like to make the excuse that I've been too busy, but I really haven't been.

The truth is, no man has caught my interest since I met Reginald. When I can get the best orgasms of my life at home, why would I go out looking?

The fucking asshole has ruined sex for me with all men.

So I've found myself spending more time with him than our contractual week a month. I say it's just for the orgasms, but my current mood implies it could be more than that. The last thing I need is to depend on someone—that's the way of heartbreak. So here I am, alone in Florida on a self-proclaimed husband detox.

The irony is, with no shoots or Pop business to keep me distracted, my mind keeps flitting back to Reginald instead of thinking about literally anything else. I need a damn distraction. Some new project to dive into.

But first, junk food.

How about that new Mexican place? What the fuck was the name of it? I'd grabbed a flyer at the food truck event last month. Where did I shove it?

Padding across the kitchen floor with purpose, I rifle through junk drawers, finally finding a stack of papers I'd shoved away. As I'm shuffling through the pile, a single black business card falls to the counter.

Henri Beaufort Gallery.

It's stark against the white marble counters, the letters masculine but elegant and foiled in gold. I shoved the card in this drawer after Christmas and never thought of it again. Sure, it's flattering that this guy wants to show my work. Could I actually put an entire collection together with the pictures I have? What the hell would I have to say? I shoot rock stars and handbags for a living.

Turning decisively on my heel, I carry the flyer back to the couch to order and then consume my nachos while watching reality shows.

Just as RuPaul is about to declare the winner, my phone dings with a text.

Kenzo

> Hey love. I want to use this photo for the album. Can you play with the colors and send a high res file to me?

I shoot him a thumbs up, flick off the TV, and head to my home office to get to work.

To be safe, and because I really needed that distraction, I mock up a few different options and email them all.

As I'm shutting down my editing program, a file I've left open fills my screen. It's the photo of Reginald and I almost kissing in front of the aurora borealis. The greens, blues, and purples of the sky swirl out from behind us, giving the viewer the sense of Valkyrie wings. The starkness of our silhouette against the dancing lights gives me an idea.

Hundreds of images flash across my screen as I look for the perfect ones in my personal files. I copy them to a new folder moments before moving on to the next. Then I edit. A crop here. Adjust the color there. Blur this area, focus that one.

When the red light of dawn spreads across my wall, I realize I've been at it all night. When was the last time a project consumed me this much?

Probably never.

Stretching to crack my back, I head to the kitchen for something to eat and drink. As I lift the glass of water to my lips for a long sip, I eye the card again and pick it up. I tap the edge against the counter twice, then bring it with me to the office.

CHAPTER THIRTY-TWO

WWFDD?

REGINALD

I'm fucking exhausted. I've had board meetings during the week, luncheons on the weekends, and an endless round of dinner parties and museum events. It's all so meaningless. How many events do these people need? The gala was so successful and so many donors mentioned their interaction with me and Nic specifically, that my parents have thrown me to the wolves full time. The irony is not lost on me.

Even the new opening of the Royal Ballet couldn't cheer me, it only made me miss Nic more. She has been distant since she left. Barely replying to my texts, sending my calls to voicemail. It's clear she's hurting because of the rumors, but I don't know what to do. We'll hash it out this weekend when she flies in.

Until then, I have no excuse to avoid dinner at Silverbrook Hall. Resigned, I trudge up the stone steps and automatically head to my sanctuary in the house—the library. Halfway across the foyer, voices drifting from the parlor draw me up short.

If the earl and countess are entertaining, this is the last place I want to be.

Silently, I turn to retreat, but my escape is foiled by the booming voice of my father. "Reginald, boy, come join us." A heavy sigh escapes, drawing a raised eyebrow from the earl.

Squaring my shoulders, I follow him through the open doorway. Any semblance of a polite smile falls as all three Wentworths come into view. Lord

Wentworth barely spares me a look from his perch in an antique wingback chair, his full attention on my father's excellent scotch. Lady Wentworth sits delicately on the settee with my mother, eyeing me with cold indifference. On my mother's other side, Serena preens as she leans forward to better display her figure.

As if today couldn't get worse.

"Reginald, you're late."

Pushing down another sigh, I cross the room to greet my mother. "Yes, Mother, hospital committee meeting ran over." I nod to my mother's longtime friends. "Lord Wentworth. Lady Wentworth. Serena." Then I hightail it to the decanter in the corner. I don't want to get sloshed in case Nic calls, but some liquid bolstering is definitely called for in this situation.

"We've barely seen you in months, son. What have you been up to?" Lord Wentworth asks.

"I've been in New York, launching a magazine with a schoolmate." That wasn't what I meant to say. I keep saying the wrong thing, my mind too wrapped up in my wife.

"Why you continue on with that ridiculous hobby, I'll never know," Mother mutters into her wineglass. "Really, Reginald, it's so beneath a man of your station."

"Where is your wife?" My father looks back through the doors like he's looking for her to appear or only now realized she's not here. "Did you come alone?"

"Trouble in paradise already?" Serena's tone is demure, but bitterness shines in her perfectly made-up eyes.

"Nic is finishing up a project back in the States. She'll join me later this week."

Mother huffs on the couch. "You don't need to pretend, Reginald."

"What are you talking about, Penny?" Lady Wentworth asks.

"It's not like they have a proper marriage." Her hand flutters in my direction.

"Mother." I take a deep breath and continue through clenched teeth, trying for a less hostile tone. "I assure you, it is an actual marriage." I squeeze the crystal in my hand until my knuckles shine white, half convinced it will shatter.

"On paper, maybe." Shaking her head, she turns back to Lady Wentworth. "They have an understanding. She needed to marry to access her trust fund. They attend events publicly, but she gives Reginald full leave to do whatever he wants. I mean, really, they don't even live together."

A thump builds at my temple, and I half pray the sound of my heartbeat will drown out my mother as my vision tinges red.

"That's enough," I yell, drawing all heads towards me. My chest rises and falls as I wait for the anger to subside. It only grows and I realize I can't spend another minute in this room. "If you'll excuse me, I believe I've had enough for one day." Without waiting for a reply, I spin on a heel and march to the entryway.

"Reggie-bear." Her heels click against the marble as she runs after me.

I stop, but only half-turn back. "What do you want, Serena?"

Her bright smile dims momentarily, then she pushes on. She walks up to me with a sway to her hips that I'm sure she thinks is seductive, and lays a pink tipped hand on my chest. "If you're stressed, I could help relieve the tension."

"What are you doing?" My lip curls in disgust.

"I understand now. I know you had to marry her for the money, but maybe there's still a path for us." She licks her lips and looks up at me with doe eyes.

My fingers encircle her delicate wrist. Hope, desire, and victory light in her eyes.

"A path?" I shove her hand off me as if burned. "What the fuck do you think is going to happen here, Serena?"

She steps back, mouth agape as she rubs her wrist. "That we could continue on as before. That you would divorce her after an appropriate amount of time and..." Her words come to a stuttering halt as I tower over her at my full height.

"And what? Marry you?"

The shock in her glare gives way to building anger. "We were good together, once."

"No, Serena." She shrinks back slightly, a twinge of guilt pangs in my chest at scaring her, but this shit has gone on for far too long and I need to make myself heard. "We were never good together. I never loved you. It was just easier to go along with what everyone else wanted than figure out what I wanted for myself."

My cell vibrates. I immediately dismiss Serena as my entire focus is pulled to the text from my wife.

Nic

I'm sick. Not going to make it this weekend.

Me

Are you ok? I'll fly to you.

I start to type 'I love you', but my fingers freeze over the keyboard. The foyer spins as the realization hits me. I love her. This foreign warmth I feel when I think about her. The sense of home, of belonging I've never felt before. The overwhelming loss when she's not near. I'm in love with my wife, and I'm starting to think I always have been.

"Is *she* what you want?"

I'd completely forgotten Serena. She still stands before me, her cheeks mottled with rage as she glowers at me. "Some artsy whore who'll never be a proper countess?"

Drawing up to my full height, I glare at Serena with all the contempt and bitterness I've buried for years. "Nic is twice the woman you'll ever be, but even if she wasn't in the picture, you'll never be my countess."

She gulps. "You'll regret this."

I highly doubt that.

My phone is already to my ear as I storm down the front steps and back into the town car—much to the shock of Foster in the front. The line rings once before going to voicemail.

"Fuck," I yell as I toss my phone onto the seat.

"Everything alright, sir?" Foster's concerned voice echoes in the confined space.

"Not really." My fingers scrape down my face as I lean my head back. "Can you take me home, please?"

"Not staying for dinner, I take it. Where is the missus tonight?" His eyes dart to me as he pulls out into traffic.

"That's the million-pound question." I sound petulant to my own ears.

"If I might be so bold?"

"You know you can always speak freely with me, Foster." Yet he still asks every time after thirty years.

"Anyone who sees you with both Miss Wentworth and Lady Ravenscourt can see the truth of it. You know how these gossip rags go."

"I'm not the one needing convincing."

A soft chuckle. "Lady Ravenscourt knows, too. But knowing something and feeling it aren't quite the same thing. She just needs some reminding."

"How?"

"Make a big gesture. That always worked with my Julia. Some of those books you are always reading should give you some ideas. What would Mister Darcy do?"

What would Fitzwilliam Darcy do? Besides throwing money at her problems, that is. First, Nic is so independent she fixes her own problems before I can help, and second, it's her money anyway, so that doesn't work. There's got to be something else.

My mobile buzzes from the floor. I scramble to pick it up, hoping it's her.

Henri Beaufort

I'm glad you convinced her to call me. Merci beaucoup.

As I'm puzzling out that message, a second arrives. The image shows an invitation to an art show at Henri's gallery next month. I'm about to close it when the artist's name stands out.

Nic Kato-Atherton.

She's actually going to do it. A complex mix of emotions flood my senses. Pride in her for putting herself out there. Disappointment that she didn't tell me herself. Jealousy that she can share this with Henri and not me. Inspiration for my grand gesture.

I smile down at the phone as an idea forms.

"Did you think of something, sir?" Foster's voice sounds as hopeful as I feel.

"I believe I did. Might need some help, though."

Like so many times in my youth, Foster listens as I talk through my thought process. A thoughtful question here, a gentle nudge there, and by the time we pull up in front of my flat, I have the makings of a plan.

April

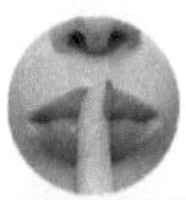 **Whisper Wire** ● ● ●

Love me, hate me, but I know when I sniff a story. Lord and Lady Ravenscourt have not been photographed together in over a month—believe me, I have bots sniffing the web for any whisper of the two of them. Lord R hasn't even left London in that time. Is his brief adventure into business now over? He appears to be the perfect little princeling again, dancing to daddy and mommy's tune. Every day he's been meeting with various boards the family sits on. Every night he's at some glittering society event.

Meanwhile, Lady R has finally vacated her Floridian sanctuary. She's back at the couple's New York townhouse, and photos place her all over the Big Apple, dinners in Manhattan, and shopping. So much shopping. She hasn't been gallivanting alone! Much of her time the last couple weeks have been spent with an utterly gorgeous French gallerist named Henri Beaufort. His website advertises a show of Lady R's work this month—under her maiden name. What are you up to?

Has the flame burned out for this fairy tale couple? Are they an utterly modern couple exploring openness? I want to know!

TTFN
Wendy

CHAPTER THIRTY-THREE

The Show

REGINALD

Lights flash as I exit the town car. I tug my cuffs to straighten the black tailored shirt across my back. Turn for the cameras. Nod vaguely. It's a dance I've done a thousand times, but tonight I want to make sure I get it right.

"Viscount Ravenscourt, over here." The vultures with cameras call my name, shouting over each other to be heard. I pivot to each, pausing for the picture.

A woman shoves to the front of the crowd, a determined glint to her brown eyes. "Viscount Ravenscourt, any comments about your upcoming publication? Why now for a new career?"

I mummer a polite "no comment" and take another step forward.

She pushes ahead along the rope, matching my pace. "How about the rumors that you and Serena Wentworth are renewing your...friendship. Got a comment on that?"

My eye twitches as red tinges my vision. That damned rumor has been dogging me for the last month.

Taking a deep breath through my nose, I wait until my voice can be trusted. "My wife is the focus tonight. I am here as Mr. Kato-Atherton, not Lord Ravenscourt. I'm happy to entertain questions that relate to her photographs or tonight's show. On any topic other than my wife's career, my answer is 'no comment'. Now if you excuse me, I'd like to head inside to my wife."

She's quickly lost as the glass doors shut behind me, silencing the crowd. The space is a cavernous room of brightly lit white walls. Three free-standing structures create an alcove in the center of the room, angled towards the front with a marble desk. A large photograph hangs with Nic's name in bold 3D letters, clearly visible from the entrance. The picture draws me in, my feet moving without thought.

Two silhouetted figures stand in the foreground, almost embracing, swaths of purple, green, and blue dance in the sky above them, as if billowing out of the female's shoulders. It's absolutely stunning. This is the photo she took on our honeymoon.

"Your wife is truly remarkable." Henri, Daniel's friend, joins me in studying the image.

"I already knew that. Is this one for sale, too?" He nods. "Not anymore. I'll pay, but no one else will be taking this one."

Henri's full lips curl, and he bows his head before calling over to his assistant. A quick exchange of whispered words and a sticker is placed on the sign under the frame.

Satisfied, I move deeper into the gallery to admire my wife's work.

The subjects vary. Here, a purple sky with flashes of lightning over a tranquil beach. There, a crane standing in a fountain. Or a vibrant flower growing between the bricks of a building.

There are landscapes and animals. Ocean views and harsh city skylines. Each photo highlights nature's raw beauty with some unexpected twist. It's all so very Nic.

As I mill through the crowd admiring the photographs, I hear murmured praise. The show is an absolute success. I finally spot her near the rear of the gallery, surrounded by a group in animated conversation.

Nic looks radiant in her black jumpsuit. The thin straps highlight her delicate shoulders and graceful collarbone and the loose pant legs draw the eye to her long limbs. The serene smile on her face wars with the excited sparkle in her eyes. She is completely in her element for maybe the first time.

She is so independent. It was one of the first things that drew me to her. Like a moth to a damn flame. She has this fire that burns bright enough to chase away my inner shadows. The emptiness when we're apart is becoming overwhelming. That flame might burn me alive, but oh, what a way to go.

The crowd parts as I approach. From this angle, I'm not sure Nic sees me until I've slipped an arm around her waist.

She startles, her eyes doing a double take. "Reginald!" Her hand flies to her chest, but she easily leans in to give me a welcoming kiss. She darts a few probing looks my way before turning back to her mini audience. "I'm sorry, Jack, you were saying?"

"I was asking where your inspiration for this show came from."

"Actually, in some ways, my husband. The first piece, Angels in the Sky, was taken on our honeymoon after he told me a myth about the Aurora. When I saw the images afterward, it reminded me of how beauty can be hidden deep inside, but it will always find a way out. We can try to shape the world around us, pretend that we control the earth, but the magic of nature can never be truly extinguished."

"That image is impressive. Surely you used software to render the picture, though." It's the same woman from out front.

"Absolutely not. All of these photographs are one-hundred percent practical effects."

"Come now, Ms. Atherton, you expect me to believe that a catalog photographer is suddenly capable of fine art photography?" She holds out her phone, eager to record every word.

"Yes, I have made my career through my skills in portraiture, although I have never artificially manipulated my work. Some manual color, lighting, or focus correction, but no digital effects. That photo is thanks to a long capture camera and patience."

"I still have the frostbite to prove it," I quip.

The group breaks into light chuckles. Seemingly more annoyed, the young woman turns to me. "Do you have any comments on your wife's work, Lord Ravenscourt? Would you prefer that she join your family foundation efforts instead?"

Nic bristles by my side. I squeeze my hand still clasped at her waist. "I have always been a supporter of the arts. It would be quite hypocritical to hold back such a gifted artist as Nicolette. I may be her husband, but I'm also one of her biggest fans. While my wife shares my passion for supporting artists, depriving the world of her viewpoint would be a crime."

The journalist finally gets the message. With pursed lips and a curt nod, she takes off, leaving the gallery completely.

The remaining group asks a flurry of additional questions about Nic's collection. Her inspirations, her process. If she plans to show again. I stand by silently, damned proud to be the one next to her.

CHAPTER THIRTY-FOUR

Jealous Husband

NICOLETTE

I can't believe he's here. That's the thought that keeps spiraling through my mind as I smile and entertain questions from the press and potential buyers. It's not that I don't think Reginald supports my work, he was the one that encouraged me to do this show after all. After the gala, I didn't think showing up in person fit in with the whole marriage deal. Bree and Anna aren't even here. That's because I didn't tell them about it.

I agreed to do this because I felt inspired in the moment and ran with it without a second thought. When it all became real, a tidal wave of what-ifs flooded my mind and I decided to keep the event to myself. I'm not even sure how Reginald knew about it, unless he got it off our shared calendar.

Yes, I let him link our calendars—it simply makes coordinating functions and travel easier.

The show has been fantastic. Talking about my photographs with like-minded individuals is invigorating. The girls have always loved my work, but they've never truly understood it. Mingling with other artists and hearing critics praise my photographs has been so much more than I ever dreamed.

Reginald's hand trails across my lower back, distracting me momentarily from the art buyer talking to me. "I'll be right back. Would you care for more champagne?"

I nod silently. His lips brush my temple in a kiss so brief I wonder if I imagined it.

The buyer hands me a card and promises to be in touch. Before I can relax, Henri has taken her place. "How are we holding up?"

I blow out a quick breath, my hair fluttering by my jaw. "Exhausted. Has it really only been a couple of hours?"

"*Oui.* I hope you regain your energy soon. Almost all the pieces have already sold. You are about to be a very busy lady, indeed."

"Seriously? How is that possible?"

"I told you, Nic, you have a unique view and the talent to capture it. This is only the beginning of a beautiful friendship. I want to put another show on the books, *mon amie. Tout de suite.*" He holds up an elegant hand, waving away any objection before I can even form them. "Now excuse me, I must go talk more buyers out of their money."

Wow. Of course I'd hoped a few of the pieces would sell, but practically all of them?

"Nic, there you are, love. Look at you, well done."

I turn to the voice, shocked to see Kenzo standing there in black jeans, a white tee, and a black leather jacket. Without his guyliner and spiky hair, I almost didn't recognize him.

After he shared my photos of his concert, he's been interacting with my posts a lot—including the video of Huck's band at New Year's Eve. We've been DMing off and on—mostly about contracts and compensation for using my pictures on the album cover.

"Kenzo, what are you doing here?"

He pulls me in and kisses both my cheeks. Stunned, I don't fight it. "I'm in the city meeting with my label before heading back out on tour. Saw the article about your show and figured I'd check it out." He motions around the room. "I like your stuff. I'll definitely be keeping an eye on you for all my future album covers."

A throat clears behind me. Reginald is standing nearby with two glasses of champagne. I reach for one. His knuckles, white where they grip the stem, take a moment to loosen. "Thanks, darling. Kenzo, I don't think you've met my husband yet."

Kenzo holds out his hand. "Good to meet you, mate. Congratulations. The news explained why I couldn't even convince this one to join me for dinner."

I roll my eyes. Turning back to look at Reginald, I expect his steel eyes to glitter with their previous dry humor, but something darker and cold shines there. Jaw clenched, shoulders rigid. This is not the same man who went for drinks. What the hell happened in the last five minutes?

"That so? And how did you meet my wife?" Reginald's hand anchors on my hip, but without the earlier softness.

"She was my photographer. Girl got me naked on the first shoot. There's no other for me since."

Waves of tension radiate off the steel arm around me. This is so not the right time for Kenzo to be himself.

"You remember the Time shoot? Then I took some candids at his concert back in July. Kenzo wants to use them for his album cover. Those are the contracts I've been talking about," I try to reassure him.

"Of course." He's still stiff, but some of the coldness has warmed. "What brings you here?"

"Just in the neighborhood and thought I'd check it out. I do need to head out to meet my manager, though. Congrats again, Nic. I'll let you know what the label says." He walks out the gallery doors to the flashes of paparazzi lights.

The show winds down. Henri stops us on the way to the door to tell us the remaining prints sold and he'll be in touch very soon.

A smattering of photographers still loiter at the door, snapping our photos and calling for comment. Ever the gentleman, Reginald opens the car door for me before walking around to the other side. The ride is silent, all the warmth of his arrival missing.

I study him, looking for indications of what changed in the last half hour. He stares out his window, but his eyes don't scan the passing city streets. His jaw is clenched so hard it appears carved from marble. White knuckles clench at his sides.

What happened while he was getting drinks? "Did Daniel call with bad news?"

"What?" He turns to me, brows pinched in confusion. "No." Shaking his head, he returns to his staring.

If this isn't about work then... Could he be jealous?

That's rich. After the Gala and his insipid maybe-ex, now he wants to act the possessive husband? Not if I have something to say about it.

I stew the rest of the short drive. My fury grows as I play out arguments in my mind.

He trails me into the townhouse and up the three flights of stairs until I finally explode.

"You're unbelievable." I burst into the bedroom, peeling off layers as I walk.

"You're mad," he says baldly.

"Ding ding ding." I whirl to face him, standing in only my underwear. "Why did you choose tonight of all nights to pull this act? Why did you even come to the show if you were going to pick a fight?"

"You didn't even tell me about it, you're sodding husband, but you invited the rock star?"

"One, I didn't invite Kenzo—he follows me on Instagram. Two, I didn't tell you because I wasn't sure you'd want to come. You've been very busy lately, and I didn't know where this fit into the deal."

He jerks back as if struck. "Fuck the deal. Of course I wanted to come—to be the one beside you, supporting you. Don't you get it by now?" In three big steps, he closes the distance until we're practically nose to nose. "You are the most important person in my life. I stopped caring about the contract long ago. Do you genuinely not see it?"

He searches my eyes, looking for some sign. His own reflect longing. His body leans forward, every atom focused on me. The air crackles with electricity.

My knees waiver, but I stand my ground, holding all my hurt and mistrust as a shield. "What about Serena?"

The muscles in his jaw flex and anger flares in his eyes, but I don't think it's directed at me. "She's nothing—she never was. My mother pushed us together as teens and I went along because it was expected. When I caught her bragging to her friends about how she could get me to buy her a car if she wanted, I couldn't take it anymore and ended things. Even if I'd never met you, I would never be with her."

My heart leaps at his words. "Does she know that?"

He searches my eyes, his lips spreading into a dark smile. "I practically screamed it in her face last week."

I lean the short distance between us and kiss him. It has the effect of a match hitting dry kindling. This isn't a pretty meeting of bodies. This is two starved people reaching for sustenance.

His hands trace the lines of my body until they settle under my thighs, lifting me up. I cling to him, all arms and legs wrapped around him, as he walks me across the room and tosses me on the soft mattress. In moments, his clothes join mine on the floor. Naked, he crawls up the length of the bed, his eyes dark with desire, until he is hovering over me. "No more running after a fight, Nic. Or I'll just have to chase you."

I run my hands up his biceps, feeling where the muscles strain to support him. "Is that a threat?"

"It's a fucking promise." His mouth descends in a bruising kiss, which I eagerly meet. My nails rake through his thick hair. I've missed this, missed him. My back arches off the bed, desperate for more contact with his heated skin.

Balancing on one hand, he snakes the other under my back. Rolling, he turns us until I land on top, straddling him. "Tonight is your night, Princess. Use me for your pleasure however you want. It's all for you."

I'm already wet, but I feel a gush at his words. His eyes burn as I hover over his thick shaft, moving my hips in small circles, not seating myself on him but rather teasing us both. He groans as my slick slit glides over his cock. I bite my lip to hide a satisfied smile, then immediately moan as I bump my clit against him.

Reaching between us, I take him in hand, giving him one pump root to tip and watch a single bead of pre-cum escape. Pushing up higher, I guide the crown to my aching center. Torturously slow, I lower myself, moaning as each inch stretches me. His fingers skirt up my thighs, sending tingles across my skin. Reginald grasps my hip bones, urging them down faster.

I halt my decent, grabbing his hands and pinning them against the headboard. "Uh-uh. Keep those hands where I can see them. Do I need to find a bow tie?"

He groans, no doubt also thinking of our first night together. "No, my lady, I'll behave."

To test him, my hips lower even slower. His legs tremble with the effort of staying still. When I'm fully seated, I take a moment to adjust to the fullness, then I begin to move. Little rocks back and forth, rubbing my clit against him as I force his cock harder into my G-spot.

"Fuck, yes, Nic. Take what you want." He clenches the headboard, knuckles white.

My eyes close, and my head falls back as I continue to rock, lost to the sensation of his body and mine. Leaning back, I alter the angle. His leg hair tickles my hands as I brace myself on his thighs, the muscles taut with strain. I rise until just his tip remains, then lower myself with a groan.

"That's it, Princess. Ride my cock, use me. I am your slave."

At his words, my pussy quivers around his length. I move my hips faster, arching my back further as my breath comes in little pants. "You may touch me now."

"Yes, ma'am," he growls. Surging up, his hands trace the curves of my ribs to my spine. He captures my nipple between his lips, the warmth and slight roughness of his tongue shooting straight to my clit and sending me over the edge. "Look at me when you cum on my cock."

My eyes fly open and I look down into his molten eyes, full of pride and satisfaction. My orgasm crashes through me and I scream his name.

"That's my good girl." With a final thrust, he swells and empties himself in me, clutching me to him as he cums.

We hold each other as the quakes still. My nails stroke his scalp as his fingers send chills along my back. With a long sigh, I dismount and collapse on the covers next to him, completely boneless. I lie there, smiling at the ceiling as I catch my breath, delicious aches pulsing through my body.

Reginald's bare feet pad into the bathroom, followed by the water running. The bed dips as he returns, one blunt finger tracing my hip. "Come on, let's take a bath and then it's my turn."

I sleepily lift my head. "Your turn for what?"

His smile is downright devilish. "I have a month of husbandly duties to make up, I don't intend to waste a moment."

My exhaustion from earlier is all but forgotten at the promise of a night in this man's arms.

CHAPTER THIRTY-FIVE

Reckoning

NICOLETTE

I kill the engine to my car and sit in the Pop parking lot, enjoying the air conditioning for a last minute before facing the balmy southern weather. All this time in New York and London is really killing my heat tolerance.

Not that the nights haven't been steamy. My lip curls into a satisfied smirk thinking about saying goodbye to Reginald last night. And this morning. I slept like a baby the entire flight here still in an afterglow.

After the show, Reginald and I are in a good place. The past week in New York has been practically idyllic. We're both busy with work, but we make time to share at least two meals a day. Our evenings are more relaxed, watching hours of shows together, or cuddled in bed reading.

I'd much rather be with him, but Bree called about some emergency at Pop, and as a partner, I need to help. A twinge of guilt twists in my belly. I haven't been around Pop lately. Anna's certainly stepped up since she invested more to become majority owner, and I don't want to step on her toes.

At least that's what I tell myself.

Barely pausing to wave at the cook staff, I trudge up the back stairs to what used to be Anna's apartment. After she moved in with David, we turned this into offices for the event space. The living room has a cozy conversation zone with photo books of our previous events, the full kitchen is useful for menu tastings or providing light refreshments to customers, and the back bedroom is storage.

"Ok, what is the big emergency that we couldn't do this over video?"

Bree and Anna sit side by side in two matching slipper chairs. Both have serious expressions as they stare at me silently. What the hell happened that has them looking like this?

"Nic, please have a seat," Bree starts.

Eyeing my two best friends cautiously, I perch on the couch across the coffee table.

Anna takes a deep breath. "We are here today, because we love you, and want the best for you."

"Is this a fucking intervention?" I stand, shaking my head, my feet already in motion.

Three steps from the door, Bree's tone stops me. "Sit the fuck down." Did she just mom-voice me? And damn if it's not working. "You've always been the tough-love one. Well, it's time for a taste of your own medicine. Nobody's leaving until we've all had a say."

I stomp back to the chair. Do I look like a petulant child? Yes. Do I care? Not particularly.

"Suga', we're worried, and a little hurt. Since when do we keep secrets from each other?"

"Gee, *Bella*, what about you never telling us you went by an entirely different name half your life or had this great lost love."

Anna flinches, and I'm almost sorry.

"That was about the past," she says, "this is different."

"Well, this is about my past."

"Really? So when you were off in London attending galas on the arm of your husband, that was the past?"

"Yes, all the shit in London and with Grandmama are tied to my past."

The silence hangs in the air. My skin prickles as I look at my two best friends. In all our years of friendship, we've never been at odds like this. It feels wrong, but I don't want to back down.

"Then what about this?" Bree slaps an article about the art show on the coffee table.

Anna leans forward, wrapping her arms around herself, looking sad. "We would have gone. We would have cheered louder than anyone else. Why didn't you tell us?"

I know they would have. "I wasn't sure I was good enough. You think everything I do is great. What would you have thought if the critics hated it?"

Anna is on her feet and sitting by me in a moment. "Oh, suga', we would have still been proud as hell of you. Then we would have taken you out to get wasted until you felt better."

"You said hell." I smile at the show of strong emotion from the ever proper southern belle.

Bree sits on my other side. "We feel like we don't even know you anymore. There's this whole other life you keep from us. We want to be there for you, but how can we if you hide things?"

"I know you don't like to talk about your parents or growing up with your grandmother. We get it, we don't exactly like talking about our childhoods either, but we'd like to know all the parts of you. To understand how to be there for you." Anna grabs my hand and holds it in hers.

"You know the real me, Nic your friend. Nicolette is fake, a persona I have to wear. Every move, every word carefully chosen, only speaking in half-truths and playing games. I'm more myself with you than anyone else." Well, almost. Reginald has quickly become that one person I can be completely free with.

"We all have different personas we have to wear in our lives. We flex to fit the situation or group of people. But that doesn't change who we are. We want to know that side of you better. The gala-attending, ballet-loving you that keeps appearing in the tabloids."

I curl my lip. "What if I don't want to be her?"

Bree grasps my arm until I meet her gaze, her cobalt blue eyes full of emotion. "You can't split yourself in two like that. Lady Ravenscourt, Nicolette Kato-Atherton, the scared little girl who lost her parents—they're all you. The good bits. The bad. It made you who you are today, and we love you. Just the way you are." She wraps her arms around me in a rare hug.

Anna joins in from the other side. "Wouldn't change a single bit of ya, darlin'."

As we sniffle back emotion, a sense of peace descends. Being at odds with these women has felt like a missing limb. They've been there for me my entire adult life. Ever since I ran away from London for a normal college experience in the States. I was so desperate to distinguish myself from the outcast teen and the grieving child,; I tried to shove my past in a box and hide it from my friends.

When my time ran out and my past caught up with me, I threw up walls to keep those parts of my life from colliding. But in reality, I was only pushing my friends further away.

"How did you two get so wise?"

"Years of therapy. I'll give you her card. Right now, though, I'm dying for some girl talk. What's it like being married to a viscount? And do you have pictures on your phone from the exhibition?"

I laugh as I wipe my eyes.

Anna bursts up and towards the kitchen. "Hold up, now. I'm making snacks, and I don't want to miss anything!"

"I'll make drinks." Bree hurries after Anna on her much shorter legs.

"Aren't you breastfeeding?" I call after her.

She shrugs as she pulls out three highball glasses. "I have a stash of milk in the freezer. I'll just pump and dump."

It's my turn to shake my head at her. "What are you making anyway?"

Anna and Bree both freeze and face the other. "ANGRY BALLS!" they yell in unison before breaking into giggles.

It's good to have them back.

I kill the engine to my car and sit in the Pop parking lot, enjoying the air conditioning for a last minute before facing the balmy southern weather. All this time in New York and London is really killing my heat tolerance.

Not that the nights haven't been steamy. My lip curls into a satisfied smirk thinking about saying goodbye to Reginald last night. And this morning. I slept like a baby the entire flight here still in an afterglow.

After the show, Reginald and I are in a good place. The past week in New York has been practically idyllic. We're both busy with work, but we make time to share at least two meals a day. Our evenings are more relaxed, watching hours of shows together, or cuddled in bed reading.

I'd much rather be with him, but Bree called about some emergency at Pop, and as a partner, I need to help. A twinge of guilt twists in my belly. I haven't been around Pop lately. Anna's certainly stepped up since she invested more to become majority owner, and I don't want to step on her toes.

At least that's what I tell myself.

Barely pausing to wave at the cook staff, I trudge up the back stairs to what used to be Anna's apartment. After she moved in with David, we turned this into offices for the event space. The living room has a cozy conversation zone with photo books of our previous events, the full kitchen is useful for menu tastings or providing light refreshments to customers, and the back bedroom is storage.

"Ok, what is the big emergency that we couldn't do this over video?"

Bree and Anna sit side by side in two matching slipper chairs. Both have serious expressions as they stare at me silently. What the hell happened that has them looking like this?

"Nic, please have a seat," Bree starts.

Eyeing my two best friends cautiously, I perch on the couch across the coffee table.

Anna takes a deep breath. "We are here today, because we love you, and want the best for you."

"Is this a fucking intervention?" I stand, shaking my head, my feet already in motion.

Three steps from the door, Bree's tone stops me. "Sit the fuck down." Did she just mom-voice me? And damn if it's not working. "You've always been the tough-love one. Well, it's time for a taste of your own medicine. Nobody's leaving until we've all had a say."

I stomp back to the chair. Do I look like a petulant child? Yes. Do I care? Not particularly.

"Suga', we're worried, and a little hurt. Since when do we keep secrets from each other?"

"Gee, *Bella*, what about you never telling us you went by an entirely different name half your life or had this great lost love."

Anna flinches, and I'm almost sorry.

"That was about the past," she says, "this is different."

"Well, this is about my past."

"Really? So when you were off in London attending galas on the arm of your husband, that was the past?"

"Yes, all the shit in London and with Grandmama are tied to my past."

The silence hangs in the air. My skin prickles as I look at my two best friends. In all our years of friendship, we've never been at odds like this. It feels wrong, but I don't want to back down.

"Then what about this?" Bree slaps an article about the art show on the coffee table.

Anna leans forward, wrapping her arms around herself, looking sad. "We would have gone. We would have cheered louder than anyone else. Why didn't you tell us?"

I know they would have. "I wasn't sure I was good enough. You think everything I do is great. What would you have thought if the critics hated it?"

Anna is on her feet and sitting by me in a moment. "Oh, suga', we would have still been proud as hell of you. Then we would have taken you out to get wasted until you felt better."

"You said hell." I smile at the show of strong emotion from the ever proper southern belle.

Bree sits on my other side. "We feel like we don't even know you anymore. There's this whole other life you keep from us. We want to be there for you, but how can we if you hide things?"

"I know you don't like to talk about your parents or growing up with your grandmother. We get it, we don't exactly like talking about our childhoods either, but we'd like to know all the parts of you. To understand how to be there for you." Anna grabs my hand and holds it in hers.

"You know the real me, Nic your friend. Nicolette is fake, a persona I have to wear. Every move, every word carefully chosen, only speaking in half-truths and playing games. I'm more myself with you than anyone else." Well, almost. Reginald has quickly become that one person I can be completely free with.

"We all have different personas we have to wear in our lives. We flex to fit the situation or group of people. But that doesn't change who we are. We want to know that side of you better. The gala-attending, ballet-loving you that keeps appearing in the tabloids."

I curl my lip. "What if I don't want to be her?"

Bree grasps my arm until I meet her gaze, her cobalt blue eyes full of emotion. "You can't split yourself in two like that. Lady Ravenscourt, Nicolette Kato-Atherton, the scared little girl who lost her parents—they're all you. The good bits. The bad. It made you who you are today, and we love you. Just the way you are." She wraps her arms around me in a rare hug.

Anna joins in from the other side. "Wouldn't change a single bit of ya, darlin'."

As we sniffle back emotion, a sense of peace descends. Being at odds with these women has felt like a missing limb. They've been there for me my entire adult life. Ever since I ran away from London for a normal college experience in the States.

I was so desperate to distinguish myself from the outcast teen and the grieving child,; I tried to shove my past in a box and hide it from my friends.

When my time ran out and my past caught up with me, I threw up walls to keep those parts of my life from colliding. But in reality, I was only pushing my friends further away.

"How did you two get so wise?"

"Years of therapy. I'll give you her card. Right now, though, I'm dying for some girl talk. What's it like being married to a viscount? And do you have pictures on your phone from the exhibition?"

I laugh as I wipe my eyes.

Anna bursts up and towards the kitchen. "Hold up, now. I'm making snacks, and I don't want to miss anything!"

"I'll make drinks." Bree hurries after Anna on her much shorter legs.

"Aren't you breastfeeding?" I call after her.

She shrugs as she pulls out three highball glasses. "I have a stash of milk in the freezer. I'll just pump and dump."

It's my turn to shake my head at her. "What are you making anyway?"

Anna and Bree both freeze and face the other. "ANGRY BALLS!" they yell in unison before breaking into giggles.

It's good to have them back.

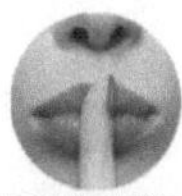

Whisper Wire

○○○

Well, well, well. Looks like our current 'it' couple may not be all that after all. Sources close to the pair have shared that appearances are not as they seem. The outwardly blissfully happy couple is in fact...FAKING IT.

Thanks to his father's love of diamonds—and hearts, spades, and clubs—Lord Ravenscourt only had dollar signs in his eyes when he proposed. Before you start feeling bad for our Lady R, she was equally materially driven. Apparently, her rebellious youth inspired a marriage clause in the heiress's trust fund and time was running out.

These two may truly be perfect for each other. Why the big show then? Is the money not enough so they wanted fame too? What do you think, faithful readers? Should we cancel #Reginette?

TTFN
Wendy

CHAPTER THIRTY-SIX

Memes

NICOLETTE

I pace as I chew on my fingernail. The incessant hum of the TV drones on in my ear, wearing my last nerve. The headline blares across the screen: Bancrofts—Fairy Tale or Fakes?

Three women sit at a curved table, debating my personal life on national television. Like a B-list actress, ex pop-star, and lackluster comedian, are experts.

"The popular gossip column Whisper Wire broke a story that the marriage between real estate heiress Nicolette Atherton and Reginald Bancroft, the future Earl of Silverbrook, have been faking their relationship this whole time. And it's all for the money." Leave it to the actress to state the obvious.

"I run a successful business, too! Who is their fact checker?" I yell at the screen as I search for a contact number at the station.

"Now, Brittani, that's a bit of a harsh summary." Thank you, Amber! I always liked her music. "They never claimed to be head over heels in love. How much of this was built up by the media?"

How the hell did this happen?

We'd been careful to curate an image of a happily married couple for the press. Sure. Doesn't everyone only post the good moments on social media? Every photo, every moment of our relationship has been one hundred percent real.

At least for me...

"Here, suga', chomp on this and give your poor finger a break," Anna calls as she pushes a plate across the counter.

Turning my back on the morning talk show, I stomp across the open-concept living room to the adjoining chef's kitchen that David remodeled when Anna moved into his house.

It really is beautiful. If I wasn't so fucking stressed, I'd take the time to compliment the way she's offset the navy lower cabinets with pops of yellow. Antique blue and white china plates hang on the wall in an abstract pattern to balance the homestead touches with modern flair.

Even decor can't distract my inner voice today.

I've been the happiest I've ever been.

Maybe that's why I'm so scared.

Lifting the pecan brittle to my mouth, the mix of sweet, crunch, and salt mollifies me slightly. The only one of our trio missing a sweet tooth, I normally bury my stress in cardio or alcohol rather than Anna's treats. None of my normal go-to's helped today. The apartment felt too quiet and memories of Reginald haunted every corner.

"You never care about what the press says. Why is this upsetting you so much?"

"I don't need this bad publicity right after the gallery show. It's going to kill any momentum I've built up."

That's not the real reason.

I shove another hunk of brittle into my mouth, hoping the loud crunch shuts up the little voice at the back of my head. Even Anna's homemade salted caramel can't work miracles though.

You're worried they're right. He only married you for the money. He's never said he loves you. You both pretended so well even you bought the lie.

Hook. Line. And Sinker.

Anna eyes me across the counter, one blond brow arched. "You sure about that?"

"What else could it be?"

"Have you talked to him?"

"No." I avoided the thirty-odd calls from him. Yes, I am aware that is not the most mature response. I need time. Time to gather my thoughts. Time to shove all these feelings into a box far in the back of my heart.

She hums noncommittally but thankfully drops it as she measures out ingredients for her next round of stress baking.

The only sound is the continued debate on the talk show. They've moved on to reading out social media posts about us. #ReginetteGate is trending.

Yay.

"Here." Anna dumps out the concoction she's made onto the floured surface with a plop. "Kneading dough is good for stress. Have a whack."

As I take my frustration out on the dough, Anna dusts off her hands and picks up her nearby iPad. "Whoa."

"What?" Her chocolate eyes dart from the screen to me, like she's unsure what to say. "Come on, Anna. What is the picture?"

Her freckled nose wrinkles up adorably. "You remember that meme where the thief is looking at Rapunzel?"

My mind goes completely blank. "Huh?"

Her brows pinch as she stares at the screen again. "How about the one about that El Dorado movie?"

The ball of dough slams onto the counter with a hard thud. "What the fuck are you talking about, Anna?"

She sighs. "It looked a whole lot like that." She slides the tablet across the island so it faces me.

Filling the screen is a photo of Reginald and me at the Red Hearts Gala. I'm looking off camera, smiling at someone. Reginald stands next to me, arm wrapped around me with one hand possessively splayed along my ribs. Instead of joining in the conversation, he stares at me, eyes filled with longing.

"The point of the meme, is that we wish so hard that someone would look at us like that, because we're too busy looking away to notice when they do."

Hope flares in me. Timid and fragile, but real.

"RoyalRobin13 says 'you can't fake this', a laughing Reginald Bancroft is definitely a new look for the previously gruff bachelor," reads Amber on the TV. The screen shows another shot of Reginald and me from that night, capturing the moment I made him laugh on the red carpet.

The next picture is from the same event, a posed picture on the red carpet. "'Fake, fake, fake. Please cancel them', says BrightonWay4. I completely agree," Brittani chirps.

A candid some paparazzi shot while we were walking downtown in New York shows next. Reginald's arms overflow with shopping bags he insisted he'd carry himself. We were both starving, so I held up a hot dog for him to bite as we smiled with chipmunk cheeks. It had been a fun day.

"I'm sorry, Brittani," Amber interrupts, "but I completely disagree. There's no way even professional actors can be this on 24-7 and there are plenty of candids exactly like this. Everything I've seen points to a happy and healthy couple."

They launch into another round of debate. No longer able to take it, I grab the remote and turn it off with a groan, shoving another square of brittle into my mouth. It does little for my mood.

Anna comes closer and wraps an arm around my shoulders. "You don't need to be strong all the time, Nic. I get that there are things you're not ready to tell us, but I hope you can tell someone."

My mind immediately goes to Reginald. How easy it is to open up to him. How much he understands me. How the unending loneliness dissipates with him. I'm scared if I let the walls down completely—if I let him all the way in—he'll have the power to break me. I never want to feel the heartbreak I felt in my childhood again.

You already do. The voice whispers. *You've never stopped feeling alone.*

"What if he leaves?" I whisper.

My cell phone vibrates on the counter, a harsh interruption to the quiet moment. Reginald's name flashes across the screen.

"What if he doesn't?" Anna asks. The phone buzzes a couple more times, then falls silent again. "So, are you in or out?"

CHAPTER THIRTY-SEVEN

Reginald Decides

REGINALD

If I wore one of those sports watches, I wonder how many steps I'd be up to. I've been pacing my office floor since my phone started ringing at three in the morning with calls from London papers.

Daniel showed up around eight, with bagels and a gallon of coffee. I've never been so happy that he reads that dreadful scandal sheet.

"Lord Ravenscourt does not have a statement at this time. He is in meetings regarding the launch of his magazine, Elysium, next week and is unavailable for comment."

We should be preparing for our first issue. Final edits, layout proofs, confirming with printers. Instead, Daniel is fielding media calls for me. It would all be great publicity for the magazine, if only I felt confident on where Nic and I stand.

Why isn't she calling me back?

I've left a dozen messages, sent an embarrassing number of texts.

"Ok, I may finally see why you hate that gossip rag." Daniel sighs as he stretches his back and refills our coffees. "This is all a bitch, but why are you so stressed? This is an inconvenience, but it's not like it's going to alter things between you. You both knew the score going in."

I wince as I take my mug from him. "Now everyone knows the deal."

"Nic is a levelheaded woman. She's no stranger to media spin. You two are perfect together. This isn't going to change that."

I stare into my coffee and say nothing. Loudly.

"What did you do?" Daniel asks.

"I never told Nic about the earl's gambling issue."

"Bancroft!" He collapses onto the edge of the desk as if the wind is blown out of him. "What were you thinking?"

"I tried to. When we were in Sweden and she was talking about not needing a prenup. She kept saying it didn't matter. Afterwards, I convinced myself it was true. I have zero intentions of divorcing her, so I figured what's the harm?"

"And then she finds out in national print and might wonder if half her fortune is worth it to get rid of a lying husband." I wince. "So I'm assuming you've never told her you love her, either."

"How did you..."

"I've been your only friend for a long-ass time. When Nic is in the room, it's like you come alive. I've never seen you happy before."

I collapse into the nearby chair. "What do I do?"

"What does the hero do to win the girl in all those novels you've read?" He tips his head at me with a smile.

"Make a big gesture? I already tried that with the art show."

He stands and pats me on the shoulder. "You gotta think bigger, mate. I'm heading home to shower and check on the team. Don't wait too long to make your move."

I'm still sitting in that chair, contemplating what Orpheus or Cyrano would do when my cell rings. I go to ignore the call but see my father's name on the screen. A lifetime of conditioning kicks in and I answer the phone.

My father's voice crackles through the speaker before I can even say a word. "What the hell have you done now, boy?"

I bristle at the accusation. "I did what you told me to. Found an heiress and married her."

"A scandal wasn't part of my instructions. Your poor mother has been in tears all day, too embarrassed to show her face."

Nearly forty years of towing the line. Going to the schools they chose. The degree they dictated. The events. The committees... When does it end?

Did I get one thank you? One scrap of praise or warmth? No, never.

That bar just got set a little higher, and I was expected to jump like a trained dog. Well, that's not quite true—at least the damn dogs were showered in affection. Well, I'm not rolling over today.

"Who's fault is it that this got out?"

"Excuse me?" Father nearly stutters. "Who do you think you're talking to like that?"

But there's no backing down now. "It was Mother who was sharing all the sordid details with the Wentworths not too long ago. My money's on Serena being the leak to the press, but I'll leave the betting in this family to you."

My father sputters. "You ungrateful rat. Sort this mess out and get back in line. We raised you better than this."

"No. My entire life, I've done everything you asked, and I'm done with it. The schools. The hobbies. I even married a complete stranger because you told me to. It's never going to be enough. I'm a grown man with my own passions and it is well past time I lived my own life."

"You hang up that phone and I'm done with you. The title, the land, all of it will go to Monty."

"Good. Let him have it. All I want is my wife." I disconnect the call and slam my cell onto my desk.

A slow clap from the doorway draws my attention. Nic leans against the doorjamb, looking gorgeous in leggings and a slouchy tee. Exactly like the day we met.

In three strides, I close the distance between us. My fingers spear her silky black hair as I cup the back of her head and pull her in. Before she can speak, I capture her lips with mine, pouring every emotion I'm dying to say but can't find the words to express.

With a sigh, she leans into me, wrapping her arms around my chest, digging her nails into my shoulders. Her mouth opens, greedily accepting everything, matching my energy and pushing for more, which I happily give.

I break the kiss, breathing heavily as I rest my forehead against hers. "The money never mattered to me. I should have told you about the gambling, but I was scared of your reaction. Divorce was never a possibility to me, so it was a lie out of cowardice, not malice."

Her lips quirk. "I know."

My head jerks back as I search her eyes. "You do?"

"Well, I didn't at first." Her cheeks bloom pink. "But after I calmed down, I thought about all the times you discussed purchases with me or tried to cheap out. If you were motivated by the money, you'd be spending a hell of a lot more of it. I mean, you fly business class, for fuck's sake." Her eyes drop to the floor. "I think I was more scared that I was the only one catching feelings."

"Listen to me." Pinching her chin, I lift her face back up to mine. "I never cared for Serena. Even when I was with her, it was what my mother wanted and I was too weak to go against it. I didn't even think to fight for myself until I met you. You taught me that I deserve to set my own terms in life."

A single tear trails down her porcelain cheek.

"I don't want independence anymore." Her mouth opens and I plow on, afraid I'll lose my nerve. "I want to be wherever you are. Here. Florida. Fucking Timbuktu if you want to go take pictures of goats."

Her lips quirk into a sardonic smile. "Pretty sure we have goats here in the U.S."

I grip her arms as I meet her smiling hazel eyes. "It doesn't matter. I'm all in. The only thing I want is you."

"I love you." Her voice rings with confidence, but I can see the vulnerability in her eyes.

Heat courses through my body, radiating outwards from my chest. I've waited a lifetime to hear those words. It was worth every torturous moment to get here. Hearing it from the right woman.

"I love you, too," I whisper against her lips before capturing them again. "Oh, in the interest of transparency. I don't think I'll be the next earl. If that matters to you."

"Dammit, guess I better cancel that custom tiara order." Her words drip with sarcasm.

"Keep it. You'll always be my princess." Her eyes darken as she bites her plump lip. I pull it free of her teeth with the pad of my thumb. "As much as I want to move onto the makeup sex portion of the evening. We have a scandal to squash and a publication to save."

"Yes, sir." My cock twitches at her response. Do I ever wish we had time to jump straight to bed. "I had an idea on the flight, but you might not like it."

She's right, I don't like it. But over a deep-dish pizza, we debate ideas and reach a solution I can live with. Late that night, as I fall asleep with my wife tucked securely in my arms, I'm completely at peace without a fear of tomorrow hanging over my head for the first time in my life.

ELYSIUM

June • • Issue 1

Letter from the Editor

The written word is a powerful thing. For centuries, it was used to preserve knowledge, to convey messages from far away. Today, we often wield it as a weapon, sharing misinformation or tearing people apart with speculation. The pen may be mightier than the sword, but it is not always stained with the truth.

Fame is dangerous. The world is a much smaller place and through online media, we think we know people we've never met because their lives are put on display. Those who seek to be public figures go into this life knowingly. My wife and I did not choose this—the world condemned us to this life because of our family names. Although we are both private people, our lives have been splashed across tabloids and gossip pages for years, culminating in the relentless coverage of our courtship and marriage over the past few months. The damage has been great, and now we feel the need to set the record straight publicly in the same court of public opinion where we have been slandered.

It is true that Nic and I both engaged a matchmaking agency, as many of our backgrounds are likely to do. It is also true that the service determined we would be compatible. However, we met organically before realizing the match had been made, and the connection was instant.

In Nic, I've found a genuine partner. She cheers on my successes, but pushes me when I need it as well. We may not carry on with public displays, but there is nothing fake about our affection. Like all couples, we have disagreements, and struggle to balance our careers and marriage. A relationship that was almost irreparably damaged by the careless accusations of a so-called journalist.

This mentality of likes and comments over truth and integrity is a blight on our society. It is exactly why I wanted to start Elysium, a publication dedicated to sharing true human interest stories about kindness and bravery—two things our world sorely needs more of.

Reginald Bancroft
Editor in Chief

CHAPTER THIRTY-EIGHT

Print and Prejudice

REGINALD

Empty coffee cups and scraps of paper cover the dining room table. We've been sitting here all night waiting for feedback on the first printed edition.

"Do you see anything yet?" Daniel is hitting the refresh button so hard the laptop might crack. He's manning the subscription portal.

"Nothing yet." The normally cool and put together Tyra hunches over her phone, hair escaping her ponytail and coffee stains on her shirt. She's scouring social media for mentions.

"How many subscriptions do we need to break even?" I ask.

"Two-Fifty. We still have the budget for a second edition and marketing as long as we hit two-hundred, though." Daniel doesn't even look up from his refreshing.

I grab for my coffee. The paper cup is lighter in my hand than I expected. The four more cups by it are equally empty. With a sigh, I slump back in my chair and massage my eyebrows. If this doesn't work... Ok, in all reality I'll be fine—I married an heiress, after all, with a booming career. But if this magazine isn't a success, I don't know what I'll do next.

It will be something, though. I will not be a trophy husband. I finally escaped my parents' noose of obligations and expectations to do something with myself, and it will not be rounds of golf and tanning on the penthouse deck.

The front door opens and closes with a bang. I lean back in my chair and see Nic with a stack of packages in her hand, and rush over to grab the pile.

"Thanks." She leans in for a kiss and I follow her to the kitchen. "Any word?" she asks.

I shake my head as I unstack the boxes and lay them out one by one on the counter.

"Well," she holds up two bottles, "I got champagne if it's good news and vodka if it's bad. And before you start pointing out that it's not even ten a.m. yet, I also got orange juice."

I laugh at the reminder of our first meeting and pull her in for a kiss. Having her against me heals more of the hole in my heart. "What did I do to deserve you?"

"Um, put up with years of abuse from your aristo-asshole parents so you'd have baggage that matched mine?" She tilts her head to the side with a mock thoughtful expression, but her eyes dance with humor. "Too soon?"

I growl at her and capture her smart mouth until she's panting. My own lips smirk in masculine satisfaction at the effect I have on this magnificent woman.

Nic shakes her head as if clearing away the lust. Too quickly, she's back to business. "Right." She marches out to the dining room and claps her hands, startling the half awake people at the table. "Ok, you both need showers to wake you up. Tyra, I'll grab you a clean shirt, dear. Bagels and pastries are in the kitchen and I'll put a fresh pot of coffee on." They stare at her, confused. "Well, go on then."

As usual, Nic is right. The break refreshes us from the all-nighter staring at screens. There's a renewed air of excitement as we sit back down.

"I, for one," Nic says around her bagel, "think the edition came out great." She holds up the glossy magazine with the other hand, the photograph I bought from her show on display.

"You're on the cover," Daniel points out. "You're biased."

She laughs. "Normally that makes me hate a magazine, but in this case, I'll make an exception. I love the story about the dog shelter. Nothing like photos of needy dogs to get people to spend money—remember that commercial that ran for years!"

"My favorite was the interview with Lord Firth about their environmental changes. Especially the way you tied it to steps people can take at home," Tyra says.

Daniel eyes the pastries before grabbing a cheese danish. "The Global Good News and Unsung Heroes posts have been trending well online. We could do more of those."

"Let's see how this edition goes first." My phone beeps. I flip it over to see a message request on social media. I'm about to ignore it when my gut tells me to check. It's from the absolute last person I expect—Kenzo.

Kenzo

> Well done, mate. I'm serious.

What the bloody hell does that mean? I'm still squinting at the words when Tyra squeals across the table, nearly flipping her chair.

"Tyra, you alright?" Daniel looks as puzzled as I feel.

"Kenzo Star just posted a photo of him reading the magazine. The caption says, 'this is the type of journalism we've been missing. Positivity. Honesty. Heart. How do I sign up for an interview?'"

Daniel and I share a shocked look.

"She's right." Nic holds her phone out to me with the post up. "It's already at a thousand likes and dozens of comments asking where to find it."

Daniel dives back to the laptop. "We have over a hundred subscribers, and it keeps going up." His wide eyes meet mine. "We did it."

Nic grabs me in a tight hug. "I'm so proud of you."

It might be the first time I've heard the words before, and damn, they feel good. Especially from this self-made woman.

The champagne flows.

Nic slips into the kitchen and returns with a sheet cake that says 'Congratulations' on it. "Come on everyone, group photo. Stand in front of the bookcases with the magazine held up." Nic poses us in groups and solo photos. We smile and laugh until our cheeks ache.

CHAPTER THIRTY-NINE

Do-Over

NICOLETTE

I turn and check my reflection one last time, the tulle frill along my right shoulder grazing my cheek. The black-and-white silk bodice hugs my body before flaring out from a dropped waist in a dazzling layered skirt dotted with crystals. My scarlet lips smirk as I scan myself down to the same rhinestone studded heels I wore that first night.

Tonight is Reginald's thirty-fifth birthday, and I've transformed myself into the black swan for him. I've arranged for dinner and the NYC ballet's rendition of Swan Lake, followed by a speakeasy downtown with rare scotches. It's going to be a fantastic night.

If I can get him out of the house.

Clutch and wrap in hand, I head down to Reginald's office. Between the two windows, the Valkyrie photograph hangs in a simple silver frame, the focal point of the room. I tried to convince him to move it to our bedroom, but he insists on keeping it here where he can enjoy it awake.

In front of the photo sits my husband at his L-shaped desk, back to the door. He's hunched over his laptop, fingers flying over the keyboard.

Quietly, I slip into the room, carefully dropping my items in a nearby chair. I sneak up behind him, bending over so my lips hover by his ear. "Don't you know hunching over like that is bad for your back?"

Quick as a snake, he turns, grabs me by the waist and sets me on the surface. The briefest flash of a grin shows before he buries his face in my neck. "I think my back is just fine."

He spreads my legs with his knee. Those hands pull me to the edge of the desk. His hardening cock rubs against me and we both moan at the contact.

My head falls back, and he uses the opportunity to nip my throat.

"Wait," I cry through the haze, splaying my hands on his chest. "What about dinner?"

"I'd rather have you." His voice rumbles and his eyes darken.

I rub my needy core against him, desperate for friction. "Fine. But I'm not missing the ballet."

Triumph flashes a moment before he dives for my neck again.

"No marks! Nibble on this side." I arch the other way, giving him full access to the side obscured by the stiff black ruffle.

His lips latch on to the skin below my ear like a man starved, serving a maddening contrast to the gentle fingers lowering the single strap.

My hands grip his shirt, pulling him even closer, then stroke down his stomach to wrestle with his belt buckle. I groan with satisfaction as I free him from his pants, his cock hard and heavy in my palm. My fingers encircle the base of his shaft, giving a slight squeeze. I gather the pre-cum at the tip before working it down his length.

He rewards me with a hungry groan. "Time to unwrap my present." Those silver eyes stare down at me as he backs up until he can lift my skirts to better view my lace covered center. "Are you already wet?" Reginald pushes the scrap of fabric aside.

I follow his gaze and see my bare pussy glistening in his office lights.

"Is this all for me, Princess?" He touches me almost reverently, then those same two fingers thrust into me, wrenching a moan as my back arches. "You're going to scream for me, and then I'm going to fuck you on this desk. Is that a problem?"

I shake my head no, unable to speak as he drives in and out of me. His palm slaps my clit with each stroke, causing a fresh gush. The sound of my wetness around his fingers is loud in the room. Every sense is full of him, my orgasm builds, and I spread wider. A silent request for him to give me what I want.

He increases the pace, curving slightly to better rub my G-spot. His other hand caresses my throat and jaw. "So beautiful. Give me your screams, Princess. I want them all." A blunt forefinger pulls my lip. My tongue darts out to swirl the tip before my mouth closes on it, sucking.

My legs tremble. I rock my hips, riding his hand. I'm close but I need something more.

Reginald removes his fingertip from my lips with a pop.

I whimper at the absence. Then a completely new sensation builds as his finger brushes my asshole, slowly pushing past the tight muscles. My entire body clenches down at the invasion, setting off my orgasm. I scream his name as my vision goes white.

My elbows give out and I lay back, panting for breath. When I open my eyes, Reginald is standing between my knees licking my cream off his fingers.

"Delicious." He hooks the sides of my thong, gliding them off my legs before tucking it into his back pocket.

"This is going to be hard and fast if you want to make the show." He grips my hips, tilting them up and entering me with one strong thrust.

My back arches off the desk, and I lock my ankles behind his back.

One hand slips further beneath my ass, holding me up. The other tugs on the bodice of my dress until my breast pops free. Reginald lowers his mouth, biting my nipple ever so slightly.

The sting of pain travels directly to my clit as I cry out. Another orgasm builds.

"Now I want to feel you gush on my cock." His hips snap, pounding into me with such force, I'm afraid I'll fall off the desk. "Touch yourself. Stroke that greedy cunt and make it cum."

My fingers rush to follow his command. Hungry for his praise.

"That's it, Princess." He stands, lifting my ass to spread me still further to him. His strokes impossibly deeper.

My pussy quivers around his length. I rub faster, looking for that peak.

"Look at me when you fucking cream," he snarls.

My eyes open, focusing in on his. The intensity in his expression sends me over the edge. I hold his gaze as wave after wave of pleasure rack my body.

"That's my good girl." His cock swells and I know he's close. I slip my hand between us and cup his sack, squeezing slightly. His eyes widen and his thrusts lose their rhythm. "Fuck. Nicolette." With one last thrust of his hips, he empties himself into me.

He lowers his lips to mine, both of us panting for breath between kisses.

When he slips from me, I whimper at the loss. His eyes rake across my still splayed form, glittering with satisfaction.

I shudder as his fingers stroke my slit, pushing his cum back inside of me. "I'm going to be hard all night knowing you're still dripping."

"Does this mean I'm not getting my underwear back?" I arch a brow.

Pouting, he pulls my thong out of his pocket and gingerly works it up my legs. "This is only because I don't want anyone stealing a peek of what's mine." He helps me up and steals a kiss as he finishes his task of adjusting my clothing. "I'll run upstairs and change. Give me five minutes."

I smile to myself as I set his desk to rights, stacking papers and gathering spilled pens. A knocked-over object in the corner catches my eye. Flipping it over, I find a hinged double frame with our wedding picture on one side and the cocktail napkin contract on the other. My heart warms as my fingers touch the glass over our signatures.

"Ready, Princess? I grabbed you a makeup-wipe, your lipstick got smudged." He doesn't sound the slightest bit sorry.

"You kept this?"

He walks around the desk, pulling me into the circle of his arms. "Of course. I'm happy we threw the terms out the window, but I never want to forget our first meeting." His lips capture mine in a sweet kiss. "Now come on. I want a redo on our second date—without my mother and brother."

I laugh as he tugs me down the stairs and out into the summer night.

L ater that night, I lay with my head on his chest, spent from another round of lovemaking, and deep in thought.

"What's on your mind, Princess? I can feel you thinking from here."

I look up at him, debating if I should voice my thoughts or not.

"What is it?"

"Did you hear from your parents today? Or your brother?" A muscle spasms in that granite jaw and I kick myself for bringing down the mood. "I'm sorry, I shouldn't have brought it up."

His large hand strokes down my naked back, sending tingles across my skin. "It's alright. You can always speak your mind with me." His chest rises and falls beside me. "Not a word. I think that ship has well and truly sailed."

I push up on my elbow and cup his tense face in my hand. "Are you ok?"

Love shines in his steel eyes as he turns and kisses my palm. "Of course, Princess."

Every bit of his body language screams his sincerity, but that little bitch at the back of my head whispers doubts. I know he loves me, but will he still in five years? Ten? What happens when he realizes he alienated his entire family for me?

My tongue swipes across my dry lips. "Do you ever regret it? I mean, if you hadn't married me, you'd still be..."

He sits up swiftly, cradling my face between his hands. His eyes are fierce as they stare into mine. "Not for one second. For the first time, I get to write my own story, and I wouldn't have had the nerve if it weren't for you. You are my beginning and end, Princess. There is no me without you."

"I haven't heard from my grandmother either. For all I know, I'll be cut off, too. What will we do then?" A traitorous tear trickles down my cheek.

He catches it with his thumb. "Then we'll dive into the lake together. I'll sell my London flat for a tidy profit. Even if we never see another penny from your trust fund and we have to scrimp and save for the rest of our lives, I'll always choose you." He kisses me, telling me without words the depths of his feelings.

I return the embrace, pouring into it everything in my heart.

When we break apart, slightly panting, Reginald lowers his forehead to mine. "Between your photos and my magazine, I'm absolutely not worried."

Laughing, I push him back down against the pillows, laying across his chest. When he rolls me under him and makes love to me again, I think life is perfect.

Well, almost.

 **Whisper Wire** ○○○

It may be true that there's corruption and greed within the Bancroft family, but it certainly did not stem from a certain gentleman I maligned most unjustly. In the wake of the #Reginettegate scandal I broke, Lord and Lady Ravenscourt have shown a unified front from their NYC home. Meanwhile, a flurry of confusing press releases have come flying from Silverbrook Hall. It sounds as if the Honorable Montague Bancroft is being pumped up as the next in line. Silly Earl Silverbrook, maybe you should google The Peerage Act of 1963—when you're done destroying your family holdings, that is.

Lord R's editorial humbled me.

I wasn't always this jaded, cynical observer of humankind—once I dreamed of becoming a real-life Lois Lane. Years of watching society's "best" do the absolute "worst" with no consequences; seeing the world around me reward bad behavior time and again, takes its toll. I told myself I was exposing corruption, holding the glittering masses accountable when no one else would, but I see now that I've become the very thing I despise. To my victims, I wholeheartedly apologize. I know these words cannot undo the damage, but I will strive to atone for my sins another way.

This will be my last column, readers. I can no longer be part of the problem.

Goodbye

Chapter Forty

Truth Rings Out

Nicolette

My legs burn as I race up the steps of our townhouse and burst through the front door. "Ren," I call out, "have you seen this?"

"Seen what?" He meets me outside his office, his eyes scanning me.

I hold up my phone. "Whisper Wire is done. She's shutting down her website."

He squints at my screen for a moment, then turns and marches to his desk. His fingers fly over the keyboard as he scans one article and then another. "It's true." Turning in his chair, he grabs my hand and tugs me between his knees. "If I accomplish nothing else with Elysium—we go belly-up in a year—it will still be worth it for this."

He pulls me closer, arms banded around my thighs. A triumphant smile splits his handsome face. Every time I see that smile, my heart gives a little flip, knowing I'm the only one who sees it.

My phone rings on the desk and I answer without looking at the name, still grinning at my husband. "Hello." The other end is silence, followed by a ragged intake of air. "Hello? Is anyone there?"

"Letty…" That one word sends me on alert. Only one person calls me that anymore, and a call from Gloria, especially with that emotion in her voice, means something catastrophic.

"What happened? What's wrong?" A pit opens in my stomach, terrified of her next words.

"It's Ms. Vivienne." Her voice breaks. "They rushed her off to the hospital."

"Which hospital?" Reginald's head shoots up and his eyes meet mine. The support and concern ground me all while I feel like the floor is dissolving underneath me.

"King Edward's in London. I don't know what's going on, though. They said I'm not family." The older woman's words are barely audible through her tears.

I stumble. "What happened?"

Reginald guides me into his chair, his hands not leaving my shoulder. A travel site is already on his computer searching for flights.

"When I brought up Ms. Vivienne's dinner tray, she seemed asleep. I tried to wake her but she wouldn't respond, so I had to call."

Grandmama never eats in her room. Why did she need a tray? "What did the responders say?" A vice tightens around my chest. I don't understand what is happening.

"She's been sick for a while, Letty. I begged her to tell you, but she ordered me not to. You should come home."

Standing, Reginald squeezes my shoulder and pulls me into him. "I got us tickets on the next flight out of JFK, and a car will be waiting when we land. Do you need me to pack you anything specific?"

Numbly, I shake my head no.

Gloria is flustered and doesn't have much more information. I promise to call her with updates on our progress and after I speak to the doctors. Reginald rushes around the apartment, packing bags and making arrangements.

I stand still at the window, watching New York bustle past as if nothing has changed. As if my entire world hasn't shifted.

I blindly follow my husband out the door and into a waiting cab. Then through security and to the gate without saying a single word. It's a wonder TSA doesn't stop us under suspicion of kidnapping.

It's been months since I spoke to my grandmother, and our argument repeats in my head. I have nothing better to do while I wait. The hours stretch on and my only thoughts are getting to my grandmother's side. My last remaining family.

Reginald grabs my hand and interlaces our fingers, reminding me that Grandmama isn't my only family after all. I squeeze his hand in gratitude and turn away as a single tear trails down my face.

Transcontinental flights are long. He tries to persuade me to eat, sleep, or have a drink, but I only shake my head.

Guilt and anticipation weave webs in my stomach. Should I have tried to make amends by now? It's been over nine months since we last spoke. Deep down, I thought we'd make up—I've never imagined my life without her in it. What if that horrible fight was our final conversation?

I gave up all pretense of religion years ago, but I pray that I make it in time.

Our relationship was never easy. It was never unicorns and rainbows, hugs and chocolate chip cookies. But even if I never understood Vivienne Atherton, she was—no, *is*—my grandmother and I love her.

The rest of the flight, deplaning, and the car ride to the hospital are another blur. Just get me there. It's a mantra I repeat, refusing to imagine an alternative.

As we pull up, I stare up at the bright lights of the emergency ward and swallow back the lump in my throat as fear roots me in place. With a mental shake, I grasp at the mask I wear in society, hoping that will protect me from what's waiting for me on the other side of those doors.

The seat dips as Reginald scoots closer to me. Looking over my shoulder, I find his gray eyes full of concern. My stomach flips a little at the support there.

Holding his hand, I approach the giant doors, once again frozen with panic, thrown back to that dark place of my childhood.

Reginald pulls me against his chest. His fingers spear the hair at my nape and pull me back until we are nose to nose. He takes a ragged breath, his body slumping as he exhales. "Whatever happens, you will get through it, but you don't have to do this alone. I'll be right here, Princess. Whatever you need. I've got you."

My heart aches at the raw emotion in his voice. How different my life would be if he hadn't sat in that airplane seat.

Sure, Bree or Anna would have dropped everything to fly here with me, but they've never quite known how to handle one of my moods. Anna would be too busy baking and Bree would be storming the castle and whipping the doctors into shape. Fuck, she'd probably be making a spreadsheet with Grandmama's test results and cross-referencing her diagnosis with clinical studies.

But none of that is what I need.

Hot tears trail down my cheeks as I squeeze my eyes shut, inhaling one last comforting scent of sandalwood before marching through the hospital doors.

Somehow, Reginald knew exactly what I needed in the moment, even when I didn't. He calmly took care of the logistics to get me here. When I voiced my needs, he immediately stopped and followed my lead. He didn't argue, didn't push, simply gave me space and offered to help.

I give my name at the front desk and am immediately whisked to a private room with a corner view on a VIP floor.

She looks pale and still in the bed, not words ever used to describe the force of nature that is Vivienne Atherton. Machines beep in the utter silence of the room. Afraid to disturb the peace, I tiptoe in to the seat by the bed. Her arms rest at her sides above the blanket and, unsure what else to do, I clasp her fingers in mine.

Her skin is so thin that it might crumble under my fingers. When did they become so spotted? Her hand is cool and slightly dry. I'll have Gloria send her Parisian hand cream. And the silk pillowcases.

A throat clearing startles me. A middle-aged man in a long white coat stands near the entrance of the room with a tablet. "Miss Atherton?"

Reginald squeezes my shoulder. Neither of us correct the doctor.

"What is wrong with my grandmother?"

"She's suffered a GI bleed as a complication from her cirrhosis." I blink at him, the words as foreign as if he was speaking an alien language. "Were you aware that she is ill?"

"No. She's always been rather secretive—especially about health matters."

He gives me a gentle smile as pity fills his eyes. "I see. Well, there is no cure, but we can treat her and give her a number of years still. I've been encouraging her to go on a medical diet, but she's refused. We have her on fluids, antibiotics, and some medicine to help with her appetite. She should be awake soon, but might be a little groggy."

"So she's not dying?" My heart constricts, waiting for him to confirm what I think I heard. His face blurs as tears burn my eyes.

"Not today. If she can get her diet under control, she won't for years yet."

I nod, unsure I can speak. Reginald's hand on my shoulder steadies me. Looking for further comfort, I thread my fingers through his, gripping tightly.

The doctor pauses at the door. "If I might be so bold. I've been treating Mrs. Atherton for several years. She always talks about you and your photographs." She does? "Your grandmother is very proud of you." He leaves me as I try to balance the Vivienne Atherton of my memories with the one he described.

The same woman who always harped on me to move back to London and settle down was proud of the business I'd built? It just doesn't make sense.

As I wait, I send texts to Gloria, giving updates. The minutes tick by and still I wait.

"Are you ok?" Reginald asks. I can only shrug my shoulder. "It's been hours since you ate. I'm going to grab you a bite and some coffee, and another chair for me." He presses a kiss on the top of my head. I close my eyes, soaking in the feeling as my lips tremble against the flood of worry.

Once alone, the adrenaline wanes and the flight catches up to me and I drowse in the chair. As my eyes blink longer and longer, I give in and rest my forehead on our clasped hands.

CHAPTER FORTY-ONE

The Truth Will Set You free

NICOLETTE

I drift in and out. Slowly, I wake to a soft hand stroking my hair. I lift my head to find her green eyes looking down at me, full of raw emotion. Pain. Love. Regret.

"Grandmama." I startle up in the chair, my back protesting the sudden motion.

"Oh, Nicolette. I'm so sorry." I'm not sure if she means the fight or not telling me she was sick.

But she's awake.

And talking.

Grateful tears slip past my mask. "Why didn't you tell me?"

Her hand shakes as she pats mine. "I haven't done much right, have I? Losing Genevieve, and so soon after my Edgar. There's nothing that can prepare you for the loss of a child—I pray that's a pain you will never know. I wasn't equipped to raise you. Most days, I was barely holding myself together and then you were with me after losing so much yourself. I was terrified that I couldn't be strong for both of us. That I'd end up leaving you, too. That's why I sent you to boarding school. To be around girls your age, form a support network in case you needed it."

"I thought you didn't want me." My voice cracks as I finally speak the truth that's haunted my heart for years.

She pales further, her soft hand cupping my face. "Oh, sweetheart, no. Wanting you and loving you was never the problem."

Grandmama sighs, looking off in the distance. "If I could do it again, I would do so many things differently. I would have held you close instead of keeping you at arm's length. We could have grieved together. Maybe then we wouldn't be so far apart now. I'm so sorry I wasn't the grandmother you needed me to be. The one you deserved."

Her words rock me, but with them a weight lightens.

I was always loved.

I was always enough.

Maybe now the healing can begin. A tentative hope rises within me. "I'd like to start over. Get to know each other now, as women."

Grandmama smiles at me as tears trace down her face. "Me too." She grows serious. "About that last fight, I was wrong about him—I see that now. He just looks so much like his grandfather."

"What are you talking about? You knew Reginald's grandfather?"

"I knew Reginald Senior when I was a girl. He was extremely handsome, and so charming." She shakes her head slightly, some color finally returning to her cheeks. "I was quite swept off my feet and got carried away. He assured me we were going to marry, that he loved me. He begged me to give him a little time to talk his family around. I believed he could do it, too. Then I saw his engagement announcement in the paper, but it wasn't to me."

"Oh, Grandmama."

"I came from an old family, land rich but not much else to offer besides our name. His wife was an heiress, new money but her father wanted to buy nobility for his grandchildren. I was heartbroken."

The pieces fall into place as I listen.

"Anyway, my parents had been threatening to arrange my marriage for months, so the next day I stopped fighting them. Edgar and I were married soon after, and I ceased believing in love. When your mother came home and told me she loved your father, I reacted badly. In trying to protect Genevieve from rash decisions, I pushed her away and to an early death."

She turns to me, regret clear in her tear-filled eyes. "I had nothing against your father, Nicolette, he was a very nice young man. But the life of an artist is fitful, I didn't want to see my baby girl get hurt like I did."

"We didn't have much, but she was happy. The house was always full of laughter and love. I think she missed you, though."

Her eyes shimmer like emeralds with unspent tears. She releases a deep breath and her shoulders sink into the pillows. "Thank you. I never asked because I didn't think I deserved to know, but I always assumed the worst."

The floodgates of my curiosity open. I want to know everything.

"Tell me about Grandpapa, I never got to meet him."

"Edgar was a gentle man—kind and patient. It was a good marriage. Not an epic love story, but we grew to care for each other very much. More importantly, he always saw me as peer and partner and appreciated what I brought to our arrangement. Which was pretty rare those days."

"It's still pretty rare in our circles," I quip.

"It's what I wanted for you, though. A stable union based on understanding and equal footing. That's why I put the terms in your trust, but I bumbled everything. Can you forgive me?"

At those words, the hole in my heart fills. A sense of peace descends as the full picture comes into focus. It will take a lifetime for the scars to fully heal—maybe never fully—but I no longer feel like the broken, unwanted orphan.

My eyes squeeze closed as burning tears flow before my lips quiver into a tumultuous smile. "Of course."

I lay across my grandmother, arms wrapped around her slight frame as she cradles my head and strokes my hair. It's new, and fragile, but I want to make the most of the time we have left.

The doctor comes back to discuss Grandmama's plan of care. I half listen, but my mind is whirling with the truth bombs that just dropped.

She wanted to give me security for after she was gone. It was never about the things I'm not, or fitting into the society I thought she valued so highly. It was about protecting me from the pain of her youth.

A tug at my hand reclaims my attention as the physician leaves. "Where's Reginald? I would have expected him by your side."

"He was." I look around, realizing he's not back yet. "He stepped out to grab me food."

She looks me in the eye. "Are you happy?"

"Yes, Grandmama, I am." I can't help the smile that splits my face.

"Good." Her velvety hand pats mine. "That boy is lucky to have you. He better stay this madly in love with you or I'll—well—I'll hit him with my cane."

A shocked laugh escapes. "Grandmama! I believe you told me violence was never the answer when they tried to kick me out of school. Though I still say Shannon Cox had it coming." She chuckles and squeezes my hand. "How did you know he loves me?"

"It's quite obvious, dear. That article he wrote about the two of you was practically a *billet-doux*. He sent me the flyer for your exhibition."

"You know about my show?"

"I wish I'd been there to see it in person, but I'm so proud of you. That Aurora piece is especially breathtaking. I called the gallery to buy it, but they said it'd already sold."

"Reginald bought it—he hung it in his office at home. I'll happily have another print made for you, though."

"Tell me more about the showcase. I want to hear all about it."

I pull up Henri's web page and my online portfolio, walking Grandmama through the various pictures. She asks questions about the subjects, the trips, and my technique. A sense of pride and peace grows with each picture we discuss, our dark heads close together.

Years of tense pain and misunderstanding can't be forgotten in a single evening, but the healing begins. A new closeness and understanding forms, which can be the basis of a completely different relationship. We may never make up for the years we've lost, but I'm confident we'll make the most of the time we have left.

CHAPTER FORTY-TWO

The End

REGINALD

My loafered feet make no noise as I exit the hospital room. I pause just outside as I work to regulate my breathing.

Powerless. It's not a word that many people would associate with the son of an earl, but it is a feeling I'm very familiar with.

Oh, I have the illusion of power. A name, money, even a practiced air of entitlement will get you far. What is the benefit of influencing others' lives when you can't influence your own? It wasn't until Nic that I no longer felt powerless.

Now here I am again and never have I hated it more.

My hand clenches and unclenches at my side, still warm from Nic's grip.

I want to be there for her. I'm not naïve enough to believe I can fix this for her. No amount of money or name-dropping is going to change the outcome ahead. Even if it could, Nic has more money and, as my wife, equal name. I know I can't physically do anything for her grandmother, but I can be there for Nic, even if it's just holding her hand, so she knows she's not alone.

With renewed purpose, I head out on the hunt for food. She's rejected everything I've tried to coax her with today, so I'm not sure what will be most appealing. Luckily we're in Marleybone and a quick search shows Indian, sushi, smoothies, and a chip shop open, all within a mile of the hospital. My lips curl as an idea forms.

My head is still bent over my phone as I exit the emergency ward doors.

"Sir." I ignore the voice, convinced it's for someone else. "Reginald."

Surprised, I turn and find Foster standing a few feet away. I don't recognize him at first—his customary suit and tie absent, replaced by faded jeans and a collared T-shirt.

"Foster? What are you doing here?" Concern for my old friend twists my stomach. "Are you alright?"

His eyes widen slightly, then he shakes his head briskly as he approaches. "I'm fine. When I got an alert you were at the hospital, I was worried about you."

"An alert?" I tilt my head in confusion.

The older man's complexion reddens. "It's one of those location tracking apps. I had them for the whole family."

A chuckle rumbles in my chest, feeling odd after the heaviness of the past hours. "That's how you always knew where to pick us up. Smart."

"Aye. Came in handy when your brother or father were too drunk to give proper directions." The disapproval is evident in his tone.

Mention of my family sours my amusement. "Do they know you're here? I'm sure you know we're not exactly on speaking terms."

"I do. Disgraceful, what they did to you—didn't sit right with me, so I quit. I don't know what I was thinking, but when that ping went off, well, I had to check on ye."

I rock on my heels, deeply touched by his words, and by the affection in his tired eyes. With two steps, I close the distance between us and wrap him in my arms. Foster pauses for only a second before he returns the embrace.

"Thank you," I whisper, my voice choked with emotion, "for being there my whole life. You were all the best parts."

He gulps and squeezes me tighter. "I stayed for you. If Julia and I had been blessed with a son, I can only hope he'd have been like you."

We break apart with wet chuckles, both knuckling away tears. "I'm sorry about the job, though. Are you going to be alright?" I wonder if Nic and I need a butler slash chauffeur—probably a little silly for a three-bedroom apartment.

"I had a tidy sum stocked away—I'll find something else." He smiles at me, then his eyes dart back to the sign behind me and panic fills his eyes. "If it's not you, it's not the missus, is it?"

"Not directly. Her grandmother has taken ill, so we flew in."

"Is there anything I can do?"

I smile and clap his back. "As a matter of fact, there is."

igh-pitched howls greet me as I approach Mrs. Atherton's door, urging me on faster. I burst through the door, arms full of takeaway containers, and freeze.

Nic is leaning on the bed with tears streaming down her face, but it's laughter and not sobs. She and her grandmother are both looking at her phone, heads tipped together. The suffocating gloom of before is absent from the room, replaced by a delicate sense of hope.

My chest heaves as I attempt to steady my heart rate.

As the merriment dies down, Nic peers up at me, a wide, happy smile on her face. "There you are, darling. Look, Grandmama is awake."

"I see that. How are you feeling, ma'am?" I nod a greeting at the matron as I place the packages on the nearby table. Nic's face tells me all is well, but I know this woman never approved of me, and despite the tubes and hideous hospital gown, she looks every inch the ferocious matriarch I know she can be.

"Much better. Thank you for getting my granddaughter here."

Hands now free, I resume my post behind Nic's chair and smooth a hand over her hair. Smiling down at her as she turns that sunny face in my direction. "Of course. I got you a little bit of everything, Nic. So no excuses, please eat something."

Foster enters with the remaining bags and drink tray, and an orderly with an extra rolling table and chairs.

Nic immediately wraps the man in a tight hug. "Oh, Foster, it's so good to see you." She doesn't even question his presence, simply grabs a smoothie from him and sets about organizing the various containers. Her shoulders relax and all the strain from the past few months eases. For maybe the first time in our year together, she's at peace.

"Oo, fries. And a spicy tuna roll?" She keeps opening cartons. "Is this vindaloo?" Her hazel eyes are wide as she looks up at me, love shining clearly. "You got all my favorites?"

I wrap my arms around her—careful of her overflowing plate—and kiss her forehead. "Of course, Princess. Whatever you need, remember? Now would you fucking eat something, please?"

She pops a sushi slice in her mouth, her eyes full of heated promise.

"Well, I'd best be going." Foster says behind us, hat clenched in his hands. "I'm glad I was able to help. Be good to each other."

"Oh no, you must stay, Foster," Nic entreats.

My chest tightens at the idea of never seeing him again. "Please, do. I may have overdone it on the food." My stomach drops as I remember the other person in the room. Slowly, I turn wide eyes to the bed. "That is, if it's alright with you, Mrs. Atherton."

The room falls silent, the faint hum of the lights suddenly loud.

"Young man," she begins. I tense for the dragon to roast me alive. "It's Grandmama." She emphasizes the last two syllables. Then her lips tilt in the subtlest of smiles as gratitude and affection shine in her eyes before she turns to her granddaughter.

We spend the evening passing food and sharing stories, the room filled with a warmth I've only recently learned a gathering can have. A sense of belonging and excitement for the future fills me.

Later, as Foster drives us to my flat, I wrap my arm around Nic as she leans into me. "I love you, Princess."

"I know," she quips, a wicked smile on her lips as she faces me.

My nose tickles her jaw as I growl against her neck. "That right?"

The husky laugh that always makes me hard vibrates through her. "I love you, too."

I know. It's the one thing in this life I'm most sure about.

Epilogue: September

NICOLETTE

"**I**s there anything else I can get you?" the air steward asks as he lowers two mimosas onto the nearby table.

I smile and shake my head as I reach for the bubbling glass.

Reginald grumbles in the cream leather seat beside me, glaring at the retreating man's back. "You had to hire a male flight attendant."

Chuckling, I curl into his side. A year of marriage and he still gets stupidly jealous. The possessiveness actually makes my inner lost-girl happy—not that I'll ever tell him that. "Missing the blond from our first flight?"

A deep V wrinkles his eyebrows as he turns to me. "What blond?"

Smiling, I stroke the creases until they relax. "I love you."

His lips spread into a full grin. "I love you, too." I see so many more of these real smiles since we cut ties with his parents. Each one still gives me butterflies. "A month of you all to myself. What should we do first?"

After a vow renewal ceremony in Friendship Springs, we're headed to Hawaii for a long-overdue honeymoon.

The last few months have been a whirlwind. Although the lack of Bancroft family obligations has cleared some of our schedules, with the recent successes in both of our careers, we've been pulled in different directions.

"Hmm, probably some shopping in Honolulu. Then maybe a hike up Diamond Head. Are you sure you can leave the magazine for a whole month?"

Elysium is up to over five thousand subscribers. They had to scramble to find additional printers and distributors to meet the demand. The second issue was just as successful, featuring Kenzo on the cover. It's a hard-hitting interview too—not a fluff piece. The publication is earning its reputation as a tough but fair source of truth.

I couldn't be prouder of him. More importantly, Reginald is proud of himself. There's an air of contentment in him that was missing before—a sense of purpose.

"Daniel has it in hand. I hired those journalists so I wouldn't have to do it all myself, remember?" I raise an eyebrow at him, knowing full well what a control freak my husband is. "Ok, I'll probably check in while you're still sleeping and give a review of the final copy."

I laugh. "That's fine. I brought my camera and you know how I get lost in the view sometimes. I'm not worried." His lips are soft as I lean in for a kiss.

"I don't mind—I love watching you work. We should do a book of your photos. I'm sure you'll have enough for two after this trip."

Between the exhibition, Elysium's cover, and Kenzo's album, my inbox has been overflowing with requests. More than I could hope to complete in a year. It's given me the freedom to be picky about which jobs I take on, only agreeing to those that I believe in. My creative well has never felt fuller. Henri has been after me to do another collection. Why not a book too? We'll see—nothing feels impossible.

Reginald reluctantly breaks the kiss as our meals arrive. "How's Grandmama doing? Is she going to be alright while we're away?"

The two have formed a strange bond since the hospital. He calls her every week to discuss books and hear her suggestions for philanthropic stories for Elysium. Reginald's never really had maternal attention before, and he's not wasting it now.

I asked her once if the resemblance still bothered her. She said Reginald was everything she wished his grandfather had been, and spending time with him reminds her of being young. "She rushed me off the phone because Foster was waiting for a game of backgammon, if you can believe it. I think they'll be just fine."

After the fallout at Silverbrook, Grandmama hired Reginald's old friend. Officially, he's a chauffeur and assistant, but he's become more of a companion. He accompanies Grandmama to her doctor appointments, manages her schedule, and takes care of the bills. This has left Glo time to focus more on the cooking—and also keeps Grandmama out of her hair so she can cook to the recommended diet plan. Foster has brought a much needed breath of fresh air into that old house.

The flight attendant returns, reaching for our half drank mimosas. "Sir, Ma'am, we're preparing for takeoff. Please buckle your seat belts."

I sigh as I settle back into the plush leather, admiring the mahogany trim throughout our new private plane. With the constant—and frequently unplanned—flights between London, New York, and Florida, we finally broke down and got one. "I should have bought one of these years ago."

Reginald glares with that grumpy look I love so much. "If you had, we never would have met."

"Mm, true." I lean in, brushing my lips against his ever so slightly.

The pressure increases as Reginald leans in, slanting his head. His tongue slides across the seam of my mouth, seeking entry.

With a needy moan, I grant it. My fingers spear into his dark hair, nails scratching his scalp.

His throat vibrates with a groan. He turns towards me, hands seeking.

My breath catches with anticipation. I know in moments his weight will press onto me. He'll whisper something filthy in my ear or a command.

His lips skim along my jaw, as if he heard my thoughts, and then...nothing. "Fucking seat belt."

Confused, I open my eyes to find Reginald jerking in his seat like a toddler in a highchair. Laughter wells up, until I'm doubled over, thankful for my own restraint keeping me in the chair.

"Laugh now, you won't be amused when the seat belt sign is off." He nuzzles the spot below my ear I love so much, the gentleness at war with the heat in his voice. "There's a reason I picked the model with a bedroom, Princess. I'm going to have you screaming my name all the way to Oahu. You'll be begging me as I bring you right to the edge with my mouth, over and over again." I squirm in my seat, imagining everything he describes. "Then I'll fuck you for hours. You'll orgasm until your legs shake for days."

His tongue traces the shell of my ear, distracting me. "But what about Diamondhead?"

"Do you actually want to hike a mountain?" he asks against my throat.

"Kind of..." What were we talking about? This man makes me lose my mind.

A chuckle reverberates through my hand on his chest. "Then I'll just have to carry you, Princess."

Ding, ding. Click. Clatter.

I blink through the haze of arousal and realize the seat belt light is off. Reginald has already unfastened his restraint and thrown the ends against the chair. His nimble fingers open my buckle and lift me in a bridal hold. Long legs haul us down the short distance to the rear bedroom, then kick the door shut behind him. He tosses me onto the bed, molten steel in his gaze as he prowls towards me.

It's funny. Only a year ago, I was mourning the loss of my independence, cursing a marriage that I was sure meant the end of my life as I knew it. In some ways, it was. I no longer jet set across the globe alone, living out of suitcases. Stopping in Friendship Springs to soak up time with the girls, but staying on the edges of their lives. Dreading my obligated time with my grandmother.

This brilliant, loyal man has taught me the true definition of freedom: the ability to be myself unapologetically and live my best life. A life with him is so much more than I bargained for. I thank my lucky stars every day that I didn't stick to the deal.

Want more Whisper Wire? The infamous gossip will return in a spin-off trilogy starring your favorite NYC bachelors: Henri, Kenzo, and Daniel. Wendy will be exposed in the final book—but you'll have to wait and see if the gang gets their revenge or not! Sign up for my newsletter or check www.RSBarry.com for the latest updates!

Not ready to say goodbye to Friendship Springs? Go back and fall in love with Nic from the beginning in *Stick to the Plan*, or catch up with the couple as they drop in during future stories. Asher is up next—will he have the quiet year he wished for? Highly unlikely!

Loving this series? If this story made you smile, swoon, or stay up way too late, I'd love to hear about it! Please consider leaving a review for *Stick to the Deal*—just a sentence or two can help fellow readers decide if this book is for them.

Also by

Want more Friendship Springs?
Friendship Springs Romance:
Stick to the Plan (Brianna & Colin)
Stick to the Recipe (Annabel & David)
Stick to the Deal (Nicolette & Reginald)

Acknowledgements

When I first thought about this series, it was these three women I pictured and only these three books. This has become so much more though, and I'm so happy to say I will keep returning to Friendship Springs with more stories and more characters. The Friendship Springs world is growing too—I plan on two spin-off trilogies, including a billionaire bachelors of New York series with Henri, Kenzo, and Daniel from this book. Henri and Kenzo's books will be set within the year of this book with more posts from Whisper Wire between chapters. Daniel's book will start just after the launch of Elysium and will reveal who Wendy from Whisper Wire is. The other spin-off will go back to Hitchcock, Georgia, from Anna's book. There's still three unmarried Bennet brothers who need love. Each book will loosely retell the classic novels the brothers are named for and feature the strong FMCs you've come to expect from me. You've already met one—did you pick up the breadcrumbs I've been leaving?

I've shared before that I started and stopped *Stick to the Plan* dozens of times over a decade, but didn't really sit down and take it seriously until my mother suddenly passed. After that, my husband dubbed this my "grief trilogy," and he was right in a lot of ways. Through book 1 I honored her memory, as the story had already been long set. In book 2, I explored my grief, bleeding it onto the page. I also gave myself the experience of saying goodbye because I never got that in real life. In this book, I relived the experience of getting that call and rushing to her side, but this time I made it. My beloved dog, Riley, also passed while writing this book, so in many ways his death brought me full circle. Writing these stories has healed a part of my soul, and I only hope that they can help readers feel seen. Put words to wounds they can't quite express. And support someone through a difficult time. Or just be a really fun escape!

You are beautiful. You are enough. You are special.

I can't believe I made it here, and I wouldn't have without so many people. My amazing editors–V and E—and cover designer, L, who were so patient and genuinely excited when I brought them this book. My best friends H and M who cheered me on. The author Discord girlies who let me ramble and give advice and support. The amazing bookish community I've found on social media (especially you, my Feral Raccoon Army on Threads). And of course my family—my kids who respected writing time (even though my daughter is still mad I won't let her read these yet), and my husband who kicked my butt every time I needed it, and urged me to have grace when so many things seemed against me.

And of course, you, the readers. Without you, I'd still write the stories—I'm compelled to—but your reactions, reviews, and messages make it oh so much sweeter. So please, feel free to email or drop into my DMs and tell me how my stories make you feel. Maybe I'm discovering an appreciation for praise like Nic. ;)

9 798990 185852